SAM CRESCENT

EVERNIGHT PUBLISHING ®

www.evernightpublishing.com

Copyright© 2018

Sam Crescent

Editor: Karyn White

Cover Artist: Jay Aheer

ISBN: 978-1-77339-653-8

SAM CRESCENT

DEDICATION

I want to say a big thank you to all of my amazing readers. For a long time you have asked for a longer book, and well, I hope you like this one. The Biker's Baby holds a special place in my heart.

SAM CRESCENT

THE BIKER'S BABY

Sam Crescent

Copyright © 2018

Chapter One

Gunner stared down at the slut that was licking his dick. She was just a regular club whore who thought she could bag herself an old man or at least a club patch. A lot of his men liked her, but he was finding her a little too bland for his taste. She was twentysomething and had a mouth like a fucking suction cup. Her mouth bored the shit out of him, and he was losing his erection fast. Her blonde hair was dyed, and the feel of it in his hand was greasy as fuck.

He usually liked to use the club whores. They distracted him from some of the tough decisions he had to make or when he just wanted a few moments of peace. Right now, that wasn't the case.

"Get the fuck off," he said, pushing her away and tucking his dick back into his pants. Running a hand down his face, he tried to clear the anger from his mind, but that didn't help.

"I can do better. Please, Prez, I want to please you." She ran her hands up and down his thighs. Since he was the Prez of the Satan's Demons MC, they all wanted to please him.

"If you don't get the fuck out of my office in the

next ten seconds, I'll make sure that you don't touch another club dick."

She was already scurrying away. Leaning back in his chair, he released a breath. He didn't know what it was. The young women used to do something for him. He liked their need to please, to make their place known. The men were all over them, including the married men.

If his men wanted to break their marriage vows, that was on them. When he had been married, he wasn't a saint. He wouldn't judge any man on how he lived his life. He had two teenage boys himself, and both of them were fucking nightmares. Even now, in high school, they were constantly after pussy like two horny teenagers usually were. It did fill him with a little pride knowing his boys liked to fuck and were not into hearts and flowers. At least they knew to bag their shit up because he wouldn't stand for anything less, not in his house. He wasn't going to have any unplanned brats around his place.

"You want to tell me why you sent that piece of ass away?" Kent asked.

He looked up at his VP, who was leaning against the door. "Wasn't interested." When it came to Kent, he didn't trust the man as far as he could throw him, which was one of the reasons he'd made him VP. Keeping his enemy close.

Kent had wanted to take the Prez's patch, but when Gunner himself got the patch, Kent seemed to step down. There were times he saw something in Kent's eyes, and that feeling in his gut never went away, not when it came to this man.

The MC were strong together, but that didn't mean there weren't men who wanted to take his place.

"I get it. She probably tasted of another man's cum. From what the guys tell me she does nothing but talk, which is why they're always putting her mouth to good use."

Gunner wrinkled his nose. "I do not need to hear that."

"Maybe you're getting old."

"I can fucking take you, so don't start that shit."

Kent burst out laughing, but there was a bitter edge to it. "That's never in question."

"Isn't it?" He stared at Kent long enough to watch the other man withdraw. So far Kent didn't have the balls to take him on. "You think I'm ready to settle down."

"Or maybe you've had your eyes on a certain brunette that comes around sometimes."

Gunner stared at the man across from him and didn't say a word. He knew instantly who he was talking about. Scarlett Williams wasn't a club whore, nor did she have anything to do with the club. She was a thirty-year-old, sweet as they come, curvy woman who was also the wife of one of the club's close friends, John.

Gunner and John had served in the military together. Rather than join the club, John continued his college education and was now an accountant with his own firm in town. He'd once had big plans of city life. That had all ceased when he caught sight of Scarlett. Gunner couldn't blame him.

Scarlett was a mystery to him.

She was all fire and sweetness mixed into one. The men adored her, though of course many believed she was way too sweet for the club life. Not only that, she *did* have a husband.

He didn't like to think of Scarlett in his bed, not when he cared about John. His friend always had his back, and there was no way in hell that he'd ever hurt his best friend.

John would have been one of the best club

members. He was loyal and fierce as fuck.

"What do you want, Kent?"

"Was wondering if you got word from John. He called an hour ago. Wants to talk to you."

Gunner sat up. He had John going through the books of all the club businesses, legal and not. The not-legal shit John was keeping to himself.

"Why didn't I get notified ASAP?" He stood up, grabbing his jacket.

For most of the day he'd been out on the road, going over his businesses, and he'd not even taken a shower.

It was late, which meant he'd have to go to John's home. Just thinking about it sent a shock of excitement through him.

"You were kind of busy, Prez. We all know that Elle wanted to give it to you." Kent gave him a wink.

This was just another reason that he didn't trust Kent. There were times when he was dealing business within the club that fine little details would slip Kent's mind. In fact, on some occasions when he'd been interrogating, Kent would shoot the bastards dead before they could breathe a word. Gunner had his doubts about Kent's loyalty, but he couldn't make a case to the club when he didn't have any solid proof to back up his … hunches.

"I don't want her anywhere near me." She was nothing more than a cum bucket, and some chicks got off on being that, but not him. He didn't want to deal with a hospital trip.

A few years ago, most of the club ended up with the fucking clap. He'd been royally pissed. He always bagged his shit up, apart from when he'd been with his wife, who was now his ex, and even then, he'd rarely dipped his dick in bare.

"She's quick and easy," Kent said. "Thought you'd like the release? Something to help take your mind off shit."

He stepped up to Kent, getting in the man's space. He had a good foot on Kent, and even though he was older, he had a lot more muscle and knew how to use it. "What you doing that needs my mind taking off shit?"

"Just being a good guy here, boss. You got a screw loose or something to think there's anything wrong."

"Fuck off, Kent." He moved the man out of his office and locked the door. Until he got to the bottom of the stealing from his stash, no one was allowed in his office. "Call me if you need me." There wouldn't be any calls. There rarely were.

He nodded at Kent and several of his men as he passed. Most of them had their dicks in women that were not their wives. They saluted him with a beer, and he nodded at them.

For the most part, this club was his life. He had his two boys, the businesses, and the club, but that was it. When he'd taken over, the club had been complete and utter shit. Drugs, booze, skanks, and Feds breathing down their neck about their personal business and their involvement with the guns and drugs. If it hadn't been for him there wouldn't *be* a club.

For over ten years he'd done the wife thing as well, but that hadn't stuck. Cherry had been an awful wife. She'd slept with more men than he'd even looked at women. It was pathetic, really.

They'd been the worst ten years of his fucking life, and he had no wish to repeat them, not ever.

Leaving the clubhouse, he headed straight to his bike, straddling the little beauty before gunning out of the parking lot. No one asked him any questions.

He was the Prez, and he did what he wanted to.

He'd earned his patch more than twenty years ago, taking the club from a two-bit drug dealer and child molester. Since he'd taken charge, the club had gone from strength to strength. The Feds couldn't pin anything on them. He kept their business locked up tight.

There had been challenges along the way. Big ones. He'd taken every single one of them. The men who'd accepted he'd won had kept their lives and moved on while still being within the club. Those that didn't accept it were buried six feet under in the clubhouse yard. In his world the only way to survive was to take out the enemy, and he'd done that. Piece by piece, the club now belonged to him.

Satan's Demons MC was his baby.

He'd brought it back from total destruction.

But now someone was stealing from him, and that shit didn't set well with him at all.

Whoever it was, he was going to make sure that they paid, and that the entire club knew of the shit that was happening.

Twenty minutes later, he found the modest house that his friend lived in. He knew John had wanted something bigger, but Scarlett didn't like for him to think she was after his money. She was happy with their home, and that was what she'd made even though John could afford bigger.

Parking his bike next to John's top range car, he made his way to the door.

Knocking hard, he waited.

And there she stood with one of the prettiest smiles on her face.

"Gunner," she said. "It's good to see you."

She stepped back, giving him room to enter. The moment he did the scent of cinnamon cookies filled his senses. "You've been baking?"

"Always. You know the kids love it." She chuckled.

She helped at the local day care center where busy parents brought their kids. The center was for kids younger than five.

"You're here to see John? He's in his office. He said to send you straight to him when you arrived."

"He didn't even know if I was going to turn up."

She chuckled. "I'll make you a drink. What would you like?"

"Coffee would be great."

"Coming right up."

He watched her walk down the small corridor. The sway of her ass in those tight jeans doing things to his cock that the young bitch's mouth hadn't been able to. Pushing aside those dirty thoughts for his best friend's wife, he found John looking through paperwork.

****

"You need to learn to get a life," Gunner said.

John smiled as he looked up. "I have a life. Not a lot of people get it."

"It's all the numbers and shit. Boring as fuck."

"To you, maybe. To me they tell a shitload of other details."

"Like?"

"Like someone is stealing from you, and it looks like it's an inside job. Not only that, they're stealing from both of your ... dealings."

John watched as Gunner cursed and entered his office. The man before him went from joking around to all seriousness. "I fucking knew it."

His friend was not one to mince his words.

"Any way of finding out who?" Gunner asked.

"I'm working on that. They're clever. Never take

too much, always odd amounts here or there. Give me time, and I'll go through the numbers every single evening."

"That's a lot of work."

"Well, you're a friend and you're paying me, so we'll call it even. It just means you're going to have to stop by here every single night, and I can go through the lists and see. What made you realize money was missing?"

"The money from the paperwork was never the same as the money in the bank or the safe. Over time it starts to add up, and I can't see that kind of cash popping up anywhere. I need to know who is stealing and why."

"Yeah, whoever it is either didn't think or doesn't have time or opportunity to doctor your main books." He looked over at Gunner, who was glaring. "I called you a couple of hours ago. This work is for someone else. Kent said you were busy with a special lady. Someone I know?"

Gunner snorted. "There was nothing special about her, believe me. Was bored and couldn't even get it up. Half the club uses her."

John chuckled. "Charming."

"That's what I thought. You know how the club is."

"I do, which is why I'm more than content with my very beautiful wife." Thinking about Scarlett dropped his smile, though. Realizing that Gunner saw everything, he forced it back up. "You need to find yourself a good woman."

"What's going on?" Gunner asked.

"Nothing."

"I saw that look. You can't keep that kind of shit from me."

They had served together, been through a lot, and

there was a time that he'd had every single intention of helping Gunner in the club. He'd have been his VP, and none of this shit would be happening right now.

He'd met Scarlett, and the rest had been history.

Marrying her, making a life with her, had been more important than joining any club.

"Are things okay between you and Scarlett?" Gunner asked.

John wasn't an asshole, nor was he blind to Gunner's interest in his wife. He also knew that his wife was completely clueless to it. She was always her usual sweet self, and he adored that about her. He loved that she was his sweet wife outside the bedroom, and when the door closed and they were alone, he got to feel and possess all of her fire.

Every man wanted one; a lady in the kitchen and a whore in the bedroom.

He got the best of both worlds.

Just lately, something had been missing though. No matter what they did in the bedroom, it would all end in tears, and it was starting to put a strain on their marriage. They'd learned that he couldn't have children.

Scarlett wanted children, lots of them.

She'd refused to grant him a divorce, and when he'd tried to leave her, she'd begged him not to, that she loved him.

Since finding out he couldn't give her children, it had messed something up inside his head, and now he couldn't … get past it. She said working at the day care center was all she needed.

When he went to visit her though, he saw the love she had for all those kids. The way she looked when she held one of them or as they talked to her. He couldn't get that shit out of his mind. She wanted a kid, and that was the one thing he couldn't give her.

A brand-new, bigger house? Yes.

A top-of-the-line car? Yes.

A newly designed kitchen? Yes.

Anything that money could buy could be hers. She didn't want it.

The money helped life, but she wasn't a woman that needed it. She'd lived a simple life on the poverty line when he'd found her.

The one thing he couldn't give her was the one thing she wanted: children.

"We're doing fine, Gunner."

"That's not what I asked, and you know it."

John blew out a breath. "I don't know what you want me to say. Scarlett and I, we're doing good. Really good. We … are just having some bumps."

"Bumps? John, for fuck's sake. I can't help if you don't tell me what the problem is, okay. I'm not wired the way you fuckers are."

"I can't have kids," John said, finally telling his friend the truth. "That's the crux of the matter. I can't have babies, and she wants them. Only now…" He stopped and gritted his teeth. "Only now she's decided not to have any because she loves me more than having any possible kids that we could have." That for him hurt more than anything.

"What about adoption?"

"We've not talked about that option yet. We're still … kind of … dealing with this new wave of information."

"Could they be wrong?" Gunner asked.

"I had three doctors tell me that I can't have kids. That I'm firing blanks and probably have been for years. I can't get her pregnant." There was a knock on the door. Scarlett always knocked when he had clients in his home. She never just barged in. "Don't say anything to her, please. She's, we're … handling it." He called for her to come in, and there she was, perfection.

He'd caught sight of her across the street nearly ten years ago. He'd been thirty-five years old at the time. Not long home from deployment, getting himself back on his feet once again. They had said it would be his last mission, but he'd been planning and preparing to put in for another assignment when he caught sight of her.

Her brown hair had been a mess, piled on top of her head. Her clothes had been well worn, and to anyone looking at her, they could tell she struggled every single day. What struck him the most was she was the only person that day to reach into her pockets and hand a homeless man some change. It was probably all the money she had on her, but she'd given it to a stranger.

John had known then that he wanted to get to know her. He'd chased her down the street, and after nearly terrifying her, asked her out to coffee.

He'd been wearing his uniform, and he honestly believed she trusted that more than his crazy talk of not being a serial killer. For a long time, he didn't think that she believed him, not that he blamed her.

He never posted the papers and retired within that week.

Accounting was his next love, after Scarlett, that was.

She placed the coffee on a small table. The view of her ass in those tight jeans was enough to make him hard. Glancing over at his friend, he saw Gunner staring at her like he had done many times.

The weird thing was, when Gunner did it, he didn't want to murder the bastard. Other men, however, he was more than ready to go fucking crazy on their ass. No one stared at his wife for long.

John didn't say anything.

"I brought you both a couple of cookies. Lasagna will be in half an hour. Will you be staying for dinner?" Scarlett asked.

Guilt filled John as he watched her.

Lasagna was something she always made to cheer him up, to help him.

Fuck!

Forcing a smile to his lips, he turned to Gunner. "There will be plenty for you. You don't mind, do you, sweetie?" John asked.

"No, I don't."

"Then count me in. It has been a long time since I had a home-cooked meal."

"You mean Cherry never served you?"

"You know my ex. She didn't serve anyone."

John had never liked Cherry. She'd been with Gunner purely for the patch, and it had shown. The only thing good to come from her were their two boys.

Another bolt of pain rushed through him.

His best friend could have kids.

Gunner had had them.

Two boys who carried his blood and his name.

Scarlett left them alone, closing the door behind her. Staring at where his wife had stood, he looked at Gunner.

She didn't know that Gunner wanted her.

John didn't like the wheels that were turning in his head, but mainly because a plan was forming, one that could end his marriage, but then, it might not either.

He held a secret, one that even his wife didn't know about.

****

Scarlett marveled at her steady hand as she served the lasagna. This was John's favorite, and it had taken her five years to get just right to how he liked it. He was a good husband, the love of her entire life. Ten years ago, when she'd just given the last of her change to a homeless man, she'd been worried.

Most people would have kept their last bit of money, but she'd seen him there, starving, looking unkempt. Her apartment had been paid up for another month, so ramen noodles were not a problem. She always wanted to help others. Then of course, John came out of nowhere.

His uniform had been so dashing, and when he'd looked at her, or at least the way he looked at her, she'd been on fire for him, and it hadn't stopped.

Of course, they'd been married for eight years before she thought about having a baby. They talked about having kids often, but they wanted to enjoy each other. The timing hadn't been right. Then she'd stopped the pill, and for over a year and a half, nothing.

John arranged the appointments at the hospital, and the news they'd been given had shattered their world. He'd not been the same since, and sex ... he'd not wanted anything from her.

The lights were always off, and he got on, rutted about a little, and that was it.

She'd never felt so ... lonely before.

He'd stopped by the day care center where he caught her with the kids, and she'd seen that look in his eyes. The one that seemed to always look a little guilty. She'd felt bad.

Yes, she wanted kids, but not like this.

Not at the expense of losing John. She'd rather not have any.

Putting the lasagna on his plate with some salad, she handed it to him, which he took, thanking her.

"Don't even think of putting that green shit on my plate."

She turned to Gunner. Even with all of his MC leather on and looking deadly like he could kill a man with his bare hands, she always found him sweet. "I wouldn't dream of it." She rolled her eyes and served him up an extra slice. "Enjoy."

"I will."

After serving herself a modest piece, she sat down. John had asked Gunner to sit at the head of the table, where John usually sat. She was on one side while John was on the other. She stared across, facing him, and her cheeks heated.

John was staring at her.

She couldn't decipher the look though.

Glancing from him to Gunner, she smiled. Taking a bite of the lasagna, she couldn't taste a thing.

The tension in the room seemed to rise, and she was thankful when he'd said that Gunner was coming to visit and they had work to do.

"How is the club?" she asked, trying to find something to distract herself with. She knew the club wasn't a hundred percent legal. Even John warned her against being at the club without him or Gunner there.

She didn't like this.

Her love for John was absolute. There was nothing she wanted more than to be with him. Only it seemed kids were a sticking point with him.

Slowly, he'd been pushing her away, and they were in this rut that she couldn't get out of. She felt at times like she was drowning. Most nights she lay awake, listening to him sleep, wondering if he was waiting for the moment to kick her out.

They'd had arguments over the years, moments where nothing seemed to go their way, but afterward they'd made love and been better for it.

Sex wasn't going to make this issue go away.

"The club is its usual self."

"Dirty, stinky, smelly?" John asked.

Gunner threw his head back and laughed. "Close. I did hire a cleaner. He's been doing a good job."

"You hired a man?" John looked shocked. "What happened to the woman?"

"She became club property as she couldn't say no to the men. She was keeping them serviced when the club whores wouldn't."

She chuckled and pressed her thighs together. Scarlett would love to get serviced at least once by her husband. It had felt like forever since they had sex or fucked really good that made them all sweaty and felt amazing.

"Don't you think, honey?" John asked.

"What? Sorry?" She hadn't heard anyone say anything.

"I was just saying that maybe if he stopped them fucking on every single surface, he wouldn't need to worry."

"Yes. I agree." Her cheeks were on fire. She couldn't believe she hadn't been paying attention to what was being said, just thinking about being fucked really good by her husband.

The rest of the meal went by without a problem. Gunner and John shared some really good memories, and she listened to them, enjoying them talk about the good old days. Once dinner was finished, she grabbed the dishes and made her way into the kitchen.

Gunner followed her.

"He's just getting me some paperwork," Gunner said when she looked behind him.

"Oh, okay. Would you like some of this to take away?" she asked, taking the lasagna from him.

"I'd love some."

She grabbed a bag and started to pack him a large slice.

Scarlett paused as he seemed to step right up behind her. "You're not afraid of John, are you?"

"What? No."

When she made to turn, Gunner stopped her, his hand at the back of her neck. The smallest touch of his fingers and she gasped, her nipples going hard. Gunner was much larger than she was, and now she realized how deadly he was.

All it would take was a single gunshot and John was gone, and she'd be completely at his mercy.

She quickly shoved those thoughts out of her mind. Gunner would never harm his friend. He loved John.

"Then what is going on?" Gunner asked.

"We're just having some trouble, is all. We're good though, and I'm not afraid of John, not at all. I promise."

"If you ever feel afraid of him, you'd call me?"

"Seriously, Gunner, we're just having some troubles with the test results. There's nothing going on."

She forced herself to turn. He released her for a second, but his hand went to her throat, and they stared at each other.

"John would never hurt me, and I love him, more than anything." She wasn't afraid of John. He'd never been physically violent to her. A few spanks in the bedroom, and the way he used to hold her down, but she'd loved that.

No, what she was afraid of most was John leaving her.

That was what she couldn't stand.

"Am I interrupting something?"

She froze, staring up at Gunner.

"Nothing. Just trying to figure out what's going on with you two." Gunner stepped back.

"He seems to think you're hurting me. I'm just letting him know that we're fine."

John chuckled.

They left the kitchen without another word. She finished the dishes and went straight up to their bedroom.

She took a quick shower, changing into a pair of pajamas. Anything sexy was off the menu right now. She was combing her hair when John entered. "Gunner's gone home."

"Okay."

He moved up behind her, taking the brush from her hands. "There are times I think he's really lonely."

"Maybe we should find him a woman or a wife?"

"It's not a wife he wants. It's … someone else."

She stared at her husband, waiting for him to say something else.

"I'm sorry about the way I was tonight and for the way I've been."

"It's fine. We've had a shock."

"You don't think I'd hurt you, do you?"

"No." She chuckled. "I can't even believe that Gunner would think that either. I guess he's on edge with club business. That's why he was here, right?" He finished brushing her hair, and he nodded. She turned around, cupped his face, and kissed him. "I know you'd never hurt me, John. You're the best man that I know."

He held her wrists and pressed a kiss to each of her palms. "You're way too good for me, and if you ever did feel afraid of me, I want you to go straight to Gunner."

She rolled her eyes and chuckled. "No, John, I'm just right for you, and stop already. You're not the big bad wolf here."

Scarlett didn't want to push him, so she waited, being as patient as possible with him.

"I'm going to take a shower. I'll join you in a second."

And the moment was gone. She nodded, pulling away. Climbing into bed, she waited and listened as he took a long shower.

Not for the first time she wondered when they were going to get back on track. She missed her husband and didn't want to spend the rest of her life living like this.

Tears filled her eyes, but she pushed them away, refusing to let them fall or to give up hope. One way or another, she'd make this work.

Chapter Two

For an entire week Gunner stopped by John's house, where he went through the accounts. They had started two ledgers. One was for each of the businesses where they took an end of day reading, and then the next morning, they took a morning reading of the money that was taken.

He noticed that there were only three places that were showing losses of up to three thousand dollars. The strip club, the sex shop, and the florist shop, which he didn't get. The club had their hands in a lot of pies. Each of his men got an equal share of the profits. He invested his own money in property and shares while the boys tended to waste it. These legitimate businesses were also a good way of cleaning their own money as well. Their businesses were successful and helped them to invest right back into their pockets, even in the stock markets but only in small quantities. He didn't like drawing attention to the club, especially that on the right side of the law.

Each night that he went to John's the tension in the house was getting out of control. Last night Scarlett didn't even share dinner with them, and he didn't like it. One of the reasons he loved to visit his friend was to see her smiling face. Only now, she wasn't smiling all the time.

Not having a baby, John's inability to give her children, was causing a rift between the two. He loved both of them and didn't want either of them to be hurt. Their marriage had always been strong.

Staring across at Cherry, he glared at his ex-wife, who was demanding he take his sons full-time.

"I'm sick of their shit. They don't listen to me. I

tell them not to party, and they do it for longer and more often. No girls in the house, and they've got the place looking like a porn studio."

Kent had seen her, and now he wanted to shoot his VP. It was moments like this that he wished he'd not organized the vote. The previous Prez was pretty gun-happy and would shoot anyone who got in his way. No one was safe. Gunner's way meant all club members were safe until proven guilty.

"What do you want, Cherry? You've raised the boys to take what they want. It's exactly what you do."

"Fuck you, Gunner."

"I'd be careful how you speak to me, Cherry. You may have been my old lady, worn my patch, but that doesn't give you any fucking right to mouth off at me. Don't for a second do that shit again." His voice was hard as he spoke to her. He'd already had enough of her while married to her. Now divorced, he still had to take that shit? Not happening.

Bennie and Carlos were his two sons. He didn't have the chance to name them himself. Cherry had done it out of spite because he'd not been there on time for the births, not that he needed to. She spent most of the two pregnancies complaining about being fat and how awful it was having brats inside her.

"You don't want to deal with our boys anymore, I can take care of them."

Cherry looked relieved. She stood up to leave.

"The money stops," Gunner said. He'd been paying her two thousand a week plus extra so that his boys had a good life.

"What? Gunner, you can't."

"I don't have to pay you shit. You cheated on me, remember."

"You had skanks riding your dick all the way

across the fucking state lines." She gritted her teeth.

"Yeah, well, you're the one that decided to go public after screwing the wrong woman's husband, Cherry. I don't have to pay you anything. That money is for Bennie and Carlos. Send them in."

"Let's talk about this."

He'd been wanting to get rid of her for some time but hadn't found a good enough reason to get her out of town and out of his life. He should have known the boys would wear her down eventually.

They were so getting a raise, and he'd pay for whatever their hearts desired. They had done in a couple of years what he'd been trying to do for two decades.

"Leave and send them right in."

Cherry's face had gone pale, and he sat back with a huge smile on his face.

Ben was eighteen, Carlos sixteen. Both were large men, bulky, and spoiled brats. They were hard-working though. He'd seen them in the club, and when someone needed help, they were there.

"Sit down."

They sat.

"Your mother said you've been causing trouble."

Neither of them said anything.

He looked between them, expecting to get lip.

He got nothing.

"You'll be moving into my home tonight. You will be attending school every single fucking day, and I better not get a single call from the principal. We go way back, and if I have to hear that bastard gloat, I will personally shove each of your heads up the other's ass, understood?"

"Yes, sir."

"Good. No parties at my place. No bitches, no whores. You disobey my instructions, we'll start with privileges. I will make your lives a misery. Is that understood?"

"Yes, sir."

"Good." He stood up, moved around the table, shook both of their hands, and then pulled them each in for a hug. He slapped them on the back. "Go on, get out of here. Get your shit moved in."

He handed Ben the keys to his car and the house. "If there's a scratch I'll make you earn me a new ride."

"I won't damage it."

"Go on then, take care of your brother." He watched his two boys leave. Both of them were excited, and he smirked.

That had been easy.

He wished everything in his life was that easy, but of course, it wasn't. Nope, he still had the issue of theft within the club. Standing by his office door, he looked out, seeing Kent with another woman. He rarely had the same one every single night, not that he could blame him. Kent was the kind of man that had a pretty face and knew what to say to have the women fawning all over him.

"You okay, Prez?" Billy asked.

Billy was a tough cookie, weird as fuck as he liked to watch multiple men fuck his wife. It was all consenting, of course. He himself had actually caught them doing it in the club, and Billy's wife had been begging for more.

They were a fucked-up crew, but within the club they all had a place.

"Yeah, I'm okay."

"People are talking a lot about you spending so much time with John and his wife?"

"They do?"

"They're wondering if John's going to try for

Prospect?"

Gunner burst out laughing. "Nah, John's not going to do that. I'm just spending time, catching up." He didn't mention what he had John looking into or that he liked staring at Scarlett. That was his own business.

"You noticed anything going on around the club? Any new faces? Anything out of place?"

"Nope. Other than the free pussy that comes in and the regulars from town, nothing new. It's all just running smooth. To be honest, the boys are getting restless. They want a ride so bad, they can taste it."

Closing his office door, Gunner flicked the lock. He'd always been doing this for as long as he became Prez.

"I'm heading out. Call if you need anything."

"Will do."

He left the guys in the club, heading out to his bike. Once outside he looked up at the building. Nothing seemed out of place, but he had this feeling someone was taking not just from him but from the club. The only problem he had was proving who it was.

Installing security cameras sounded easy enough, but he'd have to do it when the boys were away, or else try for discretion. He didn't want anyone else to know.

If he tried to bring this to the table right now, without any proof, they could vote him out, and he wasn't having any of that shit. Whoever it was, they were being sneaky about it, and he wanted to know why.

Now he just needed to head back to John's house and see how he could help his friend.

****

It was a warm night, and John had set up the barbeque for them to have some grilled steaks.

Scarlett wasn't home yet. She'd called that she had to stay behind at the day care center to help clean up after chatting with some of the parents. He had to wonder if she was avoiding coming home.

The past week he'd been watching Gunner and his wife. Scarlett didn't have the first clue that Gunner was interested in her. She smiled, joked, and was polite, but in no way tried to lure him.

John had seen women try to seduce his friend. He'd watched some of them, and they were true masters of their craft. His wife wasn't like that. She didn't seduce.

Gunner came out with a bottle of beer.

When Gunner had called to say that he was heading over, he let him know the door was open and that he should just come through.

"My two boys are now living with me," he said.

"They are? I thought you'd agreed for Cherry to have them?"

"I did, and now I've saved myself a fucking fortune. You should have seen her face, John. It was priceless. The only downside is the fact I'm not going to see it again myself."

"You really don't like your wife, do you?"

"She's my *ex*-wife for a reason. It felt good."

"Are you sure you want those boys at your house? I've heard from town gossip that they destroy everything."

Gunner laughed. "They'll be fine. They're damn good boys, and they won't test me on this. I know."

"You gave them the old daddy warning type thing."

"Yep, and it worked."

He nodded. "Must be nice."

Silence fell between them, and he checked on the coals. There were still a few minutes before he'd be able to cook over them. He didn't like having those modern gas grills. They were useless anyway. He loved food that he could taste had been cooked over a grill. All the other fancy stuff was for people who wanted to change shit.

"What the fuck is going on with you?" Gunner asked. "I know you can't have kids, but believe me, it's not the end of the world."

"You had two kids with a woman you can't even stand," John said.

"So."

"I can't even give my wife one, and I love her more than fucking anything in the world, Gunner. That's my problem, okay? I see the way she looks at those babies she takes care of, and I know I can't put a baby inside her. Her tits are not going to swell because of me, nor is she going to have a nice big, fat stomach, swollen with our kid, and it's all because of me, because I'm firing fucking blanks." He took several deep breaths, trying to gain control of his anger. Staring at his friend, he'd been planning something for a week, and he didn't see any reason to wait. "But you could."

Time seemed to freeze as Gunner stared at him. They'd been best friends all of their lives. They had done a lot of shit together, fought beside each other. Gunner had been best man at his wedding, just as he'd stood beside him, even though he'd tried to talk Gunner out of marrying Cherry.

Gunner had done the right thing though.

"What the fuck did you say?" Gunner asked.

"I can't give my wife what she wants, but … you can. You can get her pregnant for me. You can give her what I can't."

"Dude, you're so not thinking straight right now." Gunner held his hands up as if to ward him off.

"I've done nothing but think clearly for weeks, Gunner. I've seen the way you look at my wife. You want her. I bet you've even imagined her completely naked, taking your cock."

"John, enough," Gunner said.

"She wants a kid. She likes you, and I know that I want this too," John said.

"I said fucking enough." Gunner stood up and glared at John. "I'm not going to spit my stuff into a damn cup to be inseminated into your wife."

John smiled. "I didn't say anything about going to the hospital and having treatment, Gunner."

"What?"

"I want you to fuck my wife."

He didn't want Scarlett to go through the pains of having IVF or the drawn-out process of adopting. He'd done his research into everything. All of it came with problems.

"You're crazy," Gunner said.

"Crazy? No, I'm not crazy. What I am is desperate. I want to give my wife everything."

"Then do this the proper way. Get the medicine or whatnot. Go to a donor, I don't care."

"You're my best friend, Gunner. I can't … I won't put her through this. Our association with your club will cause problems for adopting. IVF is not easy either. It can also be very painful. There's no one else I'd have to help me with this. Just you."

"You do realize you're asking me to knock your woman up with *my* kid. You think I'm just going to walk away from that, John? I married Cherry because she was pregnant with my kid."

John knew this. He knew that Gunner wasn't always a good man, but he had a list of priorities. He'd fought in the fucking military to defend his country.

He's not the kind to just leave. John didn't want him to, and he didn't expect it either.

"You want Scarlett. I know you do."

"For fuck's sake, I've got to go."

"No, you don't need to leave," John said.

"You've just asked me to fuck your wife. To get her pregnant. You don't think that needs to put some distance between us?"

"No, I don't. All you've got to do is think about it. We can work everything out." John watched his friend shake his head and cuss.

"You ask a fucking lot, John."

"Just think about it." John ran fingers through his hair. He'd been thinking about it for an entire week. Each time he stared at his wife and remembered the way Gunner looked at her, it had gotten him hard as fuck.

The thought of his best friend touching Scarlett made him damn hard. They had fucked women in the military, shared women, taken turns, but like this, with Scarlett, it felt … right.

Before Gunner could leave, they both heard the sound of the door opening and closing, following by Scarlett's greeting.

"Does she know?"

He shook his head. "No. I didn't want to tell her yet in case you reacted like you did."

"Can you blame me?" Gunner asked.

They stopped arguing as Scarlett came to the door. "You're grilling?"

"I will be. Coals are ready. You want to grab the steaks? We can use up those leftovers from the other day," he said.

"Yep, sure will."

She left them alone and headed inside.

He and Gunner didn't talk.

Scarlett came out with her hands full. He grabbed the steaks, and Gunner was there to help her with the rest of the food.

"Sorry, had a completely lazy moment there," she said with a giggle. "That would teach me to make a couple of trips."

"Long day at work?" John asked, gripping her hip and kissing her cheek. He glanced at Gunner, who was watching him.

See, I'd let you touch her like this, to feel how good she is against you.

"It was. We had to have some training on how to spot and deal with abuse cases. It was horrible. They gave examples, and it was just awful."

John held her close. "I know, baby."

"Anyway, I'm home now. What did I miss?" She removed her jacket. It was still warm, one of the last days of summer that they got to enjoy.

"I finally got my boys," Gunner said, filling in the silence.

"From Cherry? She just handed them over to you? Aren't they teenagers?"

"It would seem they have no respect for her at all, and she couldn't handle them. I've just saved myself a fortune by taking them back."

"Well, congratulations, I guess." She chuckled. "What about you?"

"Just the regular day at the office."

The smile dropped from her eyes.

They were really struggling with this.

"I'll serve us something up."

She pulled out of his arms and went to the table. He watched her, aware of Gunner watching him.

Finally, when he couldn't handle the scrutiny anymore, he grabbed the steaks and began to grill them.

Gunner talked with Scarlett, and he listened to them get along great.

John had never seen this coming. Not being able to give his wife something that she wanted more than anything else in the world.

Fortunately, it wasn't brought up again. They sat, enjoyed food, talking about some of the stuff that was on the news. Scarlett yawned and excused herself, leaving him alone with Gunner, who was sipping his beer.

"You'll think about it?" he asked.

"Yes, I said I would."

"Good."

****

Scarlett had been making excuses not to go home for a few days now. It wasn't that she was afraid of John. She hated this stalemate. She'd tried to approach other options, like IVF or adopting, and he shut them down, telling her that it wasn't going to happen.

She truly believed he didn't want kids at all.

Why wouldn't he just tell her that? She'd rather have him than any kids. There were times she'd wish for them, but she had her job, and her life with him. It was more than good.

Sitting out in the cold, wrapped in a jacket, she sipped her coffee and stared up at the night sky. It had been a long day, and she told John she'd walk home, and pick up some Chinese food, which she still had to order.

Cracking her neck from side to side, she wondered how she'd gotten to be in this position right now, not wanting to go home.

He didn't make love to her like he used to. When he touched her, she felt him holding back. The other night he was talking with Gunner and they'd been having heated words. The moment she appeared, nothing.

Was he having an affair?

Was that why he didn't want to touch her?

It wasn't the first time that she'd thought about it

since last night. All day she'd been wondering if there had been any telltale signs. She'd even looked online for advice on how to be sure your spouse was cheating. Nothing helped her.

She was thoroughly miserable, and if she asked him, she didn't know if he'd tell her the truth. Then of course there was the trouble that if it came out he wasn't and she thought it, and everything was a mess.

"Hey, are you okay?"

Scarlett looked up, quickly wiping the tears from her eyes. She never wore makeup, so she had no worries about smearing it.

"Gunner, hi," she said. "I thought you'd be with John."

"I'm heading over there now. I had some business to take care of." Gunner moved to sit beside her.

She liked him. A lot of the women at the day care center didn't like the local MC, but she didn't mind it. Satan's Demons MC wasn't a bad place to be.

"You okay?" he asked.

"Yeah, I'm okay."

"Then why are you sitting on a bench drinking whatever it is you're drinking?"

"It's not alcohol. It's just coffee. Extra cream and sugar." She'd wanted the calories tonight and the comfort. Screw diets or healthy eating. They were all overrated anyway. Pushing some of her hair off her face, she blew out a breath. "I'm going to get some Chinese food. I'll be home in a minute."

"You're avoiding."

"I'm…" She was about to lie, but the look on his face forced her to keep the lie in. "Yes. I was avoiding. Do you—no, it doesn't matter." She looked down at her drink, wishing all the bad stuff could just get wrapped up in a box, and thrown away somewhere. She was tired of dealing with it.

"Do I what?" he asked.

"It's fine."

"A problem shared is a problem halved?"

"Do you think John is having an affair? Is that why you're coming around a lot more?" She laughed. "Wow, I don't sound like the paranoid girlfriend at all, do I? I've gone a step up and now the complete crazy one."

Gunner took her hand. "John is not having an affair."

"You know that?"

"There's no way he'd ever do anything to harm you. He loves you more than anything."

She took a deep breath. "You're sure?"

"The moment he saw you, I even remember the phone call. He told me that he'd found the world's only angel and that she was going to marry him."

Tears filled her eyes. "I do love him so much, and now I feel just awful for thinking this. Ugh, what is wrong with me? I'm sorry. John deserves better, way better. It's just this thing with the kids and everything. It's not fair. I don't want to lose him, and I feel like he's slipping away, and I don't know what to do to make everything better. We're not close like we used to be, and I'm scared."

"You won't lose him. John will do whatever it takes to make you happy, Scarlett. That I can guarantee."

"Thank you."

"Now, how about we pick up that Chinese food and I take you home?"

"Okay."

"No more hiding."

She nodded. Finishing her drink, she threw the cup into the trash before linking arms with him. She ordered all of John's favorites from the Chinese place, waiting as Gunner got his bike.

He secured the food on the back of his bike. The man serving them had been happy to put it in a box for them so they could ride home.

"I don't like bikes," she said.

"I'll go slow. I didn't expect to make a collection. Hold onto me. Don't let go."

She wrapped her arms around his waist and gave a little gasp as he pulled away. The vibrations of the bike shocked her. She held on tightly to Gunner, and she tried not to think about how big and firm he was.

Gunner was a catch. She wasn't blind to that. Even though the women were quick to judge the club, they had no problem saying who'd they'd love to be with. Gunner was at the top of the list.

She didn't think of him like that.

John was her husband.

He'd been the only man she'd ever slept with. John knew her better than she knew herself, and she missed him so much.

Gunner parked in the driveway, and she climbed off. Her legs were a little wobbly, but she kept herself upright, which as far as she concerned was a huge bonus.

She grabbed the food that he handed to her and was about to go in.

"He's not," Gunner said.

"I know. Thank you. It was silly of me to think it." She gave him a quick hug. "I'll go and prepare dinner."

Pushing her doubts out of her mind, she focused on food. Baby steps.

Chapter Three

"Is there a reason you asked me to come here late?" John asked the following Friday.

Gunner closed his office door and locked it so no one would enter. "I've been thinking about your proposition."

"Okay."

He watched his men in the window for a few seconds before dropping the blind and turning to his friend. It wasn't like they'd never shared a woman before. They had plenty of times, long before John had ever met Scarlett.

They'd not shared a woman since he met her or since. That part of their life had been over for a long time now.

"Scarlett thought you might be having an affair," Gunner said.

"What?"

"Yep. We talked the night I came home with her and Chinese."

"Fuck. She's not said anything. I didn't. I wouldn't."

"I know that. She's struggling with all of this, John, and to be honest, so am I." He held his hand up when his friend went to say something. "I like Scarlett. I respect her. Do I want to fuck her? Yes. I won't lie to you and pretend I don't. I want her. I want her so badly I can fucking taste it. I crave to know what she sounds like when she comes, or how her pussy feels as she does." He saw John's reaction. "You like the sound of that too?"

"I know what she tastes like and her voice as she begs for more. One taste won't be enough."

"You're asking me to fuck her without a condom,

fill her with my cum until she's pregnant."

"Yes."

Gunner ran a hand down his face. "I'll want to be part of the baby's life."

"You're going to do it."

"I want to be part of any kids you have with her, or I have with her. Fuck. I accept not being called dad, but you can't push me away. I will kill you if you think of doing that."

"I won't. You'll be part of it."

He'd been debating this for some time. Each second, he'd wanted to just go ahead, fuck Scarlett, knock her up, and be done with it. Then he wanted everything else. To feel her stomach as the baby kicked, to watch her hold their baby. It was more than just sex. It was a partnership for life.

"No one can know," John said. "We do this, it'll stay between you, me, and Scarlett."

"I want to fuck her whenever I feel like it," Gunner said.

John stared at him.

"I won't hide it either. I'll take her in front of you, and I'll do whatever you want me to do, but we do this, we do this my way. You don't get to control this. You're using me for my spunk," Gunner said.

"We used to share our women."

"I know."

"We start off like that."

"If you hurt her out of any jealousy, you'll divorce her and she becomes mine," Gunner said.

"Are we working out a contract here?"

"She can't be hurt by any of this." Gunner pointed between the two of them. "She may not even be able to handle me touching her."

John smiled. "My wife is sweet, Gunner. She was

a virgin in every single way when I took her. When it comes to sex though, she's …kinky as fuck. Scarlett will like it, especially if I want it too. I won't be jealous. I can't wait to get started."

Gunner nodded. "I've never been a third wheel."

"You won't be now."

They were silent for several seconds. He watched John, seeing the arousal in the other man, and he felt one building inside him. Not just at the prospect of getting Scarlett, but also to see his friend in action once again. He'd not seen John fuck in ten years, and he'd loved watching his best friend.

John loved to fuck. It was an art form for him, and the women they'd been with had been completely consumed by pleasure.

Gunner loved every second of it, which was another reason why he wanted to fuck Scarlett. The chance to see John in all of his glory was too good to turn down.

"Why couldn't we discuss this at my home?" John asked. "Why here?"

"Because I didn't want the temptation for tonight. I only just came to my decision today. Scarlett doesn't know what we're doing. To her, I want it to seem like an accident, like something we had fun doing."

"You don't want me to tell her?" John asked.

"No. I don't want her to think we're cutting her out of decisions."

"We are."

"We're going to make it fun for her. Do you really think she'd be able to handle me putting a baby in her after believing you could be having an affair?"

"I'd never step out on my wife."

"I know that, but this has come between the two of you. You've let it affect you."

"Tell me, Gunner, would you be happy if the only woman you've ever loved can't get pregnant because of you? How you've planned for years, talked about it often, and then at the last moment got told that there's no chance of you ever having children. It's impossible?"

He saw the pain in John's face, and wished he'd not said anything.

"I'm sorry." He'd never had that experience. In fact, he'd taken for granted knocking Cherry up, and now he felt an overwhelming guilt. He'd not cared about getting her pregnant or all the stages from the ultrasound to figuring out how the breast pumps worked. He'd left that up to Cherry, and she didn't really care either. Up to the last minute she partied hard with the club.

"You don't need to be sorry." John stood up and moved toward the window that looked outside onto the parking lot. "I've never felt like this before. I didn't know what to do. Those results were not what I was expecting. There was no warning. It was bam, you can't have kids, and with it … I felt helpless. Scarlett's amazing. No doubt about that and I want to give her everything in this world that her heart desires. I can't do everything by myself, and I know you want her."

"Any other man would have been beating the shit out of me for the feelings I have for your girl."

"I've never been like most men, Gunner. It's weird, but the thought of any other man but you touching her, and I want to kill them. I'd make it painful too. You … maybe it's the time we've served with each other or something, I don't know. I just know I trust you, and I know that no matter what, you'd take care of her."

Gunner stared at his friend. "You're not going anywhere?"

"Hell no, I'm not going anywhere, but in my will, I've written a letter asking you to take care of her in the event that anything happens."

"Fuck, man, you're so fucking miserable and got that whole doom on you shit going." Gunner shook his head. "I'm the one with the MC. I'm the one that could die any minute."

"So it makes sense to do this right away. Or you can always spill your stuff in a cup, and I'll put it in for you."

"That's just nasty." They were both chuckling as they knew none of that would happen. "I'll help you, John."

"Thank you."

They didn't linger on a conversation, and he saw him out. Gunner gave him a wave as he drove out of the clubhouse.

"Is there anything you need to tell me?" Kent asked.

"Not that I'm aware of, why? Anything *you* need to tell *me*?"

"You're spending a lot of time with the Williamses. Is something going on?"

"I'm catching up with an old military buddy, and whatever the fuck I do, Kent, it's none of your business."

"I'm your VP."

"That doesn't make you my nanny or my keeper." He stepped up close, staring into Kent's eyes. Since the theft, he didn't trust anyone. The club was his family. When that family had a traitor, he had no choice but to pull away from all of them, find the person responsible, and take them out.

The club had rules, and anyone who hurt the club, their lives were forfeit. If it was a club member, then that shit got ugly really fucking fast. These were the rules that he'd put in place.

"There's a lot of talk."

"What about?" he asked.

"About you. About the family."

Gunner smiled. "Then as your Prez, I say curb that fucking talk."

Stepping back, he headed into his office, closing the door. Dropping down into his seat, he rubbed at his eyes, feeling more tired than he had in a long time.

Screwing Scarlett would be something he'd fantasized about doing for years. Cherry had even been pissed at him for the way he'd look at her or treat her. She was different from the women, but then John was also different as well. They were the two people outside of the club world that he'd refused to give up.

He couldn't *not* have them in his life.

They were part of his family too.

****

John walked into his bedroom and saw the light was on, but there was no sign of his wife. Heading to the bathroom, he heard the shower running, along with a feminine moan, which told him all he needed to hear. He'd been neglecting his wife. Stepping forward into the room, he made sure to be silent as he started to remove his clothes.

The glass had steamed up, but there was no doubt about what she was doing behind that glass. One of her hands was stretched out against the wall, holding onto the tile. The other was between her thighs, moving against her clit.

His cock hardened at the sight, and he wanted her more than anything. They hadn't had sex in a couple of months, and that was on him. He'd gotten a knock, and it was only tonight where he'd been sitting opposite Gunner that he felt a real hope for the future. Gunner was his lifeline in giving his woman what she wanted.

He didn't think for a second that getting Scarlett

to agree would be easy. When they'd first started having sex, she'd been nervous, but being a virgin, he'd expected it. After they'd been screwing for a few months, and she still liked to fuck with the light off, or keep some of her clothes on, he'd gotten pissed.

When he finally confronted her about it, she'd nearly broken his heart. She didn't want him to be repulsed by her size. She'd always been bigger, curvier, and years of being bullied had messed with her with regards to her size. From that moment, he'd been so fucking pissed, enraged, heartbroken. So many different feelings, but he'd taken Scarlett to bed, stripped away every single layer of clothing, and kissed her body until he was sure that she knew he fucking loved her. Not only did he love her, but he wanted her all the time. Her body turned him on.

He wanted her more than any other woman in the world, and he wanted her exactly the way he could get her.

"Oh, John," she said, moaning.

With the last of his clothes now on the floor, he wrapped his fingers around his cock. Working up and down the length, he saw the pre-cum spilling out of the tip.

Stepping up to the door, he opened it, and Scarlett let out a scream, spinning around to face him.

"John, you scared me."

He stepped into the stall and closed the door. "I want to watch you."

"What?"

"I want to watch you. Continue playing with your pussy."

"John?" She nibbled her lip.

"I know you want this, and I know I've been a bastard to you, pushing you away." He closed the distance between them, cupping her face. Running his thumb across her lip, he smiled into her eyes. "That stops now. I won't push you away. This is no one's fault, baby. No one's. I want to watch you come by your own hand, and then I want to feel you come all over my cock."

Her pupils dilated, and he stepped back, watching her. The water ran down her body, making her all slick.

"You see this," he said, holding his dick once more. "This is all for you. No one else. All yours. It's got your name written on it."

She chuckled.

"Show me what you were doing."

She ran her hand down her body, sliding between her thighs. He watched her stroke back and forth across her pussy.

"You're not doing it right. Push those fingers inside you, get them nice and wet, just like I know you will be."

She did as he asked and moaned at the pleasure. He groaned, watching her, unable to take his gaze away.

Up and down he moved on his shaft, feeling his balls tighten at the sight. He slowed down his movements, not wanting to come yet. He was so far from wanting to end this right now.

Scarlett drew her fingers up and began to circle her clit, slowly at first, but then as the pleasure became too much, she sped up, and then he ordered her to stop.

She instantly did as he asked.

With his hands on her hips, he spun her around so that she was facing away from him. "Don't rush everything, baby. You've always been so impatient for more." Sliding a finger down between her thighs, he found her clit.

It was already swollen, and he nibbled at her neck. He didn't give her what she wanted though. Down he went, plunging a finger deep inside her cunt. She was so soft and tight, and wet. He fucking loved her like this. When it didn't matter what he did, she seemed to be aroused by him.

With his other hand, he cupped one of her tits, squeezing the flesh. He heard her moan, and the sound echoed around the room.

His cock pressed against her back, hard and ready for more.

"Please," she said.

"You want to come?"

"Yes."

"I'll let you come when I've touched you and I've felt how ready you are for more." Adding a second finger into her pussy, he pumped in and out, feeling her tighten around him. Drawing those fingers up, he teased her clit, feeling her body tighten. "Were you thinking about me?"

"Yes."

"Did you want me to touch you?" he asked.

"Yes, so much."

"Have you missed me?"

"More than anything, John. I hate it when you don't touch me. When you don't make love to me."

"What about when I fuck you?"

"Yes. I'm so greedy. I want everything you can give me."

"You want my cock inside your pussy right now?" he asked.

"Yes, yes."

He released her pussy, moving her forward just a little so that she could place her hands against the tile. She opened her thighs, and he gripped his cock. He found her entrance and pressed his cock against her. He felt her gasp, then cry out as he slammed to the hilt inside her. Holding onto her hips, he closed his eyes, basking in the feel of her cunt wrapped around his cock.

In that second, he realized he could save a fortune on condoms and it was such a weird thing to think about, which led him into his next one. The sight of her pussy, filled with his cum as he drove it inside her, making her take every single inch and every drop of his cum.

Pulling her back against him, he kept his dick deep inside her, loving the feel of her ass nestled against his dick. Sliding back and forth over her clit, he felt her body quiver and she moaned, thrusting against him, riding his cock and his hand to find her own release.

"You're always so responsive to me, baby. I love fucking you so much," he said.

"Yes, yes, yes, John, I've missed this."

"I want to watch you, baby."

"What?"

"I want to watch you be fucked. Damn, it gets me so hard thinking about it."

"What do you mean?"

She wasn't pulling away from him, and he smiled. She was so aroused, and he often spoke dirty to her because she loved it when he did. He loved the way she responded to him, her body always needing more, and he loved to play with her.

"Watching another man play with you. To see how fucking beautiful you are and wild. To watch you come apart as another cock is driving inside you." He saw Gunner and only him. The way that man watched Scarlett, John knew that the moment he got his hands on her, it going to be fucking explosive, and he couldn't wait.

He couldn't wait to have his friend in his bed, to watch him once again. It had been a long time, too long, and he missed Gunner. He missed so many things.

Her cunt tightened around his cock, and she

gasped as he held her tightly to him, driving inside her as he fingered her pussy.

"I'd get to watch, or I could join in, Scarlett. Having two sets of hands on you, touching your pussy and tits, playing with your ass or your pussy."

She cried out as he fucked her hard. Just thinking about it had him wanting to call Gunner up and tell him to head on over.

Scarlett came, crying out his name, and he continued to stroke her as he fucked her, finding his own release, and pushing his cock deep inside her, and groaning at the pleasure.

He saw stars and knew in the back of his mind that he'd made the right decision.

Pulling out of her pussy, he spun her around, cupped her face, and smiled at her. "You're the most beautiful woman in the world to me, Scarlett. I love you more than anything."

"I've been so scared," she said.

"Don't be. I won't do this to you again, I promise."

"I don't care about anything else, John. I love you so much. I'm so sorry. I thought you were having an affair, and I was so stupid."

"I could never cheat on you, Scarlett. Never. I promise you."

"I know. It was so stupid of me to even think it."

He held her close as her tears started to fall, not wanting to let her go. He'd pushed her too far, and that was on him.

"I've got you, baby. I'm not going to let you go. I just went a bit crazy for a second there."

She held him tightly, and the water cascaded down the two of them. When the tears finally ebbed away, he washed her body, taking care of her, loving her.

Afterward, he dried them both, and helped her into bed. Pulling her against him, he kissed her neck.

"Do you really want that?" she asked.

"Want what?"

"Another man touching me? You seemed to be really into it."

"Would you want it?" he asked.

"I've never thought of another man."

"You don't have to keep secrets from me."

She turned her head and stared at him. "I've not, John." She cupped his cheek. "There's only ever been you."

He smiled at her, kissing her palm. "I love you."

There was a risk, he knew, that when Gunner touched her, Scarlett's affections might turn. She may hate him afterward or fall in love with Gunner.

Either way, he hoped she fell in love with him because John was hoping that this arrangement could be permanent.

Right now, they were taking baby steps.

Always fucking baby steps.

****

No matter what Scarlett did to distract herself, she couldn't get John's sexy talk out of her mind. It was the first time he talked about another man being with them. She didn't mind so much, but something felt different, and the difference was with John.

Stepping into the lingerie shop, she decided to buy something nice and sexy. It was Friday night, and with John back to his old self, she wanted to celebrate, and of course to drive him crazy. She saw the delicate lace, the soft silk, and everything that was sensual on display.

Stepping around some of the sexier lingerie she paused as she came face to face with Cherry.

Gunner's ex-wife hadn't liked her. She didn't know why, and she never tried to figure it out. Some women just hated each other.

"Hi, Cherry, how are you?"

She knew Bennie and Carlos were with Gunner now, and things had settled for him and his boys. Speaking of settled in the back of her mind she made a quick note to make a pot roast for the boys.

"As if you care." Cherry sneered at her. "I can't believe you'd come here. They don't do plus size. We all know what that means, right? Fatty size."

After years of being called fat and other words, Scarlett just smiled at her and stepped away. "I'm sorry."

Why are you apologizing?

"You know I never saw what Gunner saw in you, or John. They're good-looking men, and they can do so much better than a fat bitch like you."

She pushed some hair off her face and stared at Cherry. "I've no idea what you're talking about, Cherry. I'm married to John."

"Oh, please, cut the bullshit. The way Gunner looks at you, I wouldn't be surprised if you're fucking them both."

The thought of being around this woman in this shop, with onlookers, no longer appealed, so she did no more than step out of the shop with Cherry's spite following her. The moment the door closed, and she stepped onto the sidewalk she came smack dab into a hard body, who instantly held her.

"Hey, are you okay?" Gunner asked.

"Of course." She hadn't responded to his question just that the very man that Cherry was going all spiteful over was now here. She pulled away from him, aware that his ex was watching. "I'm fine."

He looked toward the shop and then at her. "No,

you're not. What's going on?"

"It's nothing. I wanted to buy some things, but Cherry's in there and she seems to think—" She was cut off by him walking away from her, heading toward the shop. "No. No. Please, don't do that." She grabbed his arm. "No!"

She yelled the word and then dropped her head, but it did what she wanted. He stopped walking.

"If you want to shop in there for something and Cherry's ruining it for you…"

"It's fine. I don't need anything, okay. Just don't go in there and cause a scene." She tucked some of her hair behind her ear and turned to leave.

"Hey, hey, you're upset."

She looked up at him, and immediately averted her gaze. She felt bad about something, and she didn't know what, and that just confused and annoyed her.

"Are you okay?" he asked.

"Yeah, I'm fine." It wasn't the first time she'd been called spiteful names, and it sure wouldn't be the last. She hadn't been called them in a long time. They just hit her harder, and she tucked some of her hair behind her ear. "I better get going."

"Would you like to share a coffee?"

They'd shared many coffees, but now Cherry's words were going around in her head and she couldn't help but be nervous.

"If you don't I'm going to go and find out exactly what my ex said to you. You've never hesitated to have a coffee before."

Not wanting to deal with any more confrontations, she smiled. "Coffee it is."

She followed him across the road toward the coffee shop. Some people were eying up the leather cut with disdain, others respect, and some were just ignoring it. They were such a mixture of people that it made her smile.

"Do you ever get used to that?"

"Used to what?"

"People staring at you. Looking at your cut, things like that?"

Gunner shrugged. "It doesn't matter what I do or say. The moment they see the cut it divides opinion. What did you think of it the first time you saw it?"

She smiled. "That I couldn't believe I was meeting a real-life MC guy. Yes, I was totally thrilled, and it was all in a good way." Her cheeks heated.

John had found her response amusing.

Gunner laughed. "Then I must have totally blown your mind being the Prez."

"I like your club. They're a little different. Scary at times but still people. Still a family in your own way."

She'd heard the rumors about the club and knew that Gunner wasn't a good man. He was, but he did really bad things. In the back of her mind she recalled the gossip about the previous Prez, the one before Gunner. He'd gone missing and was never found. No body, no nothing.

John served with him, and she knew that Gunner was a nice guy, or at least to her he was.

He got them both coffee, and she thanked him, taking a sip of the scalding liquid.

"How is everything?" Gunner asked.

"It's great. How are things with you and your boys?"

"They're going good. Going to school, and it's about damn time. I actually got a call asking why they were always there."

She burst out laughing. "He'd rather they didn't?"

"They ask a lot of questions and are all about

putting the teachers on the spot."

"It sounds like a lot of fun."

"It is. They're good boys, but I've spoiled them. They never wanted to live with their mom though. Knowing Cherry the way I do, I wouldn't be surprised if she wasn't always saying shit about me, about the club."

She nodded. "I get it. Cherry's not your biggest fan."

"Whatever she said to you, just ignore that shit. She's a bitch."

"Don't worry. I'm used to women calling me out because of my weight. It's fine."

"What?"

"Just a few things about being fat and stuff. It's fine. I'm used to it." She took a deep breath, sipping at the hot coffee. Her cheeks were on fire.

"That shit doesn't stand, Scarlett." He went to stand up, and she reached over, grabbing his arm.

"Don't. Please. Don't. She said some things, and I don't want any more scenes. It's not like she's wrong. I *am* fat."

"You're fucking perfect. Don't let me hear you say that kind of shit again, Scarlett. I mean it."

"Gunner."

"No, so you're not a size fucking zero. It doesn't mean shit. Let me break this down to you, sweetheart. Not all men want a bag of bones in their bed, got it? Some of us like a woman we can hold onto. If we were all supposed to be the same, guess what, we would be. We're not. Some men like skinny, others like bigger, others like them larger. Big tits, small tits, tight ass, wriggly ass, it's all something we like. You just got to find the right man who appreciates you."

She smiled even though her face was on fire. "Okay, Gunner."

"Cherry's pissed because I won't pander to her needs. I never have, and I don't intend to start now. Ignore the bitch. You're fine the way you are."

She finished her coffee and felt a lot better afterward. "I don't think I'm going to be forgetting this chat anytime soon."

"Good. I don't want you to."

Gunner led her out of the coffee shop, but rather than let her go, he made her go straight over the road. This time he didn't stop as they both entered the lingerie shop together.

Turning around, she pressed her hands on his chest. "I don't want to be here."

"I watched Cherry leave. You don't want me to cause a scene, I won't. You came here for a reason, and I'm not leaving until you do what you've got to do."

"Don't you have other things to be doing right now? Like taking down a cartel or something."

"You watch way too much television. Shop, Scarlett. I'm not going anywhere until you do. Or I could start picking out outfits for you."

She stepped away from him with a squeak. There was only so much that she could take. There were a couple of women there. She noticed them admiring Gunner. Walking away from him, she made a stop at some horrible-looking things, and he tutted. Glancing behind her, she saw that he'd followed her.

"Are you going to shop with me?"

"Yes. It seems that way. John said you can be a bit of a brat."

"Are you talking to him?" she asked.

"I sent him a text. Told me to make sure you buy something nice."

She pressed her hands to her cheeks. "This day couldn't get any more embarrassing."

"You shouldn't be embarrassed. Consider me here as your husband."

Scarlett shook her head and stepped away from the ugly-looking underwear. Going back to the lace, she began to search the colors, feeling the fabric between her fingers.

"This would look good," Gunner said. He held a pastel pink that was so light and soft. She opened it up and loved it instantly.

Aware of Cherry's words, she tried not to read too much into it, or how he seemed to be close to her. One of his hands was on her hip as he leaned in close. The scent of leather was overwhelming but not in a bad way. The smell comforted her.

Over and over he suggested different colors until she finally caved and settled on a couple.

Without looking at him, she went to the counter. She didn't even need to turn to know he was there at her back. She felt him. The sales lady rang up the purchases, and she paid.

"Thank you." Leaving the shop, she took a deep breath, relieved that it was over. "I really appreciate your help in there."

"Anytime," Gunner said.

"Bye."

She walked away but couldn't help but glance back. He was there, watching her.

Chapter Four

With his boys settled for the night, Gunner made his way over to John's house. He trusted Bennie and Carlos, as he'd given them both a warning that if they tried any funny business he was going to make them pay. What he didn't want to do was push them away. They were teenagers, and they didn't need babysitters. This was his way of showing them trust.

The moment he parked up on the drive, he recalled the few hours he'd spent with Scarlett picking out lingerie. He'd not known she'd be outside the shop when he was walking down the street. He still wanted to deal with Cherry, but hearing Scarlett beg had done something to him.

His ex-wife had better not step out of line again. The last thing he wanted was for Scarlett to be upset. Cherry had been aware of his … interest in Scarlett. He'd never really hidden it from her either, but then, he'd known she'd been screwing around him. His and Cherry's relationship hadn't been a love match.

Cherry wanted a patch. The condom broke, she got knocked up, the end.

Of course, two sons down the line, and now a divorce, the end.

He'd sent John a text earlier that day, letting him know what happened. John had asked him via text to take Scarlett back into the lingerie shop and to make sure she bought something nice. His friend was starting to piss him off with these little demands, not that he had a problem with them. He liked being with Scarlett.

It beat spending his time watching Kent and looking at his club. The biggest problem with having someone steal within the club was he couldn't trust anyone. He'd never been able to trust Kent, but until now there had never been a reason for his distrust.

He'd known Kent was tight with the previous Prez, the one that Gunner put to ground. While they were in between runs, the boys were taking some down time, and Gunner was dealing with all of their legal businesses. It's what the club expected him to do. This was how they kept the law off their back. He paid them to look the other way when their *other* business came first, but also kept them off their back for all of their ventures.

Anyway, club business was the last thing on his mind right now.

Knocking on the door, he waited. John answered and shook his hand. "Good to see you."

Entering the house, he saw Scarlett in the dining room. She wore a rose-patterned dress that molded to her curves beautifully. She was setting the table.

"Hey, Gunner," she said, coming out of the dining room.

She had a sway to her hips that he found so alluring.

"Hello, princess," he said.

His cock was already tightening, and he was more than happy that his leather cut hid the evidence of that. He wondered what lingerie she had on. Did she have the pink, the white? She'd purchased several that he hoped to see her in soon.

"I've made you and your boys a pot roast to enjoy this weekend. I hope that's okay."

"It'll be interesting to see if they can even eat home-cooked food. I've only seen them eat shit I order in."

She smiled.

The sound of an alarm from the kitchen could be heard. "I'll get that." She kissed John's cheek and left.

Gunner's gaze stayed on her ass.

"Tonight," John said.

"What?"

"I want to start tonight."

Gunner stared at his friend. He didn't like this feeling that was twisting him up inside. "Fine."

"Thank you for taking care of her. Cherry said some things to her."

"She told me it was about her weight."

"There were some other things as well."

"Like fucking what?" Gunner asked.

"She spoke about you, and your interest in her. Scarlett didn't … she's not seen it."

Gunner knew she hadn't.

It wasn't like her to see other men's interest, especially as she only had eyes for her husband.

This could be a big fucking mistake.

"Are you sure about this?" Gunner asked.

"Yeah, I am. I know it's asking a lot."

"Dinner's ready," Scarlett said.

She held a casserole dish in her hands, which she placed in the center of the table.

John slapped him on the back.

Gunner once again sat at the head of the table, only this time it felt different. Knowing what John wanted, what he, himself, wanted, it was … hard. He wanted this. This family life to have his best friend and Scarlett with him.

The moment he saw Scarlett all those years ago, he'd been jealous of John. His friend had gotten a girl that was not only sweet and charming, but was everything. He'd seen the way she looked at John, and he'd known he'd wanted someone to look at him like that.

His relationship with Cherry had already started

to die, not that it had ever really been there.

His feelings for Scarlett were instant … pure.

"What do we have here?" he asked, trying to distract himself.

"Noodle casserole."

He waited for John to serve them all a portion. Conversation was light, talking about the weather and what was going on the world. The meal was amazing, but Scarlett's noodle casserole was the best.

Afterward, John opened up a bottle of wine, and Scarlett had a glass. He kept watching her to see if there was any change inside her or if John had told her something. They all did the dishes together, and throughout it he noticed John was constantly touching her, whispering in her ear, caressing her.

Gunner kept his distance, not really sure what to do right now. He noticed her arousal, the way her nipples beaded against the front of her dress. The dress hugged her figure enough to notice her thighs pressing together as well.

What exactly was John saying?

They finished the dishes, and John made his way into the living room. Some music played softly, and he sipped at the wine that he'd been given. He wasn't much of a wine man. He preferred hard liquor or beer. This was for pansies.

"Right, do you guys want to talk?" Scarlett asked, entering the room.

"Come here, baby," John said, patting the chair.

The smile on her face made his stomach tighten. She had this amazing smile that always lit up her entire face and drew everyone closer to her. Scarlett was all warmth and softness.

She sat down beside John, who placed an arm around her shoulders. Gunner watched him stroke his fingers up and down her arm. In turn, she looked up at him. Her neck was exposed, making him want to kiss her.

John leaned down, brushing his lips against hers. "Don't you think she's beautiful, Gunner?" he asked, pulling away from the kiss.

The tension in the room rose, as did his cock.

"John?"

"Shh, it's okay. Gunner likes watching you, don't you?"

"Yes, I do." He watched his friend working, and it was a sight to behold. It had been a long time since he'd seen John in action, and it aroused him as fuck to see it.

"Look at him, Scarlett." Her head turned toward him. "He wants you."

"John?"

"Don't be afraid. Feel me. Go on, feel me." Her hand reached between his thighs. She was shaking just a little, but as she gripped John's cock, he saw her confidence there. She knew her husband's body, and trusted him. "That's how hard it makes me to think of him looking at you. No one else, Scarlett. Just him, my best friend. The man I'd trust with my very life. Do you want her?"

"Yes."

"He wants you, Scarlett. He wants to see what you look like without your dress, to see those pretty, plump tits." John put his glass down, and he helped Scarlett to sit on his lap. "Look at him."

Her gaze landed on him, and Gunner sat back, watching. She truly was a sight to behold. The sound of a zipper filled the room and then he watched as the dress she wore started to sag a little.

"Trust me." He heard John speaking to her.

He pulled the dress down to her waist, and he got to see the color was in fact white, lacy. She looked almost virginal in the fabric. If she'd not been married to John for ten years he'd have been convinced she was.

John helped her up, and the dress was wriggled down her hips onto the floor.

Gunner groaned. She had the curves that he'd been dreaming about. The lace didn't hide her dark nipples, which were pressing against the fabric.

She sat down on John's lap again.

"What do you think?"

"Stunning." There really were not words for the way seeing her naked made him feel. He'd fantasized about this many times, but hadn't for a second thought that he'd get the chance to actually see her, or know what was about to come next.

"Is she making you hard?"

"Yes."

"Let her see."

Just this once he'd let John take the lead, but after that, he'd be the one giving orders. Standing up, he removed his leather cut, placing it on the back of the chair. Opening his jeans, he pulled out his erect dick. He heard her gasp. Running his hands up and down the length, he rubbed in the pre-cum that was already spilling out of the tip.

"You see how hard he is, baby?"

"Yes."

"That's for you, all for you." John released the catch of her bra, and this time, Gunner groaned. Her tits spilled forward, and they were amazing. He wanted to touch them, to feel them against him as he drove deep inside her.

John ran his hands up her body, cupping her tits, pushing them together. Gunner watched him rub his thumb across the tips. She pressed her thighs together, her eyes closing.

"Her tits have always been so sensitive. Haven't they, baby?"

"Yes, yes, please," she said.

"You want me to touch your pussy?"

"Yes."

"Gunner, do me a favor, come and touch our woman's pussy?"

He got up out of his chair. Hearing those two words, *our woman*, fuck, that did something to his head. To know that he could have Scarlett was like a gift he'd never known he needed.

Kneeling on the floor in front of her, he placed his hands on her thighs. He was much bigger than she was, and she looked small, almost fragile. "Do you want this?"

She nodded. "Yes."

Sliding his hands up her legs, he gripped the edge of the lace and peeled them down her thighs. He didn't wait or savor the moment as he spread her thighs open wide, and there was her pretty little cunt, glistening.

"Touch her, Gunner."

He slid a finger between her thighs, touching the fine hairs that covered her pussy. He'd never understood why women felt the need to completely remove all of their hair. He liked a woman to feel like a woman, not some young girl.

Spreading open the lips of her pussy, he saw her clit already swollen, peeking out from its hood.

This was what he'd been wanting, and he wasn't prepared to lose another moment.

****

John's cock was so fucking hard right now, and not just because his wife was naked, grinding on his lap.

No, it was because he'd seen his best friend's dick, but also watching him, the way he looked at Scarlett and touched her. It was fucking amazing, and he didn't want him to stop.

When Gunner slid his tongue through Scarlett's pussy, John knew it from the way she gasped, arching up and squeezing his thighs. He'd been talking to her all night, getting her ready, making her ache. Before Gunner even arrived, he'd been teasing his wife, withholding her orgasm so he knew she'd be desperate.

With Gunner now between her thighs, John couldn't help but think of the past ten years. The missed time when he and Gunner could have been sharing Scarlett.

Kissing her neck, he pinched her nipples, feeling her move.

"I want to watch this," John said, kissing her neck.

"What?"

He slid out from beneath her, and Gunner eased back. Sliding across the sofa so that he sat next to her, he helped Scarlett sit down. Taking one of her legs, he placed it over his so that she was open.

"I want to watch," he said. "I want to see him licking your pussy and driving you crazy with wanting more." He ran his hand down her body, sliding a finger deep inside her cunt. "I can feel how much you want him, baby."

She thrust up onto his fingers.

Pulling them out, he was surprised when Gunner took his fingers and sucked on them, licking them clean of her cream.

"Lick my wife's pussy," he said.

Gunner gripped her thighs, spreading her open even wider and pulling her to the edge of the sofa so that she was nearly lying down.

John had the perfect view, being able to watch his wife, and also his best friend as he licked her clean.

Scarlett grabbed his hand, and he locked their fingers together as Gunner began to lick her pussy. Unable to resist, he broke eye contact with her to watch as Gunner ran his tongue back and forth over her clit, then down to her entrance. She cried out as Gunner pistoned inside, repeatedly fucking his tongue into her pussy.

John held her hand tightly. Reaching out with his free hand, he cupped her tit, stroking the nipple. He didn't realize how much he'd wanted this until this moment. Seeing Gunner between her thighs, knowing how damn sexy she was, how giving.

This was not only about giving Scarlett what she wanted but also for him to get something that he'd been craving. When it came to Gunner, he'd been wanting a lot right now.

"Are you close to coming?" he asked.

"Yes. Oh, it feels so good. So, so good," she said.

"Then come, baby. Come on his tongue, baby. Give it to him."

Within seconds she came, screaming John's name and then Gunner's. He watched her come apart, and his own arousal went up a notch. It was one of the sexiest things he'd ever seen. Gunner didn't relent though. He didn't stop sucking on her pussy.

He looked like a starving man at his last meal, and he wanted her.

John didn't stop him.

This moment had opened up a void that he hadn't even realized that he possessed, but it was something that now wouldn't go away. He didn't want Gunner to go home at the end of the night, or for this to be a once in a lifetime thing.

He wanted Gunner to be part of his family, to share his wife, to share his life with his best friend. It was the one thing he didn't realize he was missing until right now.

Gunner thrust her into a second orgasm, and this time, he watched as she gripped the back of Gunner's head and began to thrust her pussy onto his face. He watched his friend lap it up, giving her exactly what she was desperate for.

John let go of her head and pulled his cock out of his pants. Taking her hand, he wrapped her fingers around the length, watching as she came down from her second orgasm. She collapsed against the sofa as Gunner kissed her pussy, still kneeling on the floor between her spread thighs.

Her gaze went to his cock as she licked her lips. The desire was clear in her eyes.

"I want your mouth on me."

She moved to the floor, and Gunner took her place on the sofa. She held onto the base of his shaft, her tongue peeking out, licking up his pre-cum. John watched her swirl across the tip before taking him between her lips, her teeth grazing across his flesh in exactly the way he licked. Just a small bite of pain to mingle with the immense pleasure that she was giving him. Over and over, she took his cock, sucking him hard and deep.

"Does she love sucking your cock?" Gunner asked.

"Yeah, she does. And she's so good at it. Do you want to feel it?"

"Damn, yeah."

Scarlett pulled off his cock and looked at Gunner, then at him. John nodded at her. She moved between

Gunner's thighs. He still had his jeans on, but his cock stood out, waiting to be sucked.

She took hold of Gunner's cock, and her lips moved over the head. John wanted to taste Gunner on her lips, to feel his best friend. This was his other secret that he'd been keeping for a very long time. Gunner wasn't just his best friend; he'd been wanting him for a long time as well.

He didn't know how Gunner felt, or if he was even aware of it, but there had been many times when they'd shared a woman before meeting Scarlett, that he'd touched his friend, and then wanted his hands on him.

Scarlett bobbed her head on Gunner's cock, her hands sinking into the fabric of his jeans as she took more of him.

"Don't forget about me," John said, smiling.

She was back on his cock, and just knowing that seconds before she'd been sucking Gunner's cock, he was ready to blow. Her mouth was so fucking good. She pulled off, licking down the vein at the side of his cock before taking more of him into her mouth.

He loved the sounds she made as she sucked him hard. So fucking perfect.

Her hand reached out, and she wrapped her fingers around Gunner's length, working him at the same time that she licked his cock.

John's orgasm began to build, and he groaned, tapping her head to let her know he was about to come. She didn't pull away though, and when he came, she swallowed him down, milking every single drop of his cum from his dick. He closed his eyes as she continued to work him until he was clean, her head resting on his thigh afterward.

Opening his eyes, he stared into her eyes, cupping her face. Leaning forward, he kissed her, tasting himself on her lips. When they were together, they explored, challenging each other. Every single time that Scarlett had a fantasy, he made sure to create it. The same for him. She'd always given him everything he desired.

"I want you to let Gunner fuck you, right here, on the sofa." He patted the sofa beside him and watched as she nibbled her lip.

"I don't think…"

"It's what I want to see, Scarlett." He lifted her up onto his lap. "No judgments here, baby. I'm not doing this to push you away. I'm doing it because right now, seeing Gunner driving his dick deep inside you, that's what turns me on. Seeing you be fucked and knowing you're loving it, that's what I want. Do you want to feel him sliding that big dick inside you?" He cupped her pussy, sliding a finger inside her. She was soaking wet. There was no way that she could deny that she wanted this.

"Yes. I don't want to hurt you."

"Baby, you're not hurting me in the slightest. I started this. I want to see you and Gunner together. I'm going to be right here with you every step of the way."

He sank his fingers into her hair, pulling her down for a kiss. Sliding his tongue into her mouth, he ravished her lips, wanting her more than anything. "I love you, baby," he said. "So fucking much."

"I love you too."

She gripped his shoulders, kissing him again.

John moved across the sofa so that she could lie down. Gunner stared at him, and they both knew what was about to happen. This one time could make her pregnant, but also, they had their own secret here. She didn't know that this was all on John. He hoped more than anything that when the time came for her to find out the truth, she forgave him.

****

This had to be one of the most surreal moments of her entire life. Scarlett couldn't believe that she'd sucked another man's cock while her husband watched and also had that same man bring her to orgasm twice with his mouth. Now she was laid out, legs spread, and Gunner was removing the last of his clothes. His arms, chest, and stomach were covered in ink as was his back. She'd seen the ink he had on his flesh many times.

She'd always thought about getting a tattoo, but the idea of having the needle on her skin didn't appeal to her. They were sexy though. She always thought they were, and especially Gunner's. He had that air of authority around him. People followed him. He commanded the respect of his MC, and women craved him.

He moved between her thighs, and he pressed a kiss to her stomach. She shook a little, and her need for him increased. John stroked her hair, and knowing he was there helped to calm her nerves.

This was going to change their marriage. She was scared. What if afterward he didn't want her anymore?

"He loves you more than anything in the world," Gunner said, drawing her attention back to him. "John's a sick fuck. He wants this. He gets off on seeing me giving you pleasure. He may even want the challenge to compete with the best cock you've had."

"I've only been with him, a-and now you."

"Only two cocks?" Gunner asked. He looked up to John with a smirk. "You really did land lucky, you son of a bitch."

"Never said I wasn't lucky. I know how damn special she is."

Gunner pressed a kiss to each of her tits. "You know Cherry wasn't lying yesterday."

"What?"

"John told me what she said. I look at you, Scarlett. I'm always looking at you, and I want you so badly. I'm envious of what John has. That he got to you first and I hate that I had already knocked her up, because you'd have been mine."

His cock pressed between her thighs, and she gasped as the sheer size of him took her by surprise. She wasn't expecting him to be so big. John wasn't a small man, and neither was Gunner.

Slowly, inch by inch, he began to fill her, sliding inside her. When the tip was already there, he gripped her hips, and suddenly thrust in deep, going to the hilt and making her cry out. She couldn't believe the pleasure and the pain from how hard he took her. It was just the first thrust, but that was enough.

Gunner pulled all of the way out of her, and she whimpered, wanting more. He didn't make her wait long as he slammed to the hilt inside her.

She cried out, as this time he was relentless, driving in deep over and over again. He was fucking her so hard, and she loved every second of it. When she glanced up at John, she saw her husband was relishing it as well, every single thrust as Gunner took her harder and harder. The pleasure was so intense, she felt herself building toward another orgasm.

Gunner pulled back, sitting, and his hands went to her waist, holding her steady as he repeatedly drove his cock in deep. The angle he had her at he seemed to hit every single sensitive zone within her body.

"I've wanted this for so fucking long. Wanted to know how tight your cunt is. Wanted to feel you come around my cock, and you will, baby. You will."

"Do you want me to help with that?" John asked.

"Yes, touch her clit. I want to feel her coming all

over my cock."

John reached between their bodies, and his fingers grazed her clit. The first touch had both her and Gunner groaning.

"Fuck, man, do whatever it is that you just did."

"She's so responsive, isn't she? So perfect. So beautiful."

"Yes, to everything. I don't want to fucking stop, but the way she's gripping me, I know I've got no choice."

John's fingers teasing her clit was too much, and she came, arching up, taking Gunner's cock deeper within herself as he drove higher and higher. Everything faded away until it was just the three of them.

She heard Gunner's groan, and his cock suddenly filled every single part of her as it pulsed wave upon wave of cum inside her.

Afterward, John moved to the side of her and kissed her head and her lips. Gunner collapsed on the other side. His cock was still inside her, and his head on her shoulder. She couldn't believe what had just happened.

Everything seemed surreal to her.

"Baby, you okay?" John asked.

"Yes. Erm, can I go to the bathroom?"

"Yes, sure."

Gunner eased out of her, and she winced getting up. She didn't stop though, walking as graciously as she could away from the two men. She went upstairs to her and John's bathroom and stared at her reflection in the mirror.

She didn't know what had happened there. John had been completely into it, and she'd loved it. What happened now?

Running fingers through her hair, she tried not to

think of all of her feelings rushing around her all at once. It was too much and not enough. She ran some cold water and splashed her face, not sure what to do next.

"I meant everything I said downstairs," Gunner said.

She gasped, turning around, and found him right there, leaning against the doorframe. He wore his pants again but nothing else.

Keeping her back to him, she didn't know what to do.

"What do you mean?"

"I think you're beautiful, and I've been wanting to be with you for a long time."

"Is that why Cherry never liked me? You told her that?"

"No. I never told her. She just knew. Everyone knew."

"I didn't."

"You only had eyes for John. You're a good woman, Scarlett."

"Yeah, I'm a good woman. I just let my husband's best friend fuck me."

"He wanted it. John wouldn't have done it if he didn't. He's very possessive when it comes to you."

"Why now?" she asked, looking at him.

"I don't understand."

"We've been together ten years. Why now?"

"He was ready to share you with me, I guess," Gunner took a step toward her. Her body tightened, not in fright but in desire. She liked watching him come toward her. When he was close enough he cupped her face, tilting her head back. "Don't ever for a second believe that he doesn't want you. It's just something he and I have enjoyed before."

"I really don't want to think about the other

women you've been with."

He smiled. "I rather like that little streak of jealousy." He leaned forward and kissed her lips. "Thank you for an amazing night."

She watched him walk away.

Scarlett figured he was leaving for the night, and instead of heading downstairs, she climbed into the shower. Facing the nozzle, she let the water soothe her frayed nerves.

Being with Gunner had been hot, sexy even. She'd never imagined being with him before, and feeling how hot it drove John, she was pleased that she'd done it.

Finished in the shower, she decided to push all of her doubts to one side. Drying her body, she entered the bedroom, and there John lay in bed.

He patted the empty space beside her. "I guessed you didn't want me to join you in the shower."

"You guessed right."

She put the towel back into the bathroom and walked toward the bed. Pulling back the covers, she climbed in, and John pulled her into his arms.

"You've talked about you and Gunner sharing before. Is that what I am now? Just another woman in a long line of them."

"No, you're not. You're my wife, and that made what we shared really beautiful. I wanted to watch you, to see the desire on your face, the pleasure. It was one of the best sights in the world." He kissed her cheek. "This doesn't change anything, Scarlett. I love you more than anything."

She rolled over to face him. "Do you find Gunner attractive?"

"What?"

"I saw the way you were watching me, but I also noticed that you were watching him. You've been close.

Have you ever been in a relationship with him?" she asked.

"No, I haven't."

Did she see a spark of pain there?

"Have you ever thought about it?" she asked, placing her hand on his chest. "Touching him. Putting your hand around his cock, feeling how big and how hard he is." She grasped John's cock and felt how hard he was getting.

Was that what she was nervous about?

If John and Gunner were together, where did that leave her?

John wrapped his hand around her wrist, taking her off his cock. He pressed a kiss to her hand. "We'll talk about it later."

"What does this mean now?" Scarlett asked. "Do I let Gunner touch me? Is it just a one-time thing? What happens next?"

"Do you want Gunner to touch you again?"

Not knowing what else to say, she yawned. "We can talk more later."

Rolling over, she closed her eyes. Yes, she wanted Gunner to touch her again, and John. But now she wanted her husband to have what he wanted, and that was touching Gunner.

Chapter Five

For five days Gunner had to leave town with several of his boys to complete a run with guns. It was a spur of the moment assignment that a business associate needed. He was always the messenger, taking goods from one place to another. He didn't get involved in the wars. He took care of his own turf, and anyone who tried to fight him would feel his wrath. So, from time to time, he did a bit of courier work. They currently had a shipment in a van that he was handing over to the cartel. This was his only interaction with them. He didn't do any other kind of business because getting mixed with that shit got you killed. The cartels were known for killing and taking out entire families, not just the person who did them wrong.

He'd have completely passed on the deal when he was approached, but at church all of the guys wanted the money that would come from the one-time deal. So over time they were known as good little postal boys. The cartels stayed out of their business, and that was what Gunner liked. Besides, he was friends with Carlos—who dealt as the main contact between the club and the cartels—and he had to be. The bastard had fucked his wife. Not that his son had anything to do with it. Gunner had gotten a paternity test done on both of his boys when they came out. He'd been on club business, and Cherry had already named the boy Carlos before he could do anything about it, which pissed him off.

On the way back home, he recalled the conversation he'd had with the man.

"So, rumor has it that something is going down with your boys," Carlos said.

"Now who would think that?"

"I've got a lot of ears everywhere, and I thought it was best that you knew someone is planning a takeover bid. Said that you're too old to ride, too old to fuck, and too old to see what has gone missing beneath your eyes." Carlos pointed at his own eyes and smirked. The gold tooth shone from his smile, making Gunner want to take it out. "Word has it they want to take the club in a different direction."

Leaning forward, he smirked. "You know the best way of catching a rat is to leave little crumbs, Carlos."

"Ah, so you *are* onto it."

"I never wasn't. I just need to know who else is following this rat. You been approached?"

"I've not been approached by someone from your club, but a couple of guys have said change is coming. This is all on the rumor mill. Word on the street. You know how it is. New leadership and they want in on cartel money. I'd say the rat in your club is the one that wants more business. I don't have no problem with the way you run your business, Gunner. I like that we keep this … separate. Bad news like this, it has a blood taste to it."

"I have no interest in becoming runners for the cartel. I'll deliver guns and even do the drugs, but always as a third party. I don't want this mess. I've got my boys, and I know your bosses don't ask questions until the bullets stop flying, and most of the time there's a river of blood."

"And I've got my little girls. I respect you, man. Never do no wrong. Always keep your shit locked up tight. When I heard the boys talking about this shit, I thought they were fucking trippin'. Ain't no one got a drop on you, Gunner." Carlos smirked. "You know, when I got into this I never thought there'd be a day that I regretted it. Becoming a father, now that shit … yeah, you realize how fucked-up your life has become. Ain't no out for me. Just got to keep on rolling."

"You hear anything, let me know."

"Sure as shit sticks, my man."

They shook hands and left it at that. Now back at the club, in church Gunner stared at all of his men. He had a couple of ideas who it could be.

Kent was certainly high on the list. As VP he'd been one of his enemies for a long time. He'd fought him time and time again on different deals, but Gunner had always won. As Prez he'd wanted the club to flourish, not to die due to bad fucking decisions. The cartel becoming permanent runners, partners; that shit was not going to stick, not with him. Lots of clubs got wiped out for doing bad deals with the cartels. He had to think of the best decision for the club, not just to line his pocket. He didn't know who else Kent had on his side, but he'd find out. He always did. One thing the army had taught him … patience. He would sit out on an assignment for hours and days at a time. He didn't have a problem with waiting. Sure, he fucking hated that someone wanted to overthrow his kingdom, but he wasn't about to let them take his club from him.

Planning.

Waiting.

Maiming.

Then killing.

All of them had a place, and it wasn't about acting fast.

Once again, his gaze landed on Kent. His VP had been noticeably absent of late. It would have been easier to cut Kent out of the club, but he'd not had a good enough reason to at the time.

Also, he loved the motto of keeping enemies close, and this fucker certainly was that. However, he couldn't rule out a few of the other boys that were wanting a bit of action and a large chunk of the pie.

Opening his duffel bag, Gunner dropped the money onto the table.

A round of cheers went up at the sight of the dough. It was already counted and placed in bundles for each of the men. He handed out each pile, leaving one for him, and he'd put another on the table. "This is for the club expenses. Any of you got a problem with that?"

"I don't. It's all right having the cash right now, but we've still got to keep our other investments afloat," Billy said.

All of the boys agreed, so he made his way to the safe, keeping his back to them as he put the money inside. He always liked to make sure that the club had a backup in case any of their investments had to close quickly.

"Anyone got anything they want to say to me?" he asked, looking toward Kent.

His VP just looked bored.

"No, Prez. I'd say we have everything in order. All we want to do now is fuck pussy!" There was a loud chorus of roars.

He smiled.

Gunner wasn't about to keep them from their urges.

"Right, that was our last run for a couple of weeks. Have fun. We'll be back Monday for church where we'll deal with whatever shit we need to."

It was at church that he handed out the jobs for each of the men to do the next week. He liked to share the workload so no one got pissy.

Gunner hated dealing with pissy attitudes. Their legal businesses—from the strip club to the massage parlor, and some investments in the locals as well where they got a share of the profits— all came with responsibilities, and he made sure each of them had an equal share in dealing with it. He was the one that dealt with the cash and overall running of each investment. When people heard his name, they all cowered, and that had its advantages.

His men left, and he put his money in the inside of his jacket. He stood looking out of the window, about to call John when he got a knock on the door.

Kent was there. "Mrs. Williams is here to see you."

"Send her in."

The door opened wider.

"No one is to disturb us," Gunner said.

Scarlett stuck out like a sore thumb. She wore another dress, this one blue with a flower on it.

"Do you like flowers?" he asked.

"Yes, why?"

"I just realized you always wear something with flowers."

She glanced down at her dress and chuckled. "I find them incredibly beautiful. It's why I'm always looking for a new variety to plant. I think I drive John insane with how much I love them."

"That isn't possible."

"Driving John crazy?"

"Yes."

She smiled, and damn he'd missed it for the past five days.

"Bennie and Carlos are fine. They've been staying with us, and I've been dropping them off at school."

"I bet they loved that."

Scarlett shrugged. "It's what I'd do for my own children. There's a parent-teacher conference next

Friday. It has something to do with building careers or something like that." She reached into her bag and pulled out some papers. "These are the letters they both had explaining it."

He took the letters from her, grazing his fingers against hers as he did.

Gunner watched her, and through her dress he saw her nipples harden. "Does John know you're here?"

"Yes. He was the one that told me to come here and to let you know what was going on."

"Were my boys in any way disrespectful to you?" He asked for them to keep an eye, and it had been John who said he was to bring the boys over so that they could care for them.

"No. They were really good. They eat a lot, which was really nice."

Gunner: **I want to touch your wife.**

He sent the text from his pocket. He didn't need to look at the keyboard to know where the keys were.

"They're constantly eating me out of home. I better stop off at the grocery store."

"I can do that for you if you'd like."

"We could do it together?"

"Sure. I don't mind."

His cell phone buzzed. "I've just got to see this." He pulled his cell phone out, and there in black and white was the answer he'd been wanting.

John: **Touch her.**

Putting his cell phone on the table, he stared at her. "Come here."

"What?"

"You heard."

She took a step toward him, and he removed her bag from her shoulder, placing it on the floor beside him.

Putting a hand on her hip, he pulled her closer so

that she was standing between his spread legs.

"What are you doing?" she asked.

"What I want to do." He ran his hand down her back, gripping her ass. It was so full and ripe. Fucking perfect. Her hands went to his chest but didn't push him away. "I've missed you. Five days away from you after feeling you come all over my cock is too damn long."

"Gunner … what?"

"John wants this, baby. He wants you to be mine just as you're his." He grabbed his cell phone. She wasn't a woman to stray, and as she took it from his hands, he saw her shake just a little.

"Do you like my husband?" she asked.

"You know I do. He's my best friend." Taking the cell phone from her hands, he placed it on the table beside him. Cupping her cheek, he sank his fingers into her hair, tilting her head back up. "I wished you'd been mine." He wasn't going to hold anything back.

Gripping the back of her neck with his other hand, he slammed his lips down on hers, taking the kiss he'd been wanting to take for some time, and he didn't want to let her go, not for a fucking second did he want to.

Fire consumed him, as did raging need. He wanted her more than anything else.

She opened her mouth, and he plunged his tongue inside, wanting whatever she'd fucking give him. It was like a drug he couldn't escape from, nor did he want to. His cock swelled, and the moan that escaped her just sent his need for her up another notch.

"Fuck, baby, you have no idea what I want to do to you," he said.

"What do you want to do?"

"How about I show you?"

Spinning her around, he lifted her up and placed

her on the edge of the desk, pushing the dress up her thighs. Drawing her back to the edge of the table, he pushed the dress all the way up to her waist. Gripping the edge of her lace panties, he tore them off, putting them in his pocket as he did.

"Tell me what you want," he said.

"I want you to touch me."

He slid a finger between her folds, finding how soaking wet she was. "Oh, baby, is this all for me?" He slid a finger inside her, then another. She was so tight, and he couldn't believe how fucking lucky his friend was.

Now it's your luck as well.

You've finally got Scarlett beneath you. She's wet, take her.

He sat down in his chair, very much aware that this was where he gave church. Every time he sat in this spot, he'd remember what he was about to do.

Spreading her thighs wide, he opened her pussy and licked across her slit. She cried out his name as he took her nub between his teeth, sucking it hard.

The pleasure echoed off the walls as he licked and sucked her clit, driving his fingers in deep. Over and over again, he fucked her, feeling her cunt tighten around him. He didn't want to stop, and only when she came, screaming his name, did he release her clit.

Not for long though.

Pulling his cock out of his pants, he winced at the jolt of pain from rushing. He stood up, placed the tip at her entrance, and slammed deep within her.

This time she cried out and sat up on the table.

He grabbed her hands, wrapping them around his neck as he filled her.

"Look at my cock, Scarlett. It's *my* dick inside you, fucking you, claiming you."

She glanced down, and her pussy tightened, making them both groan.

"Fuck, you have no idea how much I've imagined you being here, on this table, taking my cock. Do you like it?"

"Yes."

He pressed her down to the table, lifting her legs up so they were against his chest. With his hands on her hips, he fucked her harder, going deeper than before. He couldn't help but watch as his cock filled her. The way her pussy opened up around his cock made it difficult for him to concentrate.

Over and over, he fucked her.

Five days without her didn't have him lasting very long, and with a few short thrusts, he filled her to the hilt, pumping his cum deep inside her.

She could be pregnant now.

The moment he had that thought, he was overcome by guilt.

She took each pulse, each wave of his cum, and afterward, she smiled at him. "I guess that answers my other question."

"Which is?"

"If things would be awkward. John asked me to come over. He said I needed to see you."

He didn't want to pull out of her.

Gunner liked the way she felt around his cock.

After a few seconds had passed, and he couldn't have a reason, he placed his hand against her stomach, wondering. He'd never be able to step back if she got pregnant. That shit would be impossible.

"What is it?" she asked, placing a hand over his.

"It's nothing."

Pulling out of her, he took a seat, and then told her to wait. Placing her feet on his knees, he wanted to be the one to fill her with a child. Not IVF. Not some fucking doctor. Him. He wanted to do what John couldn't, and in doing so, create a place in both of their worlds for himself. To know that the baby they were pretending was John's, would be his.

He watched as his cum came to her entrance, and reaching out, he pushed it back inside, wanting her to keep it all.

When it came to Scarlett and to John, he was a selfish bastard who wanted a lot more from them both.

****

"Did you like it?" John asked.

He sipped at his wine, watching as his wife walked around the kitchen, putting her groceries away.

"Yes, I did." She paused with a cauliflower in her hands and turned toward him. "Do you like it? Knowing that he touched me? That he fucked me?"

"That he made you come, screaming his name?" he asked.

She nodded.

"Yes, it does. Especially the end when you told me that he pushed his cum back inside you, and then made you wear the panties again." They'd also gone shopping, but he knew what Gunner had been trying to do. He was trying to get her pregnant. It was part of their plan.

She put the last of the vegetables away and moved toward him. "You're way too kinky." She kissed his lips.

"You're worried about something."

He felt it in her kiss.

"This is all just a little scary, okay? You, me, Gunner. It's not something I was ever prepared for."

"And it has you scared?"

"Yes, of course it does. I don't … I don't want to

lose you. I love you, John."

He put his wineglass down and cupped her cheek. "I love you too. I'm not going to let this ruin us. It's what we both want. I know you got off on Gunner, that you loved his face between your thighs."

She sighed. "Fine."

"Do you trust me?" he asked.

"Yes. You know I do."

"Strip naked."

"What?"

"You heard me, strip. I want to see."

He sipped at his wine and watched as she removed the dress and clothes that he'd given her. Taking her hand, he led her out onto the dining room table. It wasn't set yet, as they planned to eat dinner in the kitchen. Gunner wasn't coming tonight because he was spending some time with his kids.

Lifting her up onto the edge of the table, he smiled at her. "He did this?"

"Yes."

Opening her thighs, he sat down on his chair. She tilted her head to watch him. "And this?"

"Yes."

He ran his fingers through the fine hairs of her pussy, knowing that Gunner had come deep inside her, that some of that was him.

His cock threatened to burst through the seams.

Secrets were much easier to keep and deny when they weren't facing you. Unable to resist, he spread the lips of her pussy open and leaned forward, touching her clit with his tongue. She tasted incredible, and his own arousal mounted, knowing that Gunner had been inside her, tasted her, and his cum was also mixed with hers.

Maybe he was a sick bastard wanting to suck Gunner's cock, to taste him as his cock was covered in

Scarlett's taste. There were a lot of things he wanted, but right now, he wanted to prove to his wife that he didn't feel jealous, that he was aroused, and he wanted her to be the same.

He slid his tongue across her clit, stroking her. He felt her shake, and he pressed a finger inside her, thrusting in deep. She was so wet, and he knew it was because of a mixture of their cums.

With his other hand, he ran it up her thighs, gripping the flesh of her hip, feeling her moan and shake against him as he bit down on her clit.

She arched up, crying out his name as he fucked her pussy with his fingers. He wanted his cock inside her.

Pulling away, he quickly opened his pants, pulling out his cock, and in one quick thrust, he was deep inside her. Closing his eyes, he felt her pussy clench around him. He knew what Gunner loved, and what he'd always loved about his wife.

She never held herself back. Even when they argued, she never made him work to please her. She wanted to be fucked just as he wanted to fuck her. This was where they could always come together, and their passion matched each other.

"You're so fucking beautiful, and I wished I could have been there, baby." He pulled out only to slam back inside. With each thrust she moaned his name. the sounds echoing off the wall, driving his desire for her even higher. He didn't want to let her go.

In and out, he pounded her pussy. Her cunt tightened around him as he felt her orgasm near.

He slid his fingers across her clit, watching and waiting for her to come apart. When her orgasm came, he held her close as she shook in his arms. Driving his dick inside her, he felt every inch of her milking him.

When it was over, he picked her up, pulling her

into his arms as he sat down in his chair. Stroking her hair, kissing her neck, he breathed in her vanilla scent. This woman, the love of his life, meant the world to him.

"I'm scared," she said.

"What about?"

"That you're going to leave me. I know I should be hard about it and not care, but I do." She pulled back and stared at him. "I love you more than anything in the world."

"I'm not going anywhere, Scarlett. You're mine. You belong to me. Most men would let you go, to find what you needed, who could give you what you wanted, but I'm not a gentleman. With you I'm going to be so fucking selfish because I don't want to lose you."

Her lip wobbled. "I like you selfish."

"Seeing you with Gunner, knowing you're with him, I'm not jealous and I'm not afraid. I like it. It makes me hot for you. You do trust me?"

"Yes."

"Good. I know I can trust him above everything else. He's my best friend."

"Why didn't you join the club?" she asked.

"It's not really my scene. I've got other commitments."

"You don't want it?"

"Gunner was away for five nights. I couldn't be away that long from you, baby. Never."

She cupped his face, kissing his lips. "Do you love Gunner?"

He stared into her eyes, knowing she was searching for something. "Yes."

"Have you and Gunner ever … done anything?"

"No, we haven't."

"Do you want to?"

He cupped her face and kissed her lips. Sliding

his tongue into her mouth, he felt her body respond to his. "I've got a few things to do. Why don't you head upstairs, get ready for bed? I'll join you in a minute."

"Okay."

She pressed her head to his. "I don't know if I'll ever look at this dining room table the same way again."

He laughed. "I've fucked you on it enough times."

"I know. This felt different."

John eased her off his lap and kissed her one last time, watching her go. He and Gunner had never fucked each other. There had been touches, but nothing like that. Running fingers through his hair, he knew without a doubt that Scarlett would continue to ask questions. He also knew keeping stuff from her like getting Gunner to make her pregnant would hurt her.

He was doing the right thing.

He truly believed that.

Glancing down at his cock, he tucked himself back into his pants before cleaning the table.

He had to be careful with how he dealt with Scarlett and Gunner. The last thing he wanted to do was ruin what he hoped to build.

****

"Thank you, Mrs. Williams," Daniel said, taking the toy out of her hand.

Scarlett smiled at the little boy and stood up. She'd just fixed the toy car for the seventh time that day, but she didn't mind. Providing all the kids were happy then she was more than happy.

Moving across the play area, she straightened the books, picking up two that had been thrown on the floor. Next, she straightened up the chairs, and finally sat down to watch as one of the girls put together a puzzle. She handed each piece to Fiona, being careful not to interfere or to show her where the piece went. The children had to learn to do the basics themselves.

She loved her job, watching kids, taking care of them, being mindful of what they needed while also being firm when they pushed too far.

"Scarlett, phone call."

Glancing over at Mary, the woman who owned and ran the day care, she got to her feet and smiled. "Did they say who it was?"

"No."

From the snooty way she responded Scarlett knew it was Gunner. Mary had made her opinions known about the MC. Scarlett didn't agree with them, but like she pointed out, her husband was friends with Gunner and they'd been in the service together. She was sure Mary was waiting for any opportunity to fire her.

"Hello," she said.

"Scarlett, so sorry to do this to you. I just got a call from the principal. Bennie's been suspended, and I need you to go and pick him up. I've already spoken to the principal, and I'll deal with him later. John's in a bind, and the boys are busy. Do you mind?"

"No, I don't mind. What about Carlos?"

"He's not been suspended."

"You want me to pick him up as well?" she asked.

"If you don't mind. I know it's asking a lot."

She chuckled. "It's not asking much of anything. I can get them. Don't worry. I'll feed them as well."

"Thanks, Scarlett."

"No problem. I better go." She didn't like the way Mary was shooting daggers toward her.

Hanging up the phone, she made her way over to Mary. "I've got to go and do a favor. Can I take the rest of the day off? I can work all day Saturday."

"You shouldn't be mingling with the likes of them. Bad news, the lot of them."

Scarlett gritted her teeth, not wanting to get into this argument today. She just wanted to leave so she could pick up Bennie.

Staring at Mary, she waited for the other woman to finish before she let her go. Mary had a bad streak inside her when it came to the Satan's Demons MC. Scarlett didn't know why it was there, or even what the cause was.

There were times she did expect Mary to fire her, but each time she waited for it, it never came. She didn't even know if Mary could fire her for an association with a club outside of work.

Either way, she didn't want to risk it, just in case she was in some way able to fire her. This wasn't about trying to piss Mary off.

Once outside, she went straight to her car. Climbing inside, she made her way to the high school without any detours. She wondered why Cherry hadn't been called. There was no reason for her to double check. The school may have already called her and then Gunner. Whatever the reason, it wasn't up to her. She just hoped Bennie didn't mind her picking him up.

She parked her car, getting as close to the main doors as she could. Making her way inside, she went straight toward reception, and as she rounded the corner, she spotted Bennie, and she gasped at what she saw. His face was a mess. There was no other word for it. His eye was already swollen, and he had a busted-up lip.

She went to her knees before him. "Bennie, honey, are you okay?"

"Hey, Mrs. Williams," he said, not looking surprised to see her.

"Did your dad tell you I was coming?"

"Yeah, he did."

"You need to sign him out." The receptionist cleared her throat, and Scarlett glared at the other woman.

"I expect whoever did that to him has already left?" she asked.

The woman paled.

"That's okay. Gunner, you know, the President of the local MC, said he'd be coming to talk with you all." She didn't care that the woman now had a tinge of green. She was so angry at the woman behind the desk that she could fucking spit. Bennie was just a boy. Admittedly, he looked more like a man, but still. They all had a responsibility to those in their care, and this was what happened. Oh, if Bennie was her son, they wouldn't hear the end of it.

A twinge of pain struck her, as she couldn't say anything. Bennie wasn't her son.

"I'm sure the principal will be waiting."

"Good. I cannot believe you wouldn't even offer him a trip to the nurse or something like that. He's an eighteen-year-old boy."

"Who started a fight," the receptionist said.

"Last time I checked that didn't stop anyone from being taken care of in this country. You should be ashamed of yourself." She signed her name, glared at the woman, and then waited for Bennie to stand.

He tried to hide the wince, but she caught it, and it only served to piss her off.

"You look like you're going to go all ninja on her ass."

"I should. I cannot believe this. No one saw you."

"I turned it down, Mrs. Williams. I didn't want that nurse poking me or shit." He glanced at her. "Sorry."

"It's fine. I'm not some delicate girl made out of

china, Bennie. I've been around grown men who swore worse than damn sailors."

He chuckled and gasped.

"Are you in a lot of pain?" she asked.

"It'll be fine. It's only because I had to sit out there, and I've tensed up. Dad told me not to move until you arrived."

She opened the car door for him. "I came as soon as I got the call."

"I appreciate it. I called Dad because Mom never picks up. Even when we lived with her, she never did."

"I'm so sorry, honey."

"Why are you sorry?" he asked.

"Your parents?"

"They've been divorced a long time. I don't have any problem with it. You shouldn't worry either. I don't. Mom's a first-class bitch, and from what my classmates like to gossip about, she's also a whore. It's like she treats her body like it's a room their dads can use for a price."

She winced, hearing the pain in his voice as he climbed into the car. She didn't think this was about the fight either.

Climbing behind the wheel, she started up the car, driving carefully to his father's place. She'd been there several times with John over the years.

"I'm sorry."

He chuckled. "You don't have to be. It's not your fault my mom's a bitch."

"It's just that … it must hurt not having your mom come and pick you up and you have to have me. I know I'm not always great company."

"I like you, Mrs. Williams. You've always got a smile on your face, and you're the first person who stuck up for me today."

"Please, call me Scarlett. I feel really old with Mrs. Williams," she said. "I'm the only one who stuck up for you?"

"I should tell you that I fought Finn Goldman today."

She glanced over at him. She knew who the Goldman family was. One of the richest families in town. "What about?"

"He was talking shit about my mom. How he'd taken her out for a test drive. That shit didn't bother me. I've been dealing with that most of my life. I've seen the men come and go from her home more times than I could count. I'm not an idiot, I know what she's doing. It was the moment he started talking shit about the club and about my dad. I don't like that kind of shit."

"Oh, what an asshole."

Bennie chuckled. "I think that's the first time I've heard you cuss, Mrs. Wil—Scarlett."

She smiled along with him. "Well, I'm glad you did what you did. You stood up for what you believe in."

"Shouldn't you be telling me that fighting is bad?"

"Oh, it is. I know the Goldmans though, and they have sticks so far up their asses they've forgotten they're normal people." She didn't like the Goldmans one bit. She'd seen them around town, and they always looked down their nose at anyone less fortunate than them. It was like they were personally offended by poverty or lack of wealth of any kind.

They made it to Gunner's house, and she climbed out, waiting for Bennie before locking the car. Bennie had his keys, and he let them inside the house.

When he made to move toward the stairs, she stopped him.

"Don't even think about it, boyo. Just because the

school didn't care doesn't mean that I don't. Kitchen, now, and I'll grab the first aid kit."

Once she had her stuff, she made her way into the kitchen, and Bennie had removed his shirt.

She saw the bruises on his chest.

"This all from the fight?"

"Yep."

"Damn, that looks like it hurt." She slapped a hand across her mouth.

"It really did," he said, laughing.

Opening the first aid kit, she grabbed what she needed and looked back at him, seeing him waiting.

Stepping up toward him, she began to clean some of the dried blood from his face. He didn't moan or flinch once.

"Your dad will be real proud that you stood up for yourself."

"He's going to be pissed that I'm suspended for two weeks."

"Let him deal with that. I still don't like that this Finn guy got to go back to class. Did he look as bad as you?"

"Worse."

"And they let him go back to class?"

"He went to the hospital. I imagine they're doing surgery to repair that pretty face of his."

"So … just out of … curiosity … was saving your father's reputation the only reason you delivered him a smackdown or was there another reason?"

She saw the look in his eyes and knew it had something else to do with it. "It's fine if it is protecting your dad and the club. I've known you some time, Bennie, and I know for a fact that you've not gotten into a fight like this over the club before. What was different?"

"He was bullying a girl."

Scarlett looked at him.

"Okay."

"She's a really pretty girl, but she's on the chunky side and … I didn't like the way he acted. I saw tears in her eyes as he pushed her, making her drop her books and stomping her favorite into the mud. I lost it. Like, totally lost it, and I was on him. I don't even think I gave him a warning. I just saw fucking red. He was hurting someone, and I had to do something."

"You're a good kid, Bennie." She smiled at him. "There, all better. Right, you will be doing homework. I will be downloading worksheets so that you don't miss class, and then I'll be making dinner before we have to go and get Carlos. How does that sound?"

"You don't have to stay."

"How does it sound?" she asked, hands on hips, giving him the best "stern voice" she could muster.

"It sounds awesome."

"Good. Go and get cleaned up."

She allowed him to leave as she got ahead with the laundry and the few odd chores around the house.

Chapter Six

Gunner saw Scarlett's car still parked in the driveway as he made it home. He shot a quick text off to John, but when he didn't get a response right away, he entered his home. For a few seconds he had to stop and just bask in the scent filling the house. He'd never been able to cook much, other than heating up some ready-made meals and frying some eggs. The smells were amazing, and his stomach rumbled.

Closing the door, he made his way toward the kitchen where he also heard laughter.

Rounding the corner, he came to a stop when he caught the sight of freshly baked cookies but also his two sons sitting at the counter with Scarlett moving between them, helping them with homework.

One look at Bennie and his anger found a new peak.

His son's face was a mash of black, purple, and other colors. Not to mention the split lip or the way that he held himself, which years of being in the military and then Prez of an MC, told him his son was hurting all fucking over.

Gunner had had to sit in the principal's office as he spoke nonstop about being a nonviolent school and all that shit. One look at his son, and he hoped whoever tried to beat on him was in more of a world of hurt.

Bennie looked up first and saw him. "Hey, Dad."

"Yeah, 'hey Dad.' Who?" he asked. He couldn't get that information out of the principal. He was going to get it now.

"Finn Goldman."

"He look worse than you?"

"They took him to the hospital." Goldman was a

name around these parts. A man with more money than he could spend who also had a cruel streak a mile fucking long. Gunner didn't like the asshole and had avoided doing business with him for a long time.

"I'll be talking to Goldman," he said.

"You don't have to, Dad."

"I don't give a fuck what you think I have to do. This shit doesn't stand. I'll be talking to the principal as well. Tomorrow your ass is going back to school. I'm not going to have this shit. You understand?"

"Yes, sir."

He moved toward his son, gripped the back of his neck, and hugged him. "You okay?"

"Yeah. Just hurts in a few places."

"They didn't even clean up his face," Scarlett said. Her hands were wringing the cloth she held so tightly. It looked like she was throttling the fabric. "I had to clean him up. He still had dried blood on his face from the fight."

He gritted his teeth, wishing now that he'd given the principal a new asshole, but as it was, he figured this was just a fight between two kids, which it was. Only his son got the sore end of the deal. Gunner had not been able to make it back to the school, and because of that, they'd pushed his son to one side.

There's no way he'd let that shit stand, and he'd make sure the principal knew about it as well. It was a good thing the principal was a male. He had no problem hurting men who hurt his family.

"How was school?" he asked, looking toward Carlos.

"I didn't hear about it until after lunch, Dad," Carlos said. He was sixteen, and already a large kid. He could take on the rest of them and still be begging for more.

"It's not your job to fight your brother's battles. Finish your homework."

"Thank you, Scarlett," Carlos said.

Both boys left the kitchen, taking one of her cookies as they did.

"Thank you for picking them up today," he said.

"It's fine. I was so angry when I saw him sitting there. I couldn't believe they could leave him alone like that. He's hurting. I didn't know if I should make him a doctor's appointment just to make sure nothing is broken or cracked. You didn't answer my call."

"You called me?" he asked.

"At the club. I don't actually have your cell phone number. I've always called the club and you've been there." She shrugged.

"Who did you speak to?" he asked.

"I don't know. It was some woman. Said that you were way too busy at the moment but she'd give you the message. I guess you didn't get it."

"What did you call about?" he asked, making a note to ask all of the women at the club. The women that were always there were the club whores. When he found out who it was, he'd make sure their asses were cast out of his club. He didn't want any of them in his club if they couldn't even deliver a simple message.

"About Bennie. That other boy is not even suspended. They left Bennie out on a bench. Didn't even let him see the nurse."

"If you can arrange a doctor's appointment for tomorrow after school, we'll get him checked over."

"I will. I'll even take him myself. You think the principal is going to listen to you? Allow Bennie back in?"

"I've got a few choice words that I can think of that will make it so. I get what I want when I put my mind to it."

She chuckled. "I bet you do." She tucked some hair behind her ears. The long length made him want to run his fingers through it. His boys had been spoiled with a day with her, and part of him was jealous that they got the chance to be with her. He wondered if he could call in sick one day and have her take care of him.

"I made some cookies. I raided your fridge and pantry and came up with dinner. You don't eat a lot?" she asked.

"Oh, we eat a lot. I don't cook. I think this will be one of the first meals we've had in a long time that wasn't brought in by telephone."

"It's a lamb hotpot. It's so good. I found a recipe for it online, and I've been meaning to try it out. I took Bennie and Carlos to the grocery store, and we filled your fridge, freezer, and pantry."

"It won't get used, baby," he said.

She rolled her eyes. "I've already called John. I'm thinking if I get here really early Sunday, I could have several meals planned and prepped for your week. You shouldn't be eating takeout food every night. It's not good for you. I can cook. I'm happy to do it, and I don't work every single day of the week either."

He knew John only wanted her working part-time.

"How come you can't be here on Saturday?"

"To make up for my shift today. I had to leave early. It's more than fine. I don't mind helping out when I can."

"You love taking care of kids?" he asked.

"Is it weird that I just love taking care of people? I think the world is one shitty place most of the time, and if I can make it happier by just being nice or helping out, I will."

He took a cookie and bit into it, tasting the peanut butter, and moaned. "You can be nice to me anytime."

The timer went off, and she quickly rushed to the oven and pulled out two round pans. "I may have also baked a cake."

"You just don't stop, do you?"

She wrinkled her nose. "Not really. I don't like taking too long a break."

He watched as she placed the pans on cooling racks he didn't even know he owned. "You bought these?"

Her cheeks heated. "I don't want to be carrying mine all over the place. This way I can bake here when you need it. Also, if you ever find yourself another woman and she wants to bake or do something nice, it's always here."

Did he see a twinge of pain flash in her eyes? He couldn't be sure, but she didn't look happy about another woman being here or using her things. There wasn't going to be another woman. If everything went according to plan, then he intended to be part of her and John's life for a long time to come.

Especially if they shared a kid together. He glanced down her body, staring at her stomach, wondering if she was right now carrying his child. His cock swelled at the thought of her stomach full, rounded, looking so fucking sexy.

He knew they were going to have a few bumps down the road. There was no doubt about it. They were planning on getting her pregnant without her even knowing about it. He didn't want to hurt Scarlett, but they had set this course in motion right now.

John had a plan, and he wanted to be part of it.

"There's not going to be a woman here," he said. "I have no intention of being with anyone else." Now that he had a taste of Scarlett, no woman would ever meet up to those standards. She was a one–of-a-kind woman, and he wasn't going to hurt another woman by pretending there was a chance.

"Oh, you're not worried about being lonely?"

"No. I'm good. Believe me, you weren't married to Cherry like I was."

She gave one of her chuckles. "You're right, I wasn't. I'm sorry it didn't work out between you two."

"It's okay. She wasn't the one anyway." *The one* had married his best friend, not that he blamed her. She was a beauty unlike anyone else.

The timer went off, and she removed the pans from the cake tin, placing them on the cooling rack. He watched as she went back and forth gathering things. On the back counter, she had a glass bowl that had some chocolate-looking stuff inside.

After about thirty minutes of walking around the kitchen cleaning up, the scent of lamb filling the kitchen, he watched as she iced the cake.

Some of the chocolate frosting got on her finger, and his cock sprang to life as she sucked it into her mouth, moaning as she did.

"Does it taste good?" he asked.

"The best. I love chocolate frosting."

Once she finished, he grabbed her hand, running her finger across the palette knife and sucking it into his mouth. "It does taste good."

Her eyes dilated, and he was about to say something more when his cell phone pinged.

John: **On way.**

"John's heading here."

"Good. I did text him early to let him know I was cooking dinner here. If you want we can go home."

"Not happening. You guys are staying for

dinner."

"Bennie, Carlos," Scarlett said, calling toward his boys. "Will you set the table?"

The sounds of their footsteps echoed around the house. They were in the kitchen, grabbing whatever they needed to take to the table. He watched as she opened the oven and pulled out a large Dutch oven. She gave a little *oomph* as she placed it on the stove, closing the oven door behind her.

She opened the lid and used a large, sharp knife to test.

"All cooked."

The sound of the doorbell rang, and it was his cue to answer.

John looked pissed off, but the moment he saw him, he forced a smile.

"You okay?"

"Yeah, I'm fine. Just a bad day at the office."

"Those numbers can really attack you, can't they?"

"And the people. They don't like what I tell them."

John always looked good in a suit. It was one of the reasons Gunner had never pushed for him to be part of the club. The leather wouldn't have suited him as much.

"Holy shit, look at you," John said as Bennie walked past.

"Goldman's kid, right?"

"Yep."

At the look on John's face, Gunner laughed. "Goldman your last client?"

"Yeah, a pissed-off one as well. He thinks he can threaten everyone in town, and it pissed me off. I had to remind him that his wealth didn't mean shit to me."

"His son's an asshole," Bennie said, leaving them alone.

"What did he want you to do?"

"Pay a large fortune to the school 'for tax reasons,' he said. Bullshit. He wanted me to make a check out to the principal. I told him that I'm not lying on his fucking tax forms." He shook his head. "I hate that fucker. I really do."

"Don't worry. I'll be having a word with him." He slapped John on the back and pressed his head to his friend's. He wanted to comfort John, to make him feel better. Stroking his fingers over his pulse, he forced himself to stop.

It was moments like this when his yearning for John came back.

He'd been fighting it for a long time, and he didn't want to ruin their friendship. They'd had each other's back all of their lives and would continue to do so.

"Am I interrupting?" Scarlett asked, drawing their attention to her.

John pulled away, going toward her. "Nope. You never interrupt anything."

Gunner watched, mesmerized, as John pulled her in close, claiming her lips. He wasn't jealous. He loved watching John and Scarlett like this.

Glancing down John's body and the way he was standing, Gunner saw that his friend was aroused, his cock bulging at the front.

Scarlett moaned, and his own dick was threatening to tear its way out of his pants.

She chuckled. "Not here. There are children."

"You do know they're pretty much grown men now," John said, kissing her neck.

"So, they're still boys." Her cheeks were on fire.

Gunner laughed. "They could probably teach us old boys a few things." He winked at John. "Especially in this day and age. We had to learn through porn mags. Now they've got all that internet stuff. Porn at their fingertips."

She covered her cheeks. "I don't want to think or know about this. You're both not helping me."

He laughed and watched as she left to go into the kitchen.

"It doesn't matter what she's cooking. It'll turn out fantastic," John said.

"Her cooking is amazing. You're lucky all around really, aren't you, John?"

His friend burst out laughing. "Your jealousy is showing."

They stood in the doorway of the kitchen, watching as she sliced some bread. Bennie and Carlos were there, and she made them use oven mitts to carry the pot to the table. He watched her with his boys, and knew she'd make an incredible mother.

She had a knack for it, and his boys adored her. Just like he did.

****

John ran over the reports once more, determined to find what he needed, what was being hidden from him. Gunner was counting on him to find the loose cannon within the club, but since they'd been spending a lot more time together, there hadn't been money going missing. Combing his way through the books, he rubbed at his temple, thinking about his friend and also his wife.

Last night, before leaving Gunner's home, his wife had started her period. She'd been so embarrassed that she had come out of the bathroom, and made their excuses to leave before he could even think of what was wrong. They'd been having a lovely time. Gunner's boys were sweet boys, and he liked their company. They also adored his wife, and he saw that in the way they were always smiling at her.

It was only when he got home that she told him the truth. They'd been in the bathroom, and she had sobbed into his jacket. He hated this part the most. The lost opportunity. She knew she felt guilty for crying on his jacket as well, seeing as he couldn't do anything about it.

Kissing her head, he'd held her throughout it.

Right now, recalling his woman sobbing, he couldn't bring himself to look over the documents.

"You okay?" Gunner asked, knocking on his door.

He jerked up, looking at his friend. "Yeah, I'm fine."

"You didn't answer any of my calls. Last night, this morning."

"You took Bennie back to school?"

"Of course. Spoke to the principal. I let him know that if he thinks of making any underhand deals when it comes to my son, he should be aware that I know everything. I see everything."

John laughed, but he didn't feel it.

Gunner closed the door, taking a seat at the desk. "You found anything? Is this why you're acting … weird?"

"Scarlett got her period last night."

"Oh." He saw the disappointment in his friend's face.

"She couldn't stop sobbing. I held her, knowing there was nothing I could do. I couldn't make her pregnant." He ran a hand down his face.

"Maybe we should tell her?"

"You didn't want her to know." John shook his

head. "I don't want to tell her. I don't want her to know yet. It has only been one month. I want to try again."

"John?"

"No, those two boys are yours, right? She wants a baby. Every single month she doesn't have one, she's going to have a meltdown like that and I can't handle that. I need … we need a baby, Gunner. I can't … it's fucking with my head." He pushed back his chair and moved to stare out of the window.

"I've got an appointment with Goldman this afternoon," Gunner said. "Want to come? It could be fun."

"And do what?"

"Let him know that if he thinks about threatening you, you're not afraid of getting your hands dirty." Gunner stood behind him, gripping his shoulders. "I'm sorry about Scarlett. I'm sorry I didn't make your dreams come true."

"Saying it like that, it sounds fucking corny even to me."

"Yeah, well, it really is corny," Gunner said.

He burst out laughing.

"You need to clear your head."

"I need to find your leak first."

"My leak will be there when you get back. Come on, it could be fun."

"Okay."

He left his office, letting his secretary know that he'd be back shortly.

Gunner had come to his office in a car, and John raised his brow. "Doesn't the MC handle business on bikes?"

"Yeah, they do. But I like to keep things fresh. If I only ride then they expect me. In a car, now that completely throws them off."

He shakes his head, completely disagreeing with his friend. "You're so full of shit, you know that, right?"

"It's good shit though. You've got to admit."

"You're crazy as well."

"Oh, come on, you know you love it," Gunner said.

He'd missed this easy banter. This was what got him through his time in the service. There had been moments when he'd feared for his life, and knowing Gunner was there with him, they'd gotten out of many a sticky situation, and that shit never got old. At least, it didn't get old for him.

Sitting in the passenger seat, he removed his jacket, loosened his tie, and ran fingers through his hair.

"It's like you're getting into character."

"I need a break and beer right now. I'm fucked in the head, and I've got to get that shit under control."

Gunner didn't say anything as he turned out of town.

"This meeting going down in top secret?" he asked.

"Yes."

They were heading down the long strip of road when John heard a feminine scream coming from the trunk of the car.

"Who is that?" John asked. He was very much aware of what Gunner was capable of.

"Oh, that, it's his mistress. You see, I've got contacts all over. Goldman is a mean old son of a bitch. But I have it on good authority that he's also got a good heart. He fell in love with one of the maids who worked for him when he was younger."

"Gunner, I don't like this."

"What? I need to send a clear message to this fucker, okay? No one, and I mean no one, messes with my boys. You always question my methods. If I've learned one thing being Prez of the MC, everyone responds to fear, to violence. You don't like it, but it's true."

"There are other ways."

"Yeah, well, when it comes to my club and my boys, this is the only way."

"Why don't you deal with your thief in that way?"

"Can't. I have to have solid proof before I point the finger. My own stupid-as-shit rule, and it was a fucking stupid one."

John rubbed his eyes. He wasn't part of the MC, and he didn't see a problem with Gunner having a woman locked in the trunk of his car. This was another part of himself he tried to hide. He wasn't always a good man.

He didn't give a shit about what society said he should be or do.

Being a businessman, he put on the façade for his clients, but the truth was, he didn't give a fuck about being prim and proper.

After serving in the military, accounting was, in fact, a relaxing day to him.

"You can't kidnap a woman."

"I have every intention of letting her go. I'm a good boy like that, John."

"She's innocent."

"Yeah, and sometimes bad things happen to innocent people. This fucker thinks he can let his kid do that shit to mine. Goldman may own half the town, but I own the entire fucking town. No one takes strikes at my kid and thinks they're going to get away with it. I don't let shit like that stand. Not now, not ever."

John held his hands up. This was Gunner's call.

He was just along for the ride.

"So how are things going at the club?" he asked. The club had never been for him, but it was part of Gunner's life, and he wanted to be there for his friend, especially now with someone actively fighting against him.

"You know I can't talk to you about club business."

"I know. I'm not interested on the runs you do or what you transport. I'm worried about you."

"Aww, ain't you sweet?"

"Cut the crap, Gunner."

"I know from a reliable source that someone from the club is reaching out. They want in on cartel business. I don't do that shit. I like my town just the way it is."

"You can't have the MC dealing with cartel shit. That's a sure way of causing some serious mess."

"I know," Gunner said. "But I can't just come out and accuse anyone. That's not the way the club works."

"Do you have any idea who it could be?"

"Whoever is stealing from the club."

"You got those security cameras I told you about?"

"Yep. I've already placed them where I need them to be. I've just got to wait for them to make a move."

John knew that the only reason Gunner didn't have security footage was purely because whatever was found on those tapes could be used against them. He'd had to work to convince them. The moment they found the rat, they could all come down and be destroyed. Every single piece of evidence.

Gunner drove up to a secure location outside of town. It was near the old haunted house that kept kids away from it, until Halloween when they all dared each other to go inside. The only reason he knew about it was because he'd gotten a call from Gunner one night when Bennie decided to take the chance.

Goldman was already there with two of his bodyguards.

"You think he's scared?" John asked.

Gunner snorted. "Probably pissing his pants." He parked the car abruptly. "There's a gun in the glovebox."

Pulling it out, John removed the safety and placed the weapon in the back of his pants as he climbed out of the car. Following Gunner's lead, he kept back, assessing the large men. They were security detail. From the way they were standing, they were not very well-trained.

To John it looked like they were more bulk than brains.

"What do you want?" Goldman asked.

"I want your kid to lay off mine. Not only that, get the charges dropped."

This was news to John.

"Your boy marked Finn's face."

"Your son is a bully and a prick. I don't care how you do it, just do it."

Goldman started laughing. "Oh, come on. You really think standing here with your pissy accountant and your attitude I'm going to give in? Please. I've got a bigger dick than either of you combined."

John winced.

He knew that Gunner took it as a personal affront to be criticized about his cock. Anyone who questioned him would always end up with a bloody nose. It was weird considering Gunner had a big dick to begin with.

Some insults were just a lot harder to swallow. *Pun intended!*

Gunner opened the trunk of his car. A feminine scream filled the air, and John raised his gun just as the two security guards did. He couldn't take them seriously. He doubted they could take him seriously dressed in a suit, next to a biker.

"How about we settle this fair and square?" Gunner said. He had a gun poised at the woman's temple. "I don't give a fuck about this bitch, Goldman. I can see that you do. You want to start a war with me, go ahead. Your entire family line would be out before the end of the day and I'd have fun doing it."

"He really would," John said.

Being in the military had hardened Gunner in more ways than it had John. They had both fought for their country, but to Gunner that didn't mean shit to every guy on the street. He fought to save his own land, not for anyone else.

"You better pick, Goldman. My hand's getting a little fucking twitchy."

"I'll drop the charges. Everything will be fine. I'll talk to Finn. He'll stay the fuck away from your boy."

"Call them now." He grabbed the girl harder, making her cry out louder.

Goldman was already on the phone, dealing with the local sheriff. Once he was done, Gunner smirked.

John raised his gun, shooting one of the men in the leg. "I'd get him to a hospital if I were you, or a doctor."

"Give her to me," Goldman said.

"As soon as your men go."

Goldman gave the two men the order, and they were gone.

Gunner pushed the girl toward Goldman. "You better be careful of the people you step on, Goldman. If I could find her, it wouldn't take long for another person who's not so patient."

Gunner climbed behind the wheel, and John did

the same. He glanced in the rearview mirror, watching as Goldman treated the woman in his arms like a delicate flower.

"Did you have any intention of killing her?"

"Fuck, no, but they didn't need to know that. I don't kill innocents unless I have no choice."

"You're crazy."

"Thanks for taking out the security guards. I think one of them did piss himself. Damn, it was good to have you by my side. That VP badge is yours, you know. You're never too old to become a club member."

"I'm sure Kent would love that."

"Kent's a fucking pussy. You always got my back. Besides, I find what I need, his days are numbered."

And he always would have Gunner's back.

****

"Are you okay?" John asked, coming into the sitting room. Scarlett had already eaten dinner. John had called her to let her know that he wouldn't be home. She didn't know how to handle it. She'd gotten her period, and he'd been out most of the night.

Feeling a lump in her throat, she looked toward her husband, wondering what was going on. He looked a little … tipsy.

"Have you been drinking?"

"A little bit. Don't worry. I called a cab from Gunner's place. It's all good."

She nodded.

"You look sad," he said.

"It's fine."

"No, it's not fine. I can tell that you've got that pissy voice. The one that's still sexy as fuck but the one that also tells me I've made you sad."

She placed the book in her lap and stared at him.

"I don't know what you want me to say."

"Tell me what's wrong."

"I start my period, and you don't come home. It's really late, and you're drunk."

He sat on the sofa beside her. "That's not why I've been out. I had to help Gunner. Did you know Goldman, the bastard, actually tried to press charges against Bennie?"

"He did?"

"Yep. It's okay though. We got it dealt with." He dropped his head to her shoulder. "I'm not avoiding you, my baby. You're the best thing that ever happened to me. I love you so much. All the time. You're all I can think about."

She pressed her lips together, trying not to smile.

John drunk was so adorable and so cute. He won her over each and every time.

"It's not going to work. I'm mad at you."

"I know, baby. I want us to have a baby so bad. I know you want it too. I feel like a total loser because I can't give you what you want." His hand pressed to her stomach. "We'll get there though. I know we will."

She frowned. He didn't make any sense.

Scarlett didn't see them getting anywhere purely because he didn't want to use any of the other channels.

Taking his hand, she pressed a kiss to his fingers. "I've got you. That is all that matters."

"Mine."

"What?"

"That's what I thought when I saw you. I thought 'mine.' You're mine. Always mine. She's going to belong to me."

She burst out laughing. "Come on, you. I think it's time for you to head to bed."

Putting her book down, he snatched it up. "Were

113

you reading a dirty book?"

She rolled her eyes, leaving him on the sofa to read her book as she checked on the house.

His cell phone was on the counter, and she picked it up, finding Gunner's name and sending him a quick text.

She didn't look at his cell phone again, placing it on the coffee table.

"*They both fucked her, taking her harder than ever before. Going deeper, fucking her with their rock-hard cocks. She wanted it, yearned for it, craved it. She wanted to be used, to be fucked, to be owned.*" John finished reading and smiled. "Kinky."

"You're pushing cute now."

"I like that my wife loves dirty things. It makes me so hot to think of you doing all those dirty things yourself."

She stepped toward him, and he placed a hand between her thighs.

"Shit, sorry, it's that time of the month." He held his hands up in surrender.

Unable to help herself, she cupped his face. "Let's get you to bed."

"You know, me and Gunner could totally do that."

"Do what?"

"Fuck you. Take you at the same time. One in your ass, one in your pussy."

She ignored the heat that flooded her at the thought.

John, however, ran a hand down her ass, cupping her cheeks. "So beautiful. I love it when I spread them wide, and you're always so responsive to me. I want to give you everything your heart desires."

"You do."

She got him upstairs and decided against the shower. John was a large man, and she didn't have the strength to get him to stand up, wash him, and then bring him back to the room.

Removing his clothes, she left on his boxer briefs and tucked him in bed.

"You'd like it, you know," he said.

She removed her gown and climbed into bed. He pulled her into his arms. "What would I like?"

"Me and Gunner, taking you at the same time. We'd drive you crazy first. Make it so that you were begging for us." He cupped her hip. "I'd take your ass and Gunner could take that pussy. So tight and hot. You make him so hard."

"Do you love seeing Gunner's cock?"

"Yeah, I do. Does it taste as good as it looks?"

She gasped at his admission, but she didn't say anything.

"I bet it does. With the tip completely covered in his pre-cum. You lick that tip, and I bet it's so soft and hard."

"Yes."

He was starting to get sleepy. His hand moved around her stomach, holding her. Seconds passed, and she heard his snores.

The way he was talking, it sounded like John had never been with Gunner, had never sucked his cock.

She thought about the two men in her life, the way they'd taken control of hers, and how one night had seemed to become more.

What would it be like to have both Gunner and John in her bed but wanting each other as well as wanting her?

She closed her eyes, thinking about Gunner touching her husband, stroking his body. John was a very handsome, sexy man. So was Gunner. She thought about them both holding each other, kissing, needing each other. More heat flooded her pussy.

Did they both want each other? She didn't know the answer to that question. Did she want them to be together? Her body was on fire at just the thought.

Slowly, she fell asleep, thinking about Gunner, John, and herself. Could they work together? Could she give her husband what he so clearly craved but refused to put into words?

It felt like she'd only closed her eyes for a minute and in the next it was morning. John was still out cold, and glancing at the clock, she saw it was a little after seven. Climbing out of bed, she was careful not to wake him.

She went to the bathroom and did her business before making her way downstairs to start with some coffee and toast.

She was buttering a slice, slathering it with some jam when John stumbled into the room.

As she placed some painkillers on the side and a glass of water, she watched him collapse into a chair. "I feel like someone is banging my head from the inside trying to get out."

"Alcohol will do that to you."

"You're happy about this," he said.

"I'm not. It's kind of funny."

"Your husband being in pain is funny?"

"Yes. What was it, whiskey, bourbon?"

"Whiskey. I don't even think it was expensive. I think it was the cheap shit."

"Well that cheap shit makes you look awful." She placed a coffee and some toast in front of him. "I know you think you're going to be sick, but you always feel better after a slice or two."

"What would I do without you?"

"Starve and feel sorry for yourself. I texted Gunner last night in case you were too busy reading my book to notice."

"What did he say?"

"I don't know. I didn't check."

"Did you look at anything else?"

"No, why?" She stared at him with a frown. "Did you not want me checking your phone?"

"No, no, it's fine. Ignore me. I'm just trying to make sure I've not thought of a present to get you or something. I don't want to spoil any of my surprises."

She shrugged. "I didn't check, and you don't have to get me anything." She took a bite out of her toast, watching him.

"What?"

"This thing going on between you, Gunner, and me, what does it all mean?"

"I don't understand."

"Well, we were together with you watching. Then I was with him, and then I was with you. I just … if I'm alone with him, are there any rules? I have no idea what to do."

"The rule is if you both want to, then do it."

"That feels a lot like cheating."

"I disagree. I'd want to know every single detail."

"You don't want to share me, but with Gunner it's okay."

"I trust him with you. He's my best friend." He took her hand, pressing a kiss to her knuckles. "I have no jealousy when it comes to him. Of course, I'd love to be there to watch. You know I love to watch."

"I know. You're kinky." She winked at him, and he smiled. This was what she'd been missing. Their time together where everything seemed to be normal. The way he looked at her, touched her. "Do you get off on thinking about Gunner touching me?"

"Yes. It makes me horny to know he wants you so much." He cupped her cheeks. "How are you feeling?"

His hand moved toward her stomach. With the counter between them it made it rather awkward.

She'd suffered with bad periods a lot in her life. Sometimes she'd had to call in work to take time off because they were so bad.

"It's fine at the moment. Manageable."

"I'm sorry I left you last night."

"You really should stop apologizing. It's fine. I'm fine." She kissed him again. "Stop stressing. You've still got work today, and so do I. I'm going to go and get ready."

"I meant what I said, baby," John said, making her stop at the doorway.

"What?"

"You want it with Gunner, I want to know about it. Every single little detail. I want you to enjoy it as well, and to know that there's no way you're divorcing me."

"You're way too kinky." She blew him a kiss and made her way upstairs.

He wanted her to be with Gunner and that was fine, but what about what *he* wanted?

Chapter Seven

Bennie returned to school, and all charges were dropped. Gunner focused on the traitor within the club, the one that wanted to take his role away from him. There was no time to spend with John or Scarlett, as that took his primary focus as well as his ex-wife constantly showing up demanding money.

"I'm used to a lifestyle. You need to pay me, Gunner. I mean it. I'm not leaving here without it."

Billy and Ford were there, watching the scene, as she stood at his desk looking like death warmed over. She'd lost even more weight in the past few weeks, and that was saying something seeing as she was already deathly thin to begin with.

"I'm not paying you another dime, Cherry. The only reason you got that other money was for the boys."

"Then I want them back."

"You were never there for them. You were a fucking shit wife and terrible mother. They're mine now. They're staying with me."

"You think that married whore is better than me, is that it? You think they've got something better with her."

He glared at her, wanting nothing more than to shoot her and bury her.

She was still his two boys' mother, and that made him hold back.

Sitting back, he stared at his ex-wife. She'd always been jealous of Scarlett, and he knew it was for a good reason as well. His feelings for Scarlett were always strong, and they were never going away.

"Billy, Ford, leave," he said.

He waited for them to go. The door closed behind

them, and he stared at Cherry.

"Come on, Gunner. I know you like it a little rough. You always liked it when we fought."

"You're fucking insane. I don't want your used-up pussy."

Cherry smirked. "You know … a little birdie told me that Scarlett can't have kids, or should I say, John."

This made him tense up. He looked at his ex, and waited for whatever it was she wanted to say.

"It's strange, but aren't you visiting them a lot more now than when you used to." She tilted her head to the side. He knew she was having fun, but he let her. "I wonder if you're going to be the one to knock her up. I can see it now, John takes claim of the baby you put inside her."

"How do you know their medical issues?" he asked.

"People talk, Gunner. I happen to know a couple of women who like to get close to the club, and, being as I was a former old lady to the Prez, they were more than happy to give me the information that I needed."

"They broke the law."

"So. Give me what I want and I won't tell a soul that you're working to putting your baby into your best friend's wife." She chuckled. "It must hurt John something bad knowing that he can't give her what you so easily can."

"You think I give a shit about you knowing about this?" he asked.

"No. But I think Scarlett and John would."

He gritted his teeth. He couldn't kill her, not yet at least, but the threat she posed was there and he didn't like dealing with threats.

"What do you want?" he asked.

"The same as you've been paying for the boys

plus a thousand. I want this to keep going for a long time. I'm going to need to remember to keep quiet."

He opened his wallet, pulling out the notes she needed.

"Until next month." She blew a kiss, and he watched her disappear.

He leaned back in his chair, his anger bubbling beneath the surface. First, he'd deal with his wife, and then he'd deal with the woman that couldn't keep personal information to herself. Either way, Cherry had started something that he was going to make sure he ended.

Picking up his cell phone, he dialed John's number.

"I hate you still. You shouldn't have let me drink," John said.

"I want to know who your doctor is and the nurse that saw you and Scarlett."

"Why?"

Gunner let him know what had just happened. John didn't sound happy at all. "I know who it was. She asked about the club. I think she's even been around the club."

He made a note of the woman in question.

"What are you going to do?" John asked.

"I'm going to pay her a little visit. Scarlett turns up pregnant you don't want the world to know it's mine, do you?"

John hesitated. "I'm ... what if it was known?"

"What do you mean?" Gunner asked.

"Forget about it. Forget I ever said anything." John hung up and Gunner stared at his cell, more confused than ever before.

"What the fuck?"

Billy and Ford came back in. "You wanted us,

boss?"

"A couple of the girls said some guys were sniffing around the toy shop. They didn't like them. Said they kept asking questions and touching them. I want you guys to go over and check it out," Gunner said.

The sex shop they owned was near an old industrial place. There were several different stores all within one unit. The club had snatched the building up, and the toy shop was booming. Sex sold more than anything else.

Some of the guys wanted to invest in a porn studio, but he wasn't into that, at least not yet. He had yet to be given proof that porn made any decent money.

He'd seen the amateur crap they were selling online, and he wasn't impressed, not in the slightest.

Once Billy and Ford were gone, he got one of his guys who could find anyone with just a name and a few details to get him an address.

Her name was Tanya, and that was all he cared about. She lived in a small apartment twenty minutes away.

With her name and address, he left the clubhouse, only to be stopped by Kent. "You need any help?"

He didn't trust Kent. Out of all of the men in the club, it was Kent he believed was the one responsible for taking the money, and for wanting cartel business. When the matter of working for the cartels came up, it had been Kent who'd been screaming the loudest. He wanted that business and the kind of money working for them would bring. What Kent didn't understand was the risks of such a decision.

"Yeah, come on," he said.

Gunner wasn't afraid of Kent, but it had been some time since he'd been with him, and it would give him a chance to talk.

"We're not taking the bikes?" Kent asked.

"Nope. It's been a few weeks since we took the time to catch up, you know."

"There's been church."

"It's not the same."

He started up the car, and he saw Kent hesitate. There was nothing for him to call this fucker out other than his gut instinct. Kent climbed into the car, and he took off out of the parking lot.

"What you been up to, Kent?"

"Screwing, drinking, partying, working. Just the same old shit over and over again."

"You don't have a problem with the last run, do you? I know the cartels were happy."

"We do what needs to be done."

"You want the extra dough from the runs?" Gunner asked.

"Getting in with the cartels is smart. They've got the drugs, the guns, the girls, and it's a party every single fucking day. No one touches them."

"You mean the Feds don't touch them. They've got men watching them at every single point. It's not smart. It's fucking dangerous. Most of the people associated with them have a very short shelf life. It's not smart at all." He glanced over at Kent, seeing the man's teeth clench. "Most of the guys voted at the table, Kent. They don't want that kind of business in their lives."

"You're right."

Gunner may be right, but the way Kent was acting, that fucker was hiding something. "You ever thought about going to them? Working for them?" he asked.

"The club is my life. It's what I wanted."

"You want the patch," he said.

He knew without a doubt that Kent wanted the

patch, the Prez's patch. Gunner had won this patch, and there was no way he'd remove it. Only over his dead body would anyone get this away from him.

Kent didn't say anything else.

Parking the car, Gunner stared up at the depressing building.

"You got a new girl or something?" Kent asked.

"Just got to take care of a problem."

"Is it a really big problem?"

He glanced at Kent. "Yes."

Checking the number on his cell phone, he made his way toward the building. There wasn't any security. People could just come and go as they pleased. Ignoring the looks of the people hanging out at the front, he took the stairs, going two at a time. Kent followed him.

Standing in front of the door that was hers, he knew from the details his guy had given him that she wasn't home.

Bending forward, he picked the lock, opening it up.

The apartment was nice. There was none of the moldy smell that had been out in the hallway.

"Have a seat," he said, pointing at the sofa. Opening the fridge, he looked inside seeing all health food, which wrinkled his nose. He didn't trust anyone who liked healthy shit.

Looking around her apartment, he wasn't impressed by what he saw.

Flicking his keys back and forth, he watched Kent. "You know anything about the books being doctored?"

Kent frowned but showed no other sign of hiding something. Gunner watched him closely. "What do you mean?"

"Money that might not have been accounted for."

"I don't know."

He stared at Kent and knew without a doubt that this fucker was the reason. Before he could take him out, he had to have proof.

"You know if money is going missing, you need to bring it to the table," Kent said, looking at him. "Boys will want to know where it's gone."

"I will."

"Why haven't you?"

"I've been working on finding out who's taking it."

"You got someone in mind?" Kent asked.

"I've got a few ideas." He didn't get to say anything else as the door to the apartment started to open.

****

"Do you want the cream or the blue?" Scarlett asked.

John looked up from his desk to see his wife holding two swatches of fabric. She'd come to visit him for lunch, just like she used to do. "What is this for?"

"The spare bedroom."

"But that's for the nursery. Shouldn't it be a neutral color?" John watched as the smile on her face dropped and he hated seeing that look in her eyes. "Baby, what's going on?"

"I don't see a reason to keep the room bare anymore. I want to decorate it. We could turn it into your office."

He stood up, and moved around his desk, pulling her close. "No."

"Come on."

"I said no. It's staying as a nursery." He pushed some hair back off her face, staring into her brown eyes.

"You're not fair."

"I am always fair. It's not going to happen."

She blew out a breath.

"I've got to go out of town for a week on business," he said.

"You have? Since when?"

"One of my clients needs me to look over his books. He works in the city, three hours away. It could take a week."

She pouted; such a cute look. "Can I come with you?"

"You'll be bored all day, and I know you hate leaving the day care center. I've talked with Gunner. I want you to stay with him."

"Wow, I'm not a child, John. I can take care of myself."

John tilted her head back, taking her lips beneath his. "This will be the first time that I'm away from you. I don't want you to be on your own." Every other time he'd been away, he'd taken her with him. She had gotten the time off. This had been a quick decision, and his client was paying him triple to get to the city to help him out. "Please, do this for me."

"I feel like a child when you want me to do this."

He chuckled. "I know you're anything but a little girl." He ran his hand down her back. "I'm going to miss you. I'll call you every single night. You won't be alone."

"I hope not." She looked up at him. "Now the colors?"

"No. We're going to have a baby, and we're going to need that room for when we do."

"We've not talked about adoption. Do you want me to book an appointment? What do you want me to do?"

"I want you to not worry at all. To wait until I get home, and then we can talk about it."

"Fine. Okay."

He helped her into a chair, sitting next to her. He gave her the lunch she'd brought for him, opening his own to enjoy the cheese sandwiches.

John watched as she ate. All the while, she looked around his office. "You're not cheating on me, are you?"

He burst out laughing. "No, I'm really not. I can even show you the details of the client I'm working for, if you want. What we're going to be looking at."

"No, it's fine. It just seems weird that you're going away and I'm staying here."

"You'll be staying with Gunner."

"And he's happy with this?"

"Of course he is. His boys are as well. They get your cooking all to themselves. What's not to love? I'd take you with me, but you and I both know that Mary's looking for a reason to get rid of you, and you don't want that, do you?"

"No."

"It's going to be a week, tops. He's got quite a few accounts to go over. I'll call you every single night. I'll even get Gunner to hug you tight for me."

She signed again, this time even louder. "I don't see why I can't be alone. I'll be fine."

"This is for me, baby. I want to make sure you're safe. Please, do this for me."

She blew a raspberry, which he did find incredibly cute. "Fine, fine. I'll do this for you. I'll go home and pack you a bag, and make sure you're all okay."

"And you won't touch our nursery. I mean it, Scarlett. I don't want you to."

"I'll leave it."

"Good girl." He pressed a kiss to her head once more. "I better get back to work."

"I'll let you do that."

She stroked his cheek with a smile and pulled away. He hated it when she pulled away. All he wanted to do was hold her back in his arms once again, but he knew he couldn't do that.

He wasn't even trying to push Gunner and Scarlett together.

A client wanted him, needed him in fact, and he had to go to help. He'd promised that he would whenever the need arose.

If Scarlett didn't love her job so much, he'd tell her to quit, and take her with him. He knew how much she loved being with the kids. She didn't have to work, but he couldn't bring himself to force her to sit around home all day, waiting around for him.

Moving toward his window, he watched her leave. Once she was gone, he sat behind his desk and began working through his endless list of clients that he'd completed accounting information for. This could go from a simple quote of dealing with their taxes, to looking over their books, to any number of things.

Hours passed before a knock came at the door.

"I got your message," Gunner said. "I don't like being summoned. I feel like I've been called to the principal's office or worse, daddy's."

John laughed. "I've told Scarlett I have to go out of town."

"Okay. Is she happy about that?"

"No, she wants to come with me, and if I didn't know that she'd go crazy without a job, I'd let her. I want her to stay at your house. I've told her you're keeping an eye on her."

"John, we're friends and all that, but on shit like this you've got to consult me."

He stepped past his friend, closing the door

behind him. "You've got a problem taking care of my woman?"

"You know I haven't."

"I didn't think you'd see this as one either. While I'm gone, I want you to fuck her." John stared at Gunner seeing the muscle tick in the side of his jaw.

"I don't fuck on demand."

"Look, she's not pregnant. You've not been around—"

"I've had club business to take care of. You know, I've got that pesky problem of a thief who wants to take my patch. I'm watching my back twenty-four seven."

"I know. We want this, Gunner. Please."

"I'm actually starting to think I should just put my stuff in a cup, and you give it to her to insert."

John winced. "I want you to be part of this."

"Man, this is … she doesn't know."

"She knows that I like sharing her with you and only you. I've given her permission as well."

"Are you like her master or something now?"

"I want this, okay? I want you and her to be able to have this without me here. I'm going to ask her to tell me everything that happens. There's not going to be any secrets here. It's not like she's cheating on me. I started all this because I can't…" He stopped feeling the emotion well up inside him. Staring at his desk, he saw the two color swatches she'd left. "Do you know what these are?" He held them both up for Gunner to see.

"Color things. I can't remember."

"Scarlett wants me to pick a color so she can redecorate the nursery. She wants to turn it into my office as it's useless right now because we're not going to be having kids." He saw the pain in Gunner's eyes. "She wants babies, Gunner. I can't give them to her. I can't even … I won't let her hurt for this. Please."

"Okay, I didn't … I'll do it."

Gunner stepped toward him, gripping his shoulder and pulling him close. John allowed himself the pleasure of resting his head on his shoulder, but that was all. He didn't allow anything else, and he closed his eyes as he did it, not wanting to give anything away. How could leather and grease have such a heady combination?

He was going insane.

It was the only word for it.

"This is on her though. I won't make her do anything."

"I know, and I wouldn't want you to."

John reluctantly pulled away. "I know I'm asking for a lot."

"Yeah, well, as friends, we're supposed to ask a great deal of each other." Gunner ran fingers through his hair.

"Still nothing on Kent?"

"Nope. The security feeds are showing nothing."

"Your books are clean as well. The money has been going missing for two weeks before you noticed it. Now he knows you're onto it."

"I want to know what he did with that money," Gunner said.

"Only way of doing that is by looking through his room or his stuff."

"I can't do that."

"Why not?"

"We're a club, man. A fucking team. I start going through his shit on a hunch and I find jack, he gets this patch, and then the only thing I recommend is leaving town. He'll tear this entire place apart. Cartels and shit. He'd make this place a circus within twenty-four hours. He thinks this patch gives him immunity or shit." Gunner shook his head. "He can't have it."

"Sleeping with one eye open?" he asked.

"Yes."

"When I get back I want you and your boys at my place."

"Why?"

"Because you've not stepped out of line. What if Kent was hoping you'd accuse him? You accuse him without any evidence that it was actually him, they vote your ass out, and he gets the patch as VP. I imagine the table was divided over the cartel problem."

"Some were unsure, but they voted to remain out," Gunner said.

"Then I won't put it past Kent to try to take you out. I wish I didn't have to go away for this shit."

"I can take care of your woman."

"*Our* woman, and I know you can." John ran his fingers through his hair. "I don't like either of you vulnerable."

"I'm not. I've got my shit locked tight. I'll keep us good. Promise."

"Good." He didn't want anything to happen to his friend. A life without Gunner it just didn't seem right, not to him. "I better head back. I don't like to be gone for long."

"Think about what I said."

"I will."

John once again watched his friend go. It was only going to be a matter of time before Kent made his move. When that time came, John would be ready. Most of the men and women in town believed he was just an accountant who was friends with Gunner. He never bragged about the badges he'd won or his training in the military. Whenever he was asked what he did prior to accounting, he told them he went traveling. They didn't know his experience at taking out targets, or how deadly he could become with a gun. Gunner knew, and that was why he wanted the element of surprise.

To protect his family, he'd do just about anything.

****

Scarlett stood in Gunner's doorway, feeling a little nervous. She'd never stayed the night.

"Are you okay, Mrs. Williams?" Carlos asked.

"Yeah, yeah, I'm fine."

"Dad, Mrs. Williams is here." Bennie shouted over the loud music. Seconds later the music went off, and she made her way toward the kitchen where Gunner stood. He was washing his hands. It seemed strange to see him in the kitchen. She kind of liked it.

"I was cleaning potatoes. Boys, go and get your homework done. Are you ready to see your room?" he asked.

"Yes."

Gunner took the suitcase from her and carried it up his staircase. Gunner had a nice home. It was much bigger than hers and John's. She didn't need a big house even though John kept trying to convince her to move. They had plenty of money, he'd always say to her. She didn't want him to think she was after him for his money.

He opened a door to the guest bedroom, going straight to the bed to put her suitcase on it. "Carlos and Bennie are down the hall. That's my room, and we share a bathroom." He pointed at the room that adjoined, opening the door. She stepped inside with him as he used the other door, showing it was his room.

"Why do you have two connecting rooms? Did your wife stay here?"

Gunner chuckled. "Cherry was already long gone from my life by the time I bought this place. I'd divorced her. This place wasn't on the market until about a month after. I snatched it up, modernized it, and here we are."

"I always have liked your home."

"Thank you." He stepped out of the bedroom. "If you need anything just give me a call."

"You're cooking dinner?" she asked.

"No. I'm cleaning potatoes for you. John said you make really good steak and potatoes, but you hate washing them."

She chuckled. "Yes. Okay. I'll put the few things I've got away, and then I'll be with you."

He moved toward her, and she gasped at how handsome he was. She stayed perfectly still, waiting for him to say something, anything.

Suddenly, he stopped, and left her alone. Her heart was racing, her nipples hard. Licking her dry lips, she didn't waste any time, putting her few items of clothing into the closet. Once that was done, she ran her hand over the bed. The sheets were so soft, and she thought about Gunner, the way he'd fucked her that first night with the roughness of the sofa beneath her.

Pushing those thoughts aside, she pinned her long tresses up and made her way downstairs. She passed Bennie and Carlos in the living room. They both had their heads in a book, writing away. She didn't bother to disturb them and found Gunner in the kitchen up to his elbows in water, washing like crazy. This made her chuckle especially as she saw the mountain of potatoes already waiting for her to take care of.

"Have I done too much?"

"It's fine. We can dry them and store them. It means I don't have to wait around for a potato scrubber." While he finished off what he was doing, she got to work on the potatoes. She rubbed each of them with a little oil and placed them on a baking tray.

Scarlett knew from previous experience that all the men had large appetites in this family, so she was sure to put in extra.

Once they were baking in the oven, she took out the steaks, pricking them with a fork before rubbing seasoning all on them. Instead of placing them back in the fridge before grilling, she placed them on the counter, away from the oven, so that they could get to room temperature.

With each job done, she got to work on clearing away the potatoes.

"The boys were really happy that you decided to stay for the week," Gunner said.

"They were?"

"Yep, they were missing your cooking."

"I stocked your fridge three days ago." She'd been making double batches of everything so that they had more than enough food to keep them going.

"We kind of ate it all."

"Wow, okay. You eat more than anyone I know." She laughed. "Don't worry about it. I'll figure something out."

They worked together to finish cleaning up the kitchen. When it was all done, Gunner opened himself a beer while she grated cheese and fried up some bacon. The potatoes didn't take long. She pulled them out of the oven, splitting them open and scooping out the flesh. All the time that she worked on making loaded potatoes, she was aware of Gunner watching her. Her body felt overly warm.

Her pussy was already on fire, especially as John had asked her to tell him everything that happened. She didn't know if he was hot at the thought of her being with Gunner, or at the man himself.

She still hadn't said anything, and she didn't

know how to bring the two men together. She truly believed they both wanted each other. Their need for each other was there, and so easy to see in the way they held each other or looked at each other.

It was a lot easier to read with John, as she'd been with him for a long time. When it came to Gunner, he was a lot harder to read.

Once the potatoes were back in the oven, she heated a griddle pan and waited.

Staring at Gunner's blue eyes, she was caught by how mesmerizing he was. They were beautiful, clear, startling, shocking.

Biting her lip, she forced herself to move away. Going for the steaks, she picked them up, feeling him move behind her. "I don't want you to be nervous while you're here."

"I'm not."

"I can see it in your eyes. You're a sucky liar, Scarlett. Has John told you?"

"He's told me that if it happens, it does. He wants to know about it."

"Kinky bastard." Gunner's lips grazed her neck, and she closed her eyes as the pleasure shot through her body. He held her arms and breathed in her scent. "Do you want me to stop?"

She shook her head.

"I'm going to need actual words."

Biting her lip, she opened her lips, and spoke. "No, I don't want you to stop."

"Are you wet for me right now?"

"Yes."

His hand rested on her stomach and she bit her lip, trying to focus on what she was doing. "I need to cook the steaks," she said.

"I know. You're not afraid of me, are you?"

This made her frown. "No, of course not." She turned to look at him, seeing the worry in his eyes, which he masked within a second. "What would make you think for even a second that I would be afraid of you?"

He held his hands up. "I scare a lot of people."

"You don't scare me." She stepped around him, feeling the arousal ebb away at his words. "Does it bother you that people are scared of you?"

"When I need to scare them, no. When I don't want to scare them, yes."

"I'm not afraid. I've seen you drunk." It had been many years ago after he got his divorce. Both he and John had celebrated the night at their house, and she'd put them both to bed.

It had been cute.

Putting the steaks on the grill, she called for the boys to set the table, which they did really quickly.

"I'm starving," Carlos said.

"Too fucking right," Bennie said.

"Watch your language," Gunner said.

"You never told us to watch our language before," his oldest, Bennie, complained. "Not even in front of Mom."

"That's because we've got a lady present, and your mom is no lady." Gunner grabbed the plates and put them on the counter. The steaks were cooked to how they liked, and she put them on a plate to rest.

Within minutes, she'd put the potatoes and steaks on a plate with a good helping of salad. She saw each of the boys wrinkle their noses at the salad, and Gunner didn't look impressed either.

She just smiled as they sat around the table eating.

"So good," Carlos said. "You're a good cook, Mrs. Williams."

"Thank you, and you know you can call me Scarlett. It won't kill you or anything."

They glanced at their father, and he nodded.

The rest of the meal went by without a hitch. Gunner got each boy to talk about their homework, what they'd done that day, what they'd learned. She saw that he really cared about the boys as he asked them both questions and made sure they knew what they were doing.

Afterward, they told her to go and relax while they did the dishes.

Gunner poured her a glass of wine as she was flicking through the television. He didn't linger, and she didn't ask him to. As the minutes passed, turning to hours, and with night falling, she knew what was coming.

She'd already gotten a text letting her know that John had landed, and he'd gotten to his hotel safely. He'd told her he was getting an early night so that he could get started with a clear head.

The boys watched a bit of a movie with her after the dishes were clean, but they went up before ten. Feeling sleepy herself, she ignored the look Gunner gave her. Cleaning her empty wineglass, she placed it on the draining board, making her way up to her room. Closing her door, she stepped back, taking care of the curtains to give herself some privacy.

She grabbed a towel and some of her conditioner, and made her way into the bathroom. The door to Gunner's room remained closed.

Stripping off her clothes, she felt so aware of him, of being in another man's house with her husband's permission to fuck. She tried not to think about it, but it was impossible. Stepping into the shower stall, she stopped. There on a small tray was the shampoo, conditioner, and body wash she always used.

She found it incredibly sweet that he'd gone out and got what she liked.

Picking it up, she opened the cap, giving it a sniff. If Gunner wanted her the way John had claimed did he do this in the shower? Had he had the scent that she loved for long?

So many questions and she didn't know if she wanted any of them answered.

Chapter Eight

Gunner rested his head against the door of the bathroom. He heard the sounds of the shower running, and he wondered if she'd seen the bottles he'd bought some time ago. When he'd leaned in close, he couldn't get the scent of her out of his mind. He'd gone straight to the store and bought the shampoo she liked. It had gotten his need at the time under control.

Damn it.

He wanted her so fucking bad.

John had given him permission to fuck her, but it was like a lifeline to what he wanted. For a long time, he'd craved Scarlett. He'd seen how happy his friend was and seen them both together to know that she was a special woman. She was the kind of woman people wrote stories about, why men went to war.

To a lot of men, she was too curvy, maybe even going so far as to call her fat. To him though, those curves were a temptation he found hard to resist. He didn't want to resist them. His cock was hard as fucking rock, and he wanted her so badly.

Removing his clothes, he stood by his door completely naked. Even at his age, nearing fifty, he was looking good. He took care to work out, to keep at his peak of health. Years of being trained by the military had kept him at a point of fitness he didn't want to lose. Especially with the dangers that surrounded the club at every turn, he didn't want anyone to take his place.

Gripping the handle of the door, he knew without a doubt that this would change everything for all of them. The moment he got her pregnant, things would change.

For several seconds he just held that door handle, waiting. A better man would walk away. Would tell John to do this the right way, but he wasn't a better man. He wanted to get Scarlett pregnant. To put his baby deep inside her. To know that no one else could do what he did.

Turning the handle, he entered the bathroom, closing the door behind him. She was already in the shower, the water running down her body, and she didn't show any signs that she'd heard him.

When he opened the shower door, she turned with a gasp, her eyes going wide as she stared at him.

"Tell me to leave. Tell me to walk away," he said. He'd let her go.

He wasn't a rapist, would never be one.

She didn't say a word.

Stepping into the shower, he closed the door. Taking the cloth from her hands, he placed it on the counter.

Putting his hand on her hip, he drew her to him. It had been a couple of weeks since he'd felt her against him, and like a drowning man, he craved it like one would air.

He held her against him, feeling every part of her soft body. The weight of her tits pressed against his chest. His cock lay against her rounded stomach. Running his hands down her back, he gripped her curvy ass, pulling her against him.

She wrapped her arms around him, her fingers holding him tightly.

He kissed her shoulder, feeling her shudder.

"I want you, baby."

"I want you too." Her voice was so soft it was merely a whisper.

Taking the soap he'd gotten for her, he squeezed some onto his hands, and spun her around so that her back was to him. Cupping her breasts, he lathered her body in the soap, taking his time, learning every inch of her, committing it to his mind so he never forgot a part of her.

She sighed against him. Her hands moved between them, reaching behind her back to touch him, cupping his aching cock. She worked his dick up and down, her movements slow.

"You know I've thought about this for a long time. About how good you'd feel in my arms. How I'd get you off." He kissed her neck, right over her pulse, flicking his tongue across it. She released a whimper, and he sank his teeth into her flesh. Not enough to hurt but to create enough pleasure to drive her wild. "Do you want me, Scarlett?"

"Yes."

"Good. I tried not to be happy about having you all to myself, but I can't lie. I wanted this, and I was so fucking happy when John said you'd be with me." He washed her body completely.

"He wants to know everything."

"And we can both tell him together. I don't mind."

"Does the thought of telling John make you hot? Do you think about how hard his dick is going to be knowing yours is balls deep inside me?" she asked.

Her words made him moan, thinking about John's dick, how hard it would look. How he'd want to touch him, goad him into doing it.

His feelings for John had always fucked him up, but he kept them under wraps. No one needed to know how he's thought about pushing John to his knees, gripping the back of his friend's neck as he drove his dick in deep, making him gag on the sheer length of his cock.

These were fantasies he'd put away for a long

time, and they shouldn't be coming out right now. He wouldn't let them.

Pressing Scarlett up against the wall, he ran his hand down her stomach, pressing between her legs, finding her heat. She cried out, his name on her lips as he ran his finger through her slit.

"Does thinking about John's cock make you wet?" he asked.

"Yes."

"What about mine?"

"Yes."

"Do you want us both, Scarlett? Do you want to feel us both driving inside you, fucking you, taking you?"

"Yes."

He groaned against her flesh. The closer they were to Scarlett, they could touch. He'd feel John's cock inside her as he fucked her.

"You want that too?" she asked.

"Yes. Fuck yes, baby. I want to feel you come apart as you're on both of our cocks."

He slid his finger down, pressing two fingers inside her. Her cunt tightened, and he added a third, stretching her for his cock. He wasn't a small man, and tonight he intended to have his fill of her.

For a long time, he'd been wanting her, and once or even twice wasn't enough.

Fucking her with his fingers, he drew them back, teasing her clit, feeling her come alive beneath his touch. She screamed his name, yelled it even.

He didn't let up, stroking her nub.

When he couldn't take it anymore, and he felt like he was going to come over her back, he bent her forward, pulling her ass back.

She opened her thighs, and he found her heat,

sliding his cock in deep in one hard thrust. Her pussy clutched his cock, squeezing him as he went as deep as he could go. Pulling out of her, he slammed inside again. Over and over, he fucked her harder, making her take his length.

She cried out his name, the sounds echoing off the wall as he took her.

Reaching between her thighs, he teased her clit.

With a few strokes she came apart.

Gunner gritted his teeth as the pleasure was unlike anything he'd ever experienced. Driving inside her over and over, he fucked her harder than ever before.

"Fuck, baby. You're so perfect. So tight. So hot."

He gripped her hips, pounding her pussy one final time, going to the hilt. In the back of his mind, he wondered if this time would be the one that got her pregnant. He didn't say anything. Running his hands up and down her back, he allowed the pleasure to consume him as he pumped his release inside her pussy.

Pulling out of her, he distracted her by cleaning her hair, first with the shampoo and then with the conditioner. He loved doing these small things for her. They felt strangely intimate.

With no other reason to linger, he turned the water off, climbing out of the shower. Grabbing a towel, he opened it up waiting for her to step inside.

She did, taking his hand.

He didn't lead her to her bedroom.

Gunner didn't have any intention of her sleeping in that room. He wanted her in his, in his arms and in his bed.

"Gunner?"

"Don't be nervous." He took her hands, placing kisses on her knuckles.

"I'm not."

"Don't lie to me, baby," he said.

"I'm a little bit. I don't know how this is supposed to work."

"You're feeling guilty?"

"Yes."

He nodded. Running his hands up and down her arms, he pressed a kiss to her lips, and pulled away. Taking his cell phone out, he dialed John's number, being sure to put it on speakerphone so that she could hear.

"He was going to sleep," she said. "We can't wake him."

"I want to. I don't want you worried about what we just did."

"Hello," John said, sounding sleepy.

"Hey, John. Gunner here. You're on speakerphone."

"What's wrong? Is Scarlett okay?" His friend had gone from sleepy to alert.

"She's fine. She's … we just fucked in the shower." Scarlett went to step away from him, but he caught her hand, stopping her. She glared at him.

"Did she come hard?" John asked.

Scarlett's eyes were wide.

"She did, but now she feels worried."

"You there, baby?" John asked.

"Yes."

"Did you like it?"

"Yes." Her gaze was on his, and he saw her lip wobble.

"What did he do?"

"He touched me all over. Then he bent me over, and fucked me."

"Did his cock go in deep? Was it good?"

From the way John's voice changed, and the

rustling of fabric, he knew what John was doing.

As Gunner moved up behind her, his own cock was already starting to harden. He opened her towel, letting it drop to the floor.

"I'm just going to get your girl ready again, John. That okay with you?" he asked.

"Tell me everything, Scarlett."

Gunner smiled against her neck.

"He's kissing my neck."

"How does it feel?"

"He's not shaved yet, so it's a little rough and I like it. My nipples are so hard, and it feels good in my pussy," she said. She gasped as he cupped her breast and pinched her nipple. She told John everything as Gunner caressed her body, taking each of her tits in his hands, stroking them. Down his hand went, moving to her pussy. This time she cried out, and he took over.

"I'm touching her pussy."

"That you already came inside?"

Scarlett was too far gone to realize the question. "Yes."

"Good. Stroke her, get her all wet. She loves it when you fuck her with your fingers. Make her take it. She doesn't mind a little rough, just so long as you make it real good."

Gunner fucked her with his fingers, driving inside her at the same time as he teased her clit, feeling the answering arousal in her cunt as he did.

Gunner learned her body as she spoke to John. Everything that made her tick. Each little moan or gasp as he teased her. Every now and again, he'd take over talking to John, especially as he had her crying out from the pleasure, her responses driving his own arousal higher.

"Fuck her, Gunner. Drive your cock so deep

inside her."

He grabbed his dick, pressing it at the entrance of her cunt. Slowly, achingly slowly, he thrust inside her. Each pulse, each quiver he felt it inside her.

John's moans came over the line, letting them both know that he was finding his own kind of pleasure at the same time.

It turned Gunner on, drove him harder inside Scarlett to think of his best friend playing with himself.

Over and over, he pounded inside her, giving Scarlett every single inch of him at the same time wanting John there, to watch him, to touch him.

Giving Scarlett a baby had awakened something inside him that he'd long thought was dead.

The moment he came, he felt Scarlett shudder with her own release, and they heard John find his.

"I love you, Scarlett. That was incredible."

The call ended, and Gunner held Scarlett in his arms, complete with the sweetest as fuck smile on her face.

****

Scarlett opened her, eyes aware of the hard, muscular arm wrapped around her stomach. Last night's events rushed through her, and she glanced behind her to see Gunner still sleeping. He looked … calm.

After John ended the call, she'd been so exhausted. She hadn't tried to go back to her own bed, and instead, stayed snuggled up against Gunner. Rolling over, she looked at him. At her movements, he opened his eyes.

"Morning."

"You're a light sleeper?"

"Had to be. Always have to keep one eye open."

"That doesn't sound very nice."

"I don't live in a nice world."

She ran her hand up his arm, taking in all of his ink, and just the sheer force of the man. He reminded her of John. They'd served together and been brothers in arms.

Thinking back to the past few weeks when she'd talked to both John and Gunner, she wondered if they even realized that they wanted each other. Was it their secret with each other? She didn't know.

She knew for certain that neither of them had acted on it, and she didn't know if that made her sad or not.

She wanted them to both have what they both needed and craved. What she didn't want was it to cause them all pain.

"The wheels are turning in your head."

"I'm just thinking."

"I'm trying not to be sexist."

She giggled. "But…"

"When a woman thinks, it never works out for the guy."

"You pig." She lightly slapped his side, and he chuckled, capturing her hands, and keeping them locked between them.

"What do you have to do today?"

"Not a lot. Today is my day off. I was going to prepare lunch for you and the boys, and then think about getting started on stocking up your fridge and freezer. I don't like the thought of you guys living on takeout or those rancid ready meals."

"You're going to take care of us?"

"I'm going to try and take care of you all."

"Cherry never cooked."

She didn't like the jolt of pain she felt at the mention of Cherry's name. The other woman once had it all. Cherry had a husband, the kids, the house,

147

everything, and she'd thrown it all away.

Scarlett loved John more than anything, but she knew not being able to have kids was changing them. He wouldn't even let her redecorate the nursery. They weren't going to be able to use the damn room unless they actually talked about their options, but again, they couldn't do that because he didn't want to talk about it.

"You've got that frowny face again. What's up?" Gunner asked. "Come on, you can talk to me."

"I was just thinking about John and the nursery."

"What made you think about that?"

Did he tense up? "Cherry. She had you and the kids, and she threw it all away."

"I wasn't a very good husband."

"Not ever?"

"No. She was just there, you know. I didn't care about it. Probably because I knew half the club had gone for a turn inside her."

She stared at him amazed. "Why marry her then?"

"Seemed like a good thing to do at the time. She was pregnant with my kid. I did make sure of that as well with both of them." He shrugged. "It just kind of happened. I hated every second of it, but I got two amazing boys out of it."

"They seem really good kids."

He chuckled.

"What?" she asked.

"They're good kids because I've got them to get their heads down. I've seen them. They're not sweet, innocent teenagers, Scarlett. Don't let them fool you into thinking that."

"They're wonderful."

"I didn't say they weren't. They're great kids. They're my boys, so I don't have a problem with them," he said. He had that smirk on his face. "What is it about the nursery? Let's not lose track."

She sighed. "I want to redecorate it. We don't have any furniture there. It's a blank room other than the yellow walls. I went with a neutral color just in case. Pink is for girls, blue for boys, but yellow, that's different. That says it doesn't matter. John and I, we're not talking about what we can do to have a kid. We're not talking about it at all. It's like it didn't exist, and … I don't want that room to become a bad cloud over our marriage. We can't have kids, and I've accepted that. He doesn't want to talk about it, so I don't want to just wait around."

Gunner's hand ran across her stomach. He didn't linger as he slowly stroked over to caress her hip.

"He'll talk about it when he's ready."

"It just seems all weird. We can't have kids, then he's inviting you into our bed, not that it's a big problem or anything. I like when we're together. I just … something doesn't feel right at times."

Gunner's hand moved up to cup her face. "Everything is fine. You'll both get through this."

"How can you be so sure?"

"It's John. I remember what he was like that first day he saw you. How happy he was. He told me that he'd found an angel and that he was going to marry her. John's not going to go anywhere. I promise."

He pressed a kiss to her lips.

"Then why is it me in the bed with you, Gunner?"

"Did he ever tell you about us sharing before?" he asked.

"He told me everything. We don't have any secrets from each other."

"Did he only tell you recently?"

"No. He mentioned it before." John would tell her

tales about his time with Gunner in the force, about how close they were. When it came to his stories of sharing, she would always get aroused by the visual he'd give. She wanted that, wanted him.

Gunner's thumb went back and forth. "It's just something we've done. The women, they meant nothing until you."

"Did you leave Cherry because of me?"

"I left Cherry because she was a waste of space and I couldn't stand her. You had nothing to do with it. Yes, I wanted you, Scarlett. I'm not going to deny that. I'll never lie to you." He pressed his lips to hers. "Please, believe that."

"I do." She heard sounds of the boys waking up and looked at Gunner. "I better get ready to take them to school."

"Would you like to spend the day with me?"

"I can?"

"Yes. I'll be at the club all day. You can come, see some of the guys, how it works. Would you like that?"

She smiled. "Yes, I would." John always told her to never go to the clubhouse unless she was there with him or with Gunner. The men were always sweet and polite to her. She didn't see a problem, but John had warned her the men were always on their best behavior.

Gunner kissed her one final time before letting her leave his bed. She made her way into the bathroom, taking a toilet break and other morning rituals.

Entering her own room this time, she grabbed some jeans and a sweater before heading downstairs.

The coffee pot was already on, and the boys were crowded around the toaster. She grabbed a pan and quickly made herself some oatmeal.

No one spoke for the longest time.

"I'm taking you in to school today," Gunner said.

Both boys groaned.

"I'm not hearing it. I'm taking you and picking you up."

There was no argument, and she glanced at Gunner. "Do they behave this way when I have to pick them up?"

"They're boys. Everything is always ten times harder to do. Don't take it personal," he said.

She chuckled. "I imagine I completely ruin their street cred."

"Nah, I bet you're one of those milfs."

"Milfs?"

"Mom I'd like to fuck."

She pushed him away as he'd wrapped his arms around her. "Not happening. That's gross."

"Didn't you ever fall for a dad?"

"A dilf? No, absolutely not." She wrinkled her nose. "I really don't need to hear about all this dirty talk."

They finished their breakfast, and it wasn't long before they were in the car heading toward the high school.

It was so busy. She noticed a group of people glaring at the car. Recognizing Finn Goldman in the center of the group, she squared her shoulders as the boys got out.

"Stay safe, okay," she said.

"Yeah, we will." Bennie bumped her fist, stepping away and heading into school, his brother by his side. She noticed a couple of the other MC brothers join up with him as they made it the entrance.

"They're all told to stay out of trouble," Gunner said. "It makes life a lot easier if they do as they're told."

"I can imagine."

"So, what's on the agenda for the day?"

"We're heading to the clubhouse."

She leaned back in the seat watching the town go by. The drive wasn't a long one, and she noticed several people already milling about. Quite a few scantily-clad women were hanging around, smoking.

Tucking some of her hair behind her ear, she followed Gunner into the clubhouse. Compared to all the women there, she stuck out like a sore thumb.

Several of the guys gave her a hug and said hello. She smiled at all of them, and in the corner, she was sure she spotted one man getting a blowjob. He'd pushed a woman's head into his lap, and was groaning.

Scarlett wasn't a prude, but right now, it felt way out of her comfort zone.

Gunner went straight to his office. She sat down on the sofa, watching as he opened up his office, and went through some items on his desk.

"Why do I feel I'm here because you don't trust me being alone at your house?" she asked.

He glanced up. "I've got some things going down. Some people know that I care about you, and I don't want you to become a target for that shit."

"So, I couldn't stay at your house?"

"No. You're safe with me. I promised John I'd take care of you. This is the only way I know how."

"You care about me?" she asked, looking at him.

"You know I do. I care a whole lot."

She looked away, not able to handle the intensity of his stare. "Is there anything you need me to do?"

"No. You can just relax. Take it easy."

"That's boring."

She lay down on her back, staring up at the ceiling. It had been a long time since she just lay around doing nothing. It felt odd to be doing it now.

It wasn't long before her eyelids started to droop and sleep claimed her.

****

The week passed in a blur. By the time he arrived at Gunner's house on Sunday, John was more than ready to see his wife. The moment he parked, the door was open, and she was out of the house rushing toward him. He noticed her wearing one of Gunner's shirts with several buttons secured in the middle, along with a pair of her jeans. Her long brown tresses were flying free.

The moment she was in his arms, he didn't care. Breathing in her scent, the smell of home, he just wanted her in his arms.

"I've missed you," he said.

She chuckled. "Missed you too."

He gripped the back of her neck like he'd done many times before, locking his lips with hers. "I want you," he said. "Are you wet for me?"

"More than anything."

Even though he'd been away, they'd talked all the time on the phone, and he'd been there at nighttime when Gunner had been fucking her. He wondered if his friend had finally done what he needed him to do. Cupping her cheek, he smiled down at her. "I'm not leaving you home again."

She ran her hands up his chest. "Did it get lonely?"

"So lonely." He pushed some hair off her face, smiling down at her. "I thought about you constantly."

"How about you stop letting out all the hot air and let's take this inside," Gunner said, calling out to them.

"Dinner is ready," she said.

"It is. I'm starved."

She kept hold of his hand, and he passed Gunner,

aware of the easy way he watched them. He'd thought often about what Gunner was doing for them, and seeing him now, how relaxed and ready he was, John felt that swirling pit of need begin to build within him. He usually had it under control, but right now, it felt like a fire had started where before it was just embers.

Gunner gripped his hand, pulling him in close, and slapping him on the back. "It's good to have you back."

He nodded at his friend.

"I better go and serve up." Scarlett gave him one final kiss before moving away toward the kitchen. He watched her go, admiring the lush curves of her ass. He'd missed her so much.

"How is everything?" John asked.

"Let's talk in my office."

Gunner led the way in the opposite direction. He heard Scarlett talking and figured it was Gunner's two boys.

"Did you have a good week?" John asked.

"Did you get everything you needed to do done?"

John stared at his friend. "Yeah, I did." He watched Gunner. "Did you do what I asked you to do?"

"I fucked your wife every single chance I got. I took her at night, during the day, in my clubhouse. I rode her pussy and filled her cunt with my cum. Is that what you wanted to hear?" Gunner ran a hand down his face.

"Does she suspect something?" John asked.

"She talked about the nursery and stuff like that. Asked me questions about the boys, and she just wants to be your wife, John. To be honest, I don't know if I can go through with this."

He stared at his friend. Gunner was a hard man. It had taken a lot of people to bring this motherfucker to his knees, but from the look on his face, something else was eating him up. "What is it?"

"It'll be mine," Gunner said.

"I know."

"That baby will be mine, and she'll belong to you. I can't … I care about her," Gunner said.

"You love her," John said.

His best friend stared at him with a frown. "I tell you that I care about your wife and you take it to the next level?"

"I'm being realistic. You love my wife, Gunner, admit it. You love her, and you want her."

Gunner stepped away from him, running a hand down his face.

"She's too young."

"You and I are the same fucking age. Her age doesn't have anything to do with this. That's a bullshit reason. You know it, and so do I."

"I know if you don't want to do this anymore. I get it, I do. She could already be pregnant."

"What do you think is going to happen after? There's a shitload of problems we've opened up right now."

"You've taken care of the nurse, and you're dealing with your wife."

"Shit, John. I wanted to fuck her. I wanted to be with her, but I didn't want this."

There was a knock at the door, and John gritted his teeth. He counted to ten inside his head. He was arguing with his best friend, but what made this even more complicated was the fact he was aroused. His cock was rock fucking hard.

He loved Gunner's aggression, his passion. It always aroused him, and mixed with the thought that he loved Scarlett, it just completed their little circle.

They were not the everyday, average normal

couple. With Gunner this could bring something to his marriage with Scarlett that he didn't even know was missing.

"We can make this work," he said, gripping Gunner's arm as he passed. The feel of Gunner's arm beneath his fingers had him tightening his hold.

His friend pulled away first, going to the door.

Running fingers through his already messy hair, John spun to see that Bennie was there.

Dinner was ready.

His wife sat on one side of the table while he and Gunner sat on either end. Carlos and Bennie took the other side.

Conversation was light, but he kept catching Scarlett's gaze. She'd look at him then back at Gunner, then back again.

Before the meal was over, Gunner let them all know that he had to go to the club for some last-minute business.

He wasn't an idiot. The fucker was running, but that was fine.

"You want us to watch your boys?" Scarlett asked.

"Yes. Are you staying the night?" Gunner asked.

Scarlett looked toward him.

"Yes, we're staying the night."

The moment the meal was over with, Scarlett and the boys did the dishes. He helped to clean the table, and while they went off to do homework, he watched his wife.

"Did you and Gunner argue?" Scarlett asked. "You both looked pretty pissed at the table."

"It's fine. Honestly. Gunner and I always had disagreements." He held his wife as she stepped into his arms.

"I don't like it. It made for a rather tense dinner, and you know I love for everything to be perfect."

"We'll make up, I promise."

"Good. I don't like either of you arguing. It doesn't seem right." She pressed a kiss to his lips, then another.

Sinking his fingers into his wife's hair, he felt his cock begin to stir once more.

"I don't suppose we could take this to the bedroom?"

"After we let the kids go to bed. It doesn't feel right having this here with them still working."

He groaned but relented. There was time for him soon.

Chapter Nine

Gunner couldn't remember a time when he'd ever been jealous of another man. He had a life he always wanted, even if it was a bit flawed at times, but this was what he wanted. The club, being the Prez. He'd earned his patch and not just because he'd killed the Prez before him. He'd proven himself to the club time and time again. It's why he'd fought so hard to become who he was. No woman had ever been important to him. Most of his life they'd always had their uses, always gave him the means of getting off, but that was where the usefulness ended.

When he'd married Cherry, not once did he adapt to the married lifestyle. He didn't sit at home, hugging her. He was dealing with club shit and club business. Yes, he stayed faithful as that seemed to mean something to him, but when Cherry first cheated that was when his loyalty ended.

That first time had been like a dam, and he'd fucked everything with a vagina.

Then ten years ago, he'd met Scarlett. A beautiful brunette who stared up at his best friend as if the sun shone out of his fucking ass.

It was the first time he remembered being jealous. He'd looked at Cherry, and knew he'd fucked up. They already had Bennie and Carlos by then. He didn't want any more kids, so he stopped screwing his wife. It was that simple. The jealousy had gone as with all things. He'd been happy for his best friend.

Then there had been the wedding. He'd stood by John's side and watched her walking down the aisle. He'd not known until recently that John had been her first. There had been jealousy on that day. To see their happiness shining through, to listen to their vows as they joined each other.

Over the years, he'd come to terms with his feelings for Scarlett, always keeping them hidden, but he'd fucking failed when it came to others seeing them. Scarlett had never had a fucking clue, but clearly John had, and so had Cherry.

He wondered if it was in the way he watched her?

Gunner didn't know. It was late as he let himself into his home. There was silence, and he removed his jacket, placing it on the back of a chair. Seeing no reason to linger, he made his way upstairs, checking on both of his boys. Entering his room, he heard the feminine moan. The bathroom that connected the rooms was open.

His cock sprang into action at the sound she made.

Did she know he'd come back?

Closing his door, he made his way toward the bathroom, and stepped over the threshold into the room he made up for Scarlett.

The sheets were on the floor, and Scarlett's eyes were closed as she rode John's cock. His friend's hands were on her hips, repeatedly driving her down onto his cock. There was a sheen of sweat covering the both of them, and he also noted the tube of empty lubrication on the floor.

"Open your eyes, baby," John said, whispering to her ear.

Her eyes opened, and as she saw him, a moan escaped. "Gunner," she said with a moan.

"Tell him what I'm doing," John said.

"He's fucking my ass."

"And why am I fucking your ass?" John asked.

"Because you said he'd come home and he'd want to use my pussy. That I had to save something for him."

"Are you wet?"

"Yes." She cried out the word, and Gunner was already removing his clothes. His cock sprang free, and he wrapped his fingers around the length as he watched her.

"Do you want his cock, baby?"

"Yes, I want it. I want it so bad."

John pulled her down hard, making her squeal. "Then open your mouth. Get him nice and wet so he can fuck your pussy."

Gunner climbed onto the bed so that she didn't have to move. One of her hands went to his waist as the other cupped his dick. Her mouth was on him, and he released a hiss at the pleasure that rushed to his balls.

"Her mouth is so fucking perfect, isn't it, Gunner?"

He didn't answer. There was no need to. His groan, and gripping the back of her head, was all they needed to see.

Her tongue swirled the tip then began to lick down his length before she went up and took him into her mouth. When he hit the back of her throat, she pulled up, and bobbed her head up and down the length of him before sucking more of him.

"She's been treating me while we've been waiting for you," John said. "She was worried that you wouldn't come back, and I told her you would. That there's no way you'd walk away after having a taste of her tits and her pussy. How you liked hearing the sound of your name as she called it." John groaned. "I'm touching her pussy, and she's so wet. I probably didn't need the lubricant, she's so wet. You want me, baby. You want me to fuck your ass while Gunner watches?"

"Yes."

Pulling back, Gunner watched as John lifted her up, only to pull her back down again. She let out a cry, but it was one filled with pleasure as he repeatedly fucked inside her, going deeper with each thrust.

When he was to the hilt, he'd grind her down on his cock, rubbing her off at the same time.

"She's so needy, Gunner. I think she needs a nice fat cock in her cunt. How do you feel about that, baby?"

"Yes," she said with a moan. "Yes."

Dropping down onto the bed, John leaned back on the bed, moving her so that he could see them both. The light from the lamps creating a soft glow to the room, he watched John's cock. His friend moved just a little, driving their girl crazy.

Reaching out, he slid a finger into her cunt, going in deep. She cried out, his name echoing off the wall. Drawing his finger up, he circled her clit, pinching the bud, and listening to her scream as the pleasure rushed around her body.

Down he went, going past that tiny piece of flesh between her ass and pussy, and then he did something he'd never done before. He touched John's cock as it slid inside her. At first, he simply traced the puckered hole of her ass where she took the cock, but that one touch wasn't enough. Wrapping his fingers around the cock that was exposed, he looked at both of them.

"I can feel how deep he is inside you, baby. How much he wants you. He's so hard, isn't he?"

"Yes." Her voice sounded far away, almost distant. Heat filled her cheeks, and her tits quivered from her indrawn breaths.

Gunner teased John just a little more, feeling him pulse in his hands, and thicken.

"Does it hurt?"

"Just a little."

"You ever had a cock inside your cunt while he's taking your ass?"

"No."

Releasing John's cock, he pressed his own dick to her opening. With the angle they were, he was able to look at Scarlett's eyes, and then turn to John's, his best friend. The only man he'd ever wanted to fuck.

Whatever had happened in the past few months, it had opened up his desire for John. He'd kept it carefully guarded, his own little secret that he'd been able to hide from everyone, including Cherry.

No one knew, not even John.

Slowly, he began to thrust inside her. Inch by inch, she took him, and through that thin membrane, he felt John.

This was as close as he'd ever dare take it.

Gripping her hips, holding John as well as Scarlett, he slammed to the hilt inside her. The pleasurable sounds came from her, echoing off the walls as he fucked all of his inches inside her.

"Fuck, baby, do you feel him?" John asked.

"Yes."

"She's so damn tight," Gunner said. It still amazed him how tight she could be. Now she was even more so with both of their cocks inside her.

Running his hands up her body, he cupped her tits, pressing them together as he lathered each nipple with his tongue.

Pulling out of her tight pussy, he kept up his ministrations on her tits as he began to rock inside her. With John, they both found a pace that drove her arousal higher. Her pussy was so slick that it made him easy for him to slide in and out of her.

Over and over again, he fucked her.

He'd done nothing but fuck her, expecting to

become bored or to find a reason not to enjoy it. Every single time was like the first fucking time.

Her body only served to drive his arousal even higher. Releasing her tits, he sat back on his knees, his cock still within her. Sliding his fingers against her clit, he remained perfectly still, stroking her nub. "I want you to come before I do. Come all over my dick, Scarlett."

She gasped. John caught her arms and held her as he fucked upward, taking her ass while Gunner teased her pussy, his cock still inside her but waiting for her orgasm to come. He wanted her dripping.

This woman was as much his as she was John's. He couldn't give her up.

He wouldn't.

Scarlett came hard, her pussy clenching down on him as she gave him what he wanted. He teased her clit until she couldn't take anymore, and she was nothing more than a mass of nerves.

Holding her hips, he fucked her hard, not showing her any mercy as he took the cunt that belonged to him. Scarlett was his, just as she now owned a piece of him, and it wasn't something he was going to give back or take away any time soon.

He wanted to own part of her, and he'd been wanting to do this for ten years. The only part missing now was the part he wanted of John. He couldn't deny it anymore, nor could he hide from it. His feelings for his best friend had been getting stronger for years. They were not going to disappear, and he didn't want them to.

Over and over, he fucked her, only pausing to bask in the feel of John coming. It was a sight and feeling that turned him on even more.

He drove inside her, feeling his balls start to tighten and his need build. He joined them both, flooding her pussy with his cum, knowing in the back of his mind that he'd gotten her pregnant. He had to have. There was no way she wasn't pregnant.

Wave upon wave of his orgasm, and he wished that she was.

She wasn't his wife, but she'd claimed a piece of his heart, and he wasn't going to let go.

****

Several days later John stood inside the nursery at his home. He'd not been back here since arriving in town. After work, he'd go back to Gunner's. They would all sit down to a meal, his sons included, and then they'd spend the entire night fucking.

Each night, they'd take Scarlett on a ride of pleasure, making her completely surrender to their needs. He loved watching her come apart, the way Gunner touched her body, igniting a fire. Seeing the two people he loved more than anything in the world coming together turned him on.

"Why are you here?" Gunner asked.

John turned to see his friend watching him. "I stopped by to pick up a few things. Scarlett said you didn't mind."

"I don't. With the way she cooks I'm more than happy for you two to move in." Gunner stepped close and looked into the bedroom. "This the nursery?"

Before John could say anything more, Gunner had already stepped over the threshold. He'd not entered this room since he'd gotten the doctor's results. "Yes."

"There's no furniture."

"We were going to buy some after we got the results. Scarlett believed it was bad luck. It makes me wonder if painting this room gave us bad luck."

"You're being miserable again, aren't you?" Gunner asked.

John gritted his teeth. "It's a little hard at times to

know that I can't take care of my woman. That I can't give her what a normal man can."

"Hey, man, this is not some kind of competition here," Gunner said.

"I know. I'm not trying to make it so. Believe me." John ran a hand down his face.

"Do you want us to stop?"

"What? Hell no. I don't want this to stop. I love sharing Scarlett with you. Have you had enough? Is that it?"

"What? No, of course not. I fucking love being with Scarlett and not just for the sex either. That shit is just a bonus. She's a one-of-a-kind woman."

He nodded. "Yeah, she really is."

"You're going to get that kid, John. I promise."

Gunner stepped up to him. A second later Gunner pressed his head against his, and John felt his breath on his face. His cock responded in kind, swelling at just the closeness of Gunner. Closing his eyes, he allowed himself to bask in the pleasure of having his friend close.

No one could take this away from him. He had to keep remembering that.

"We've got this, John. You and me. I've got your back, just like always."

"Thank you."

The tension in the room seemed to mount, and as John looked up at how close Gunner was the urge to kiss him completely swamped him. He wanted to. To hold onto Gunner's face and take what he wanted more than anything.

Don't ruin what you've got.

He could live with the touches they shared when they were with Scarlett. He loved his wife. When he'd been away, he'd craved the smallest of touches. Being able to be with Gunner through Scarlett, he could live with that.

Pushing down his desire, and his own wants and needs, he took a deep breath. Closing his eyes, he counted quickly to ten, and reopened them.

"Any news?" John asked.

He was aware that Gunner was going through shit at the club. The security cameras showed them nothing, and the money was all accounted for, apart from the amount that had gone missing prior to his and John's investigation.

"Kent's stayed particularly close to the club of late. Any chance I've got of checking out his room it's not happening."

"What about his apartment?" John asked.

"Again, not been able to do that either. He'd not been back at his place for some time. Also, I need a lookout."

"You want me to come with you?"

"Yeah, I do. There's no one else I'd trust but you."

John nodded. "Well, I'm on a break. Let me grab the few things we need and I'll come on over with you."

"I've only brought my bike," Gunner said.

"I can drive my car." He smirked at his friend, and any tension that was there disappeared. Heading to his bedroom, he entered the closet and started to pack a few more clothes. The room they were sharing at Gunner's was bigger than his room. No matter how many times he tried to get her to move, she wasn't having any of it.

He knew without a doubt that his woman loved him, and it didn't have anything to do with the money.

Gunner entered the room and picked up one of the pictures on the nightstand. It was of John with Scarlett. They were both at the beach on their honeymoon. It was so long ago, but he still remembered the feel of her in his arms as if it was yesterday, and also the way her head tilted back as she laughed. Someone had offered to take a picture and they'd both accepted. Scarlett rarely liked having her picture taken, but it would have been rude for her to refuse.

"You both look happy," Gunner said.

"We were on our honeymoon. It would have been even more weird if we weren't happy."

"That's fair."

"You never went on a honeymoon with Cherry, did you?"

"Nah, there was no need to. She had all the drink and cock she could have back at the club. Like I've said before, the only good things to come out of my relationship with Cherry are those two boys."

"How are they getting on at school now? Anything from Goldman?"

"Bennie says not, but Carlos tells me that he notices Finn and some of his crowd watch Bennie a lot. He doesn't like the way it feels. Like they're planning something." Gunner put the picture down. "I'll deal with it."

"You think your son is in danger?"

"From getting beat up by a couple of kids? Yeah. Bennie's strong though, and I've got the boys training him so he'll be able to handle his own shit soon."

"You're sure about that?"

"Yes. Besides, if Finn so much as hurts a hair on my son's head, I get to pay another trip to his asshole of a father. I've been wanting any reason to hurt that son of a bitch. If it is because of our sons, then I don't care. I'll fucking take it."

With the case packed, he watched as Gunner picked up the picture again. "Let's take this."

"Are you moving us in?"

"You both look happy in this picture. I like seeing it."

John took the picture from him. "We don't have any with you and Scarlett."

"That can be easily fixed. Just pick up a camera as I'm fucking her. You'll get plenty then."

There was something in his voice, but John didn't know what. Pushing it aside, like he'd been doing with a lot of his questions and feelings lately, he carried the picture to the car. Putting the case in the trunk, and the picture in the glove compartment, he climbed in and nodded at Gunner to lead the way.

Following behind Gunner's bike, every now and again, John thought about the picture. He'd not seen Gunner or Scarlett together all that often when he was around. They stood together, but they didn't have the closeness that he shared with her. It was perfectly reasonable though seeing as he'd married her, but still, he didn't know what to do.

He didn't know if Scarlett could fall in love with Gunner. They'd not talked about it. The sex was out of this world, and each morning he woke up, he saw Scarlett and Gunner together. She was always lying between them, her hand around his waist and Gunner holding her close.

His friend loved Scarlett. There was no doubt about it. John didn't know when it had started, but it had been going on for some time, and he'd been too blind to see it happening. Now, he knew it was there. It wasn't a little love either that was slowly growing. Gunner loved Scarlett. Was that why he wanted the picture? For it to be another reason why he had to keep his distance?

This wasn't supposed to get complicated.

What do you expect when you know you want it

but keep that a secret from the two people you love?

Gunner pulled into a parking lot, and John followed behind him, glancing up at the apartment building. There were several around town, and they could house nearly a thousand people in one block.

Opening the glove compartment, he didn't look toward his friend as he grabbed his gun. He always kept weapons close.

Tucking it away into his pants, he put his jacket over the bulge and followed Gunner inside the apartment building. Neither of them spoke as they made their way up to the twentieth floor. Neither of them was out of breath.

Gunner bent down, working the lock, opening the door with ease. Staying outside, John looked left and right, keeping a look out. The door was partially open, and John noticed a window overlooking the parking lot. Keeping the apartment in his sights, he watched the comings and goings of the people in the building.

Fifteen minutes passed before Gunner came out. He locked the door, and once again, they left.

Traveling in his car, John made his way to the office. Gunner followed him in and closed the door.

"Anything?" John asked.

"There's nothing there. His place is fucking clean." Gunner stepped back. "Cartel Carlos called me with information."

"When?"

"This morning. It's why I finally decided to go looking in Kent's house."

"What did he say?" John asked.

"They've been approached. He said that they'd been told new leadership was coming to the Satan's Demons. They want a new deal, all inclusive. No messenger, they want a real piece of the pie. They're setting up a meet in three weeks."

John's heart raced. "In three weeks they're hoping you're dead?"

"Or they're hoping to show enough of a rival that I'm going to be voted out. The club is only as strong as the leader, John. You know that."

No matter what you did or where you went in life, if the leader wasn't strong, then everything crumbled.

"What do you want to do?" John asked.

"I can't just come with Carlos's word and nothing else. I've got proof the money is gone. I just need proof that it's Kent."

"And if it's not?"

"Then I'm fucking screwed because I don't know who else it is. I know he's got a few fans at the club. That a couple of the boys wanted to be part of the bigger network." Gunner took a deep breath. "Your office is way too fucking neat."

"You want to destroy it?" John asked. "Mess it up?"

"Yeah."

"Scarlett decorated it."

All of the pent-up anger evaporated. "Fuck."

"Yeah, she came in, painted, picked out all the artwork, the furniture, the lot."

"You know I can't destroy something she created," Gunner said.

"I know. It's why I want to ask you something." John sat on the edge of his desk. "How long have you been in love with my wife? Don't bullshit me either. I don't need some shitty answer. I want the truth."

Gunner stared at him. "You knew."

"It's kind of hard to deny. You want a picture like the one I'm bringing back to your place, don't you?"

"I'm not going to try and steal your girl."

"She's *our* girl, Gunner. When did it happen?" John asked.

"I think it could have been the first day I saw her. Don't get me wrong, I knew it wasn't love. She's beautiful, but it's that kind of beauty you don't really think much about. She's striking. It's the way she talked, how beautiful and calm she always looks. It's everything that she is. It wasn't until recently, watching her with my sons that I realized that I was in love with your wife."

"Good," John said.

"Good?"

"Yes. It's good that you love her. Scarlett deserves a lot of love in her life."

"You're a crazy asshole. Anyone ever tell you that?"

"You do all the time."

****

"Smile!" John flashed his camera once again.

"What is it with you and taking pictures all of a sudden?" There were little lights flashing behind her eyes, and she had to blink them away.

"It's a new investment. I figure it'll be a lot of fun to document our life, you know. We don't take nearly as much. I know. I know. You hate having your picture taken, but I don't care. I want photos of my very beautiful wife."

"And I'm cooking."

"Keep on cooking, Scarlett, baby. My stomach is empty."

Scarlett rolled her eyes but couldn't help but laugh as he kept on snapping away. "When did you pick that thing up?"

"I saw it today. I bought it straight away."

He kept on clicking away.

Click.

171

Click.
Click.
Click.

The sound suddenly became quite comforting. She noticed he took pictures of everything. The food, the kitchen, he even took one of the windows overlooking the yard. When Bennie came in, he snapped away, then for Carlos as well.

"Not cool, man. You cannot post them up to any of my pages and don't fucking tag me."

"Tag you?" John asked, looking confused. Carlos had already left.

Picking up a pepper, she took a bite and watched her husband. "It's social network stuff. They're all on it tagging each other, hash-tagging like that." She shrugged.

"Kids today are so weird."

She laughed. "You're so cute."

"Yeah, do you remember when an app was just short for appointment? Now it actually means something. There's a whole shop of things you can buy shit from."

"I really do love you." She finished chewing her pepper, rounding the counter, to press kisses to his lips. "You're so adorable."

"Yeah, can I tag you?" he asked, winking.

"John, you can tag me anytime."

"That's a perfect picture," Gunner said. He came close, taking the camera from John. With a few clicks, he had the pictures of them, and she smiled up at her husband.

"Your turn," John said, snatching the camera away.

She made to move, but John caught her arm. "No, baby. Go and give Gunner a little hug."

Scarlett stared at her husband, but took a step

toward Gunner. The way Gunner looked at her sometimes made her nervous. It was like he had so many different feelings, and he found it hard to contain them all.

Wrapping her arms around his neck, she stared up at him and smiled. "Did you have a good day?"

"It's just getting better. You have a good day at work?" he asked.

"For the most part. Mary kept telling me how bad it was to spend time with another man when my husband wasn't around. I told her that John and I are both spending time with you."

"You want me to kick her ass?" Gunner asked.

She burst out laughing. "No, don't be absurd. I can handle her. She'll just fire me anyway." She shrugged. "There's not a lot I can do really. People in town have their views about the club, and they're not all great."

"We're not all good people."

"I know, but you're good to me, and that's all that matters." Her gaze dropped to his lips. His hand moved from her back curving down to her ass. He started to lean in closer, his mouth so close.

"When is dinner happening? I'm starved," Bennie asked, coming into the room.

She pulled away from Gunner and smiled at her husband. Moving around the counter, she tossed the last of the salad together, then got the grilled chicken out of the oven.

Seconds later they were sitting around the table. She watched Gunner and John, looking for any signs of jealousy, or something else. While she'd been away from them, at work, watching other kids, and dealing with paperwork because Mary had demanded that she do that, she'd been thinking, a lot.

Both men always came off as so calm. When she was with them and during sex, she saw the way they looked at each other. The yearning in both of their faces was so clear.

"Are you working tomorrow?" John asked.

"No. I've done my Saturday chore."

"Carlos and Bennie are staying at a friend's tonight," Gunner said. "I've already cleared it with their parents. They wanted to have some teenage time or something like that. I'll be dropping them off after dinner."

She nodded, glancing at John and Gunner. Neither of them was staring at the other. It was only when she watched them when they thought no one was looking that she got to see that they wanted each other.

Tonight, she had a plan to do something, but it could completely backfire, and she was so fucking nervous. When dinner was finished, she served them all up some apple pie. Even though everyone complained they couldn't move from all the food, when Gunner said he was ready to take the boys, they all left, getting into the car.

She went to the kitchen, cleaning away the dishes.

"It's just going to be the three of us tonight," John said.

"It is." She smiled at him. Gunner had called her earlier to let her know that Bennie and Carlos wouldn't be home tonight. That was when her plan had started to form.

"Do you like this kitchen?" John asked.

"Yeah, it's nice and big."

"I've been trying to get us to move out of our small house."

She laughed. "It's a house that is more than

suitable to our size, John."

"You're happy here."

"I'm cooking for Gunner, Bennie, Carlos, us. We don't need a bigger house," she said.

Finishing up the dishes, she put everything away and turned to look at her husband.

"I know you're not after my money," he said.

She chuckled. "I totally am. I want your money and the house and everything."

It had become like a tease between them.

"Am I interrupting something?" Gunner asked.

"Nope. That was fast," John said.

"They didn't have to go far."

John claimed her lips, and she moaned. Her body was setting on fire, and it would have been so easy for her to cave to their touch. Instead, she pulled away. "Who would like to play a game?" She went to the fridge, opening it. Pulling out some wine and beer, she held them up.

"Drinking is not a game," Gunner said, taking the bottle from her.

He downed it in a few short swigs, and she chuckled. "Perfect." Taking the bottle from him, she rinsed it out. "Now we have a perfect game. Spin the bottle?"

"Okay. Is this where we kiss in the corner or something?"

"No. How about we play truth or dare with it?" she asked. She could only do so much. Luring them into a game of spin the bottle was the easy part. Now she had to build up, and make sure they picked the right option.

So far, everything was going to plan.

Taking another beer out of the fridge, she handed it to Gunner.

"What do you boys say?" she asked. "We're

alone in this big house. We can have a little fun."

"I'm game," John said.

"You know we're not kids," Gunner said.

"Are you being a chicken?" Scarlett asked, chuckling. "Come on, Gunner. It's a bit of fun on a Friday night. Please."

"Fine, fine. Let's go and play."

Heading toward his sitting room, she got the two men to move the coffee table out of the way. Her hands shook a little as this could seriously backfire in more ways than one.

Taking her position, she waited for her men to sit down, and then she placed the bottle in the center. Pouring them out some wine, they waited as Gunner spun the bottle first. It landed on her.

"Truth or dare?" Gunner asked.

"Truth."

"Have you ever faked an orgasm?"

She chuckled. "No. My turn." Reaching out, she spun the bottle and it land on John. "Truth or dare, John."

"Truth."

"Have you ever stuck your dick in a vacuum nozzle?"

They all burst out laughing, and John answered no.

Around and around they went. John finished his first glass of wine, and she poured him a second.

They changed from truth to dare, and it started out as silly things. Gunner asked John to kiss the floor. John wanted her panties. Then Gunner dared for John to give him his boxers. After an hour of giggling, it was now her turn to spin the bottle. Several empty beers were on the floor, and the wine was down halfway, and she'd had two glasses, tops. The bottle spun, and it landed on John.

"Truth or dare?"

"Dare?"

Do it. Do it.

"Kiss Gunner for two minutes." She smiled at her husband, but she saw it. For a split second she saw that yearning that need he tried so hard to hide. Right here, right now, it was open for her to see.

It was only for a second or two, but she'd seen it. Sipping at her wine, she watched as John looked at Gunner.

"What?"

"You asked for a dare. Kiss Gunner for two minutes, and not a peck on the cheek either. Lips, the works." She waited and watched.

While John and Gunner looked at each other, she saw the outline of their arousal. They could deny it all they wanted, but they both wanted this.

"You've got to kiss me," Gunner said, opening his arms wide.

She watched, unable to look away.

John moved up close to Gunner, and she held her hand up in the air as if she was going to count.

"You want me to count down?" she asked.

Her pussy was on fire. They were both large men, both sexy, handsome, and hard. Biting her lip, she watched.

Neither of them told her to count down, so she didn't.

John's hand went to Gunner's cheek, and she watched as he sank it into his hair, holding him steady as his lips slammed down hard on Gunner's.

Warmth flooded her pussy as she watched.

This wasn't a friendly kiss.

Gunner and John were like two men that had been drowning and the only way to survive was to kiss each other, to completely take air from the other. Gunner gripped the back of John's head, his tongue tracing across John's lips.

She licked her own lips watching as the two men deepened the kiss, taking what the other wanted to give. Neither of them was fighting that want, that need.

The kiss lasted a long time.

It consumed them all, and she couldn't call time. Not even when it went past the two minutes.

They were amazing, and she watched them.

Finally, Gunner was the one to pull away first. They stared at each other, and she watched them.

"How long have you both been wanting to do that?" Scarlett asked.

They both turned to her, and the shock on their faces was clear to see. She sipped her wine watching each of them.

John shook his head as if to deny it.

"Don't lie. I've seen the way you both look at each other. You both want each other. How long?"

"Scarlett, this doesn't affect…"

She sighed. "You asked me to fuck your best friend. I've done that because I love you. I care for you, Gunner." That was putting her feelings very lightly. "But I've watched you two. I've seen the light caresses. The way you both look at one another. I don't doubt that you want me, but what about what you want with each other? Doesn't that matter?"

She watched both of them, seeing how nervous they were.

There was no denying this anymore. She wouldn't let them walk away from it, she couldn't.

Chapter Ten

For the first time in his life, Gunner had no words. He didn't know what to say to make this better or even if he could.

Scarlett sat on the sofa looking at both him and John. She wouldn't let either of them touch her. There was no anger in her eyes though. She wanted answers.

Gunner sighed. "I don't know."

"What?" John asked.

"I don't know when it started or when I found myself attracted to you. It has been harder to deny since we've been with Scarlett." He sat back, grabbing his beer and taking a seat in the chair opposite Scarlett. John did the same, looking at both of them. "You want to know the stupidest thing?"

"What?" Scarlett asked.

"I'm not interested in anyone else. I've looked at men. Every now and again I've gone out of town, wondered if I'm bisexual or something. No other man does it for me. I can't bring myself to touch anyone else. Yet when I'm with John, it's like I can't have anyone else. I figure it's down to trust."

"And love," Scarlett said. "You both do love each other. The one thing I noticed about the two of you is that in the last ten years neither of you ever referred to yourself as brothers. You were always best friends, partners, never brothers." She looked at each of them.

"We couldn't be brothers," John said. "The feelings I had for him, they were *not* brotherly."

"You ever wanted another man?" Scarlett asked.

"No, and this doesn't mean I don't want you."

John reached out and took her hand.

Gunner watched them.

"I know it doesn't, and this isn't about not wanting me. I know you both do." She looked toward him.

"We do," Gunner said. "I want you both."

"Then I don't want either of you to hold back," she said. "When we're together, I want you both to touch, to explore, to kiss, to fuck each other."

He couldn't not look away from her. "You planned this."

She didn't dispute it, and he turned to look at John.

"I thought this was weird with the game, the alcohol, and stuff like that, but it was more than that, wasn't it?"

Scarlett looked at him. "I knew that both of you would deny the feelings you have for each other. I didn't want either of you to deny anything. I don't … I want this."

"You want your husband and his best friend to fuck?"

"Yes."

This time he laughed. "You're crazy."

Scarlett stood, putting her glass on the floor, as she stepped toward him. Gunner watched as she wriggled out of her jeans, then took his hand, placing it between her thighs. Her panties were damp, and as he slid his fingers across her pussy, moving beneath the band of her panties, he found her slick.

"That's what seeing the two of you did to me."

He slid a finger inside her pussy, finding her even more wet.

John moved up behind her, cupping her tits, and he watched his friend remove her shirt and cup her tits.

"You were a very naughty girl," John said.

She reached behind her. "And yet you're hard as

rock. I needed to be naughty for you both today." She rested her head against his shoulder. "You wouldn't have acted on it, and I wanted to see this. To be with you both."

Standing up, Gunner held his slick fingers out to John. "Taste her."

John looked at her, then at Gunner.

"Taste me, John. Taste what you've both done to me."

Reaching out, he ran his fingers over John's lips. His friend finally opened his mouth and sucked his digits inside.

His cock pulsed in arousal, and he watched John. There was no reason to deny it.

"It doesn't have to leave this room," Scarlett said. "All three of us together."

Flicking the catch of the bra, Gunner freed her tits, and John held them up.

Leaning forward, Gunner took one nipple into his mouth, tasting her. He bit down on the hard bud before soothing out the sting with his tongue. She cried out his name.

Cupping her naked pussy, he slipped a finger between her sweet folds, finding her clit. Round and over, down, and around, he played with her clit while sucking her tit.

John held her body as he played with her.

Suddenly, Scarlett pulled away, breaking all contact with her. "Get naked."

Her voice was a little shaky and so was her body. She pushed some of her hair out of her eyes, and she stared at them. "Both of you, completely naked."

Gunner's nostrils flared. He wasn't used to being the one that was ordered around. He liked doing the commanding.

Removing his clothes, he stood, like John, completely naked, at her mercy.

"Look at each other," she said.

Gunner's eyes turned to John. His best friend, his secret yearning.

"Touch each other."

It was like her words unlocked that barrier that had been holding them captive for so long.

Reaching out, Gunner gripped the back of John's neck, pulling him close to his body. He'd done this so many times with Scarlett. It felt only natural to do this with John. Pressing his nose against John's neck, he breathed in the scent of his friend, finding his arousal once again.

For so long he'd kept his distance, hiding what he really wanted, that it seemed strange to be acting on it now.

With his other hand, he trailed his fingers down John's back, cupping his ass. So firm, completely different from Scarlett's soft flesh. Glancing over at her, he saw her smiling at him. She gave him a nod, and he saw something in her eyes—he didn't know completely what, but it was something that struck him hard. She wanted this, wanted the two of them together.

She wouldn't make either of them choose.

Out of the corner of his eye, he watched as Scarlett leaned back, her legs opening and her hand trailing down her body. He couldn't look away even as he reached out, taking hold of John's cock. Running his hand up and down his friend's length, he watched as Scarlett teased her pussy.

"Look at her," he said. "She's wanting to watch us fuck."

John's head turned to look at his wife.

"You don't have to hide from me," she said. "I'm

here, and I'm not going anywhere. I want you both to want each other."

"Slide a finger into your cunt," John said, his voice firm as he gave her the order. "Add a second finger."

Scarlett pushed a second finger deep inside her cunt, and Gunner ran his thumb across John's tip.

"I think it's time you did something as well," Gunner said. He pressed down on his friend's shoulder, and John didn't put up a fight. With his mouth inches from Gunner's cock, he gripped his flesh, running the tip across his lips. He'd thought about this moment for many years, so often, refusing to give himself the chance to go any further than just a thought or a secret fantasy.

"You like seeing this, Scarlett? Your husband on the floor, worshiping my cock."

"Yes."

John wrapped his fingers around Gunner's dick, working up and down the length before finally taking the tip into his mouth.

Gunner groaned the moment John's lips were on him. They were hard, firm, and he used just a little teeth to make it almost painful.

The sound of movement had him looking toward Scarlett. She moved from the sofa and came to kneel down beside John.

"Do you mind me joining in?"

She was a little fucking minx. He couldn't believe that she'd gotten them to this point, when neither of them had been able to do that.

Sinking his fingers into her hair, he wrapped it around his fist, and guided her close. John came off his cock, and Scarlett took her turn. She bobbed her head onto his shaft, taking him as deep into her mouth as she could before gagging. She pulled off his cock, and with his dick between them, he watched as John and Scarlett both kissed. They did so even with his cock there, stopping them.

Gripping the back of John's head, he held them both. Glancing down, he saw that Scarlett was also touching John's dick. They were all connected, all being pleasured.

"That feels so fucking good," he said, watching them both. "Suck her tits," he ordered John. With Scarlett taking care of his cock, he was able to enjoy watching John play with her tits.

Her moan vibrated up the length of his shaft, and he felt so fucking needy. So possessed by everything that she could give him. She wasn't just giving her body to them, she'd brought them both together, and he didn't want to lose that.

Seeing and feeling John at his feet, loving his cock, and also touching their woman, he wanted so much more. He didn't want this to be a one-time thing. The look in John's eyes told him straight, this wasn't one time. There were going to be many times.

Tugging on Scarlett's hair, she got to her feet, and he took possession of her mouth. John, needing no further instruction, took over sucking his cock.

"Do you like that?" she asked. "Do you like having his mouth on you?"

"You know I do. You're the only person who has ever seen through all our bullshit." Tilting her head back, he cupped her cheek. "You're not jealous?"

"No. You both get to share me, and now I get to watch and share the two of you." She cupped his face. "You've both been wanting each other for a long time. I get it. I know how it feels to want. I can give this to you. To both of you."

He saw it in the eyes, the pain of not being able to

have children, of wanting them.

Soon.

He knew that soon he'd fill her with his child.

They could be happy with their life together, and he was more than ready to take a chance.

He'd even give up his patch if that was what was needed.

"Let's move this to the bedroom," he said.

"I agree." Scarlett pulled out of his arms, and he watched her ass as she walked away. John stood up, and Gunner caught him, holding him tight. "I had no idea you wanted this."

"I didn't know you wanted it either. I've fought it for so long I kind of just figured it would never happen."

"Does it bother you that she knows?" Gunner asked. "That she was the one who did this for us?"

"No. It bothers me that she doesn't know what we've tried to do. I don't want to tell her. Not yet."

"It'll solve all of our problems." Gunner didn't like lying to her.

"Or it could ruin what we're about to share. Let us enjoy this, Gunner. If you're not happy, start using condoms, but the end result is the same. I want her pregnant. I don't want to keep going home to an empty nursery. I'm a bastard for wanting the things I want, but I'm doing it because I love her. I love her more than anything." John kissed him hard, almost punishing. "Just like I love you, and I have for a long time."

Hearing those words, Gunner kissed him back, needing him unlike anyone else. "I love you too, and your wife." He'd fallen for Scarlett hard, and he didn't want to be without either of them.

"She loves you too. She just doesn't realize it."

****

John entered the bedroom and found his wife in a

position that turned him on. Kneeling on the bed, he took her face between his hands, and kissed her hard. "How long did you know?"

"I got a few clues when we first started. Then you were drunk and you said some things. I put two and two together and thought it would be best to see," she said.

"And you're okay with it?"

"John, you've been sharing me with your best friend. How can I not be okay with it?"

"There's no other woman in my life. No one else I'd ever want. I love you more than anything in the world."

She silenced him with a kiss. Gunner had yet to arrive, but that was fine. John knew he would.

"You don't have to worry about anything. This is … different, but we always promised each other when our needs changed or if we wanted something more, we'd get it. I want you to be with Gunner. I want to watch and see the two of you together. I don't want you to be afraid. I'm going to be here. You're not going to get rid of me that easily." She placed her hand over his heart. There were only two people he loved in this world, and one of them was right in front of him.

In the back of his mind he knew he should tell her about his agreement with Gunner. She wanted kids so badly, and he couldn't give them to her. Would she be hurt? He didn't know. There was a chance of it, and right now, when he was about to get everything he ever dreamed of, he didn't want to risk losing it.

He was a selfish bastard, and he knew he'd regret this, but he didn't see any other way.

Gunner entered the room, and John turned to look at his friend. His cock stood hard and proud, the tip glistening with pre-cum. His mouth watered, recalling the taste of him. He wanted him again, and again.

"This is my bedroom," Gunner said. "This is my domain, and what I say, you do."

"Yes," Scarlett said.

John nodded, and then voiced his response.

"Good. John, spread her legs and lick her pussy. I want you to get it nice and wet for me."

John eased Scarlett to the bed. Moving between her thighs, he opened her lips, sliding his tongue across her clit, then down to her pussy. Drawing it back up, he circled her clit. Gunner moved across the room and out of the corner of his eye, he watched his friend go to a drawer. He pulled out a tube of lubricant and came back to the bed. He also held a couple of condoms, placing them on the bed. John didn't let up licking Scarlett even as Gunner moved between her thighs. He didn't put a condom on either. With his face so close, John watched as Gunner filled his wife, making her take every single inch of his cock.

Running his tongue down her slit, he licked Gunner's cock as he entered her. Everything came naturally to him, how to touch, to lick, to draw more of an arousal out of Gunner. They'd been sharing women for years, and he didn't see anything wrong with using his skills and knowledge of their time together to his advantage.

Gunner pulled out of her pussy, and John was there, licking his cock, sucking it, working the length, moaning as he filled his throat with both of their tastes. He pulled out, and Gunner fucked Scarlett. John used either his fingers or tongue to get him off.

"Fuck, you feel so good," Gunner said. "I can't wait anymore."

He pulled out of Scarlett, leaving her whimpering.

"John, I want you to fuck your wife, to take her

hard, and make her beg for it."

Grabbing his cock, John stood between her legs. Finding her entrance, he slid in deep. He moaned at the feel of her tight cunt wrapped around him. He didn't want to move as her pussy pulsed around him, each little ripple turning him on even more.

Gunner took one of the condoms, tearing into it.

Part of him wanted to change places to have Gunner fucking Scarlett so that they had a higher chance of getting her pregnant, but he didn't want to ruin this moment.

So much he wanted to do and say and he couldn't. This was all because of his own actions. Gritting his teeth, he slammed to the hilt inside her, watching her tits bounce. Damn, he loved this woman. He'd loved her from the first moment he'd seen her.

He'd craved her more than anything else.

Gunner touched his back, and he stopped. Fingers stroked across the puckered hole of his ass, and he closed his eyes.

"Is he touching you?" she asked.

"Yes."

"It feels a little weird, doesn't it? Like you want him to stop but then continue."

He saw the wicked smile in her eyes, and knew she was having fun with this. When they first tried anal sex, she'd been nervous, and he'd told her everything would feel fine. "You're getting your own back?"

"Just a little."

He slammed inside her, and she groaned.

John stopped as the tip of Gunner's cock pressed against his ass. He'd never done this before, and even as he was unsure, he needed it.

So many different feelings were rushing through him, and not all of them entirely certain. He wanted it so much.

Slowly, Gunner pushed against his ass, and he gritted his teeth.

Scarlett moved up, taking hold of his ass and spreading the cheeks. She kissed his chest. "Don't forget to push out and to relax, baby. It's supposed to fit, and you'll love it. Those first inches are always the worst."

"Using my own words against me is not cool."

She chuckled. "But it's a lot of fun."

Sinking his fingers into her hair, he pulled her head back, taking possession of her lips. He groaned as Gunner worked his cock inside him, and they both gasped as they were suddenly all together.

Scarlett would be able to feel it as Gunner's body touched her fingers. He felt them around him.

Fuck, it was the best feeling in the world, and he didn't want it to end. He didn't know it could be like this.

Closing his eyes, he felt everything. Scarlett's cunt on his dick, Gunner's cock pulsing in his ass. Everything was on fire, but it was the good kind of fire. The kind that he didn't want to put out.

"Fuck, that feels good," Gunner said, his hands going to John's hips.

Pulling out of Scarlett's pussy, John drove inside again. He held still as Gunner started to work his ass, going in and out, testing him, driving him wild as his cock seemed to stroke a part of him that made him ache.

"Touch yourself," Gunner said. "I want him to feel your tight cunt wrapped around his dick as you come. You're always so tight and feel so fucking good."

Scarlett touched her pussy, and John felt as her cunt started to clench around him. His own release wasn't far, and he wanted to come so badly. To fill her pussy with his cum, to make her pregnant. Together he and Gunner could do anything and had done everything and now he wanted her.

"You want to come," Gunner asked, thrusting in deep.

"Yes."

"You get to wait until our lady comes. She looks so pretty when she does."

"Please," she said.

Her body was getting tighter as he fucked her. She came hard, her cunt so incredibly tight as he filled her. Her pussy milked him, but he held back. Gunner was the one in charge. He made the rules, not him.

Gunner held perfectly still within him. They both watched Scarlett as she came.

"Now you can come," Gunner said.

Together he and Gunner fucked, John driving his cock into her pussy while Gunner owned his ass.

Both of them were together, fucking harder than ever before, and he took it. He took everything his friend had to give him and relishing the bite of pain as it came.

When his release came, he did so with a shout, slamming inside her, filling her with his cum as he felt Gunner do the same. Each pulse was like a brand within him, telling him who owned his body.

Gunner owned him.

Scarlett owned him.

Just like he owned them.

Collapsing over her, he rested his head on her breasts, exhausted, sated, and just fucking happy.

Scarlett stroked her fingers through his hair just the way he loved.

Afterward, Gunner pulled out of him and left to go and run a bath. He heard the sounds coming from the bathroom, and Gunner had a pretty big bathtub that would easily fit all three of them inside.

Pushing some of his wife's brown hair out of the

way, he stared down at her, seeing her smile.

"You okay?"

"Yeah, I'm okay. Are you?" she asked.

"Yeah, I'm on cloud nine right now."

"That's good to know. I was so worried that you'd hate me," she said.

"What for?"

"For manipulating you both. I didn't know what to do, but I knew you needed each other, and if there was anything I could do to bring you both together I wanted to. I didn't want either of you to go without." She was still stroking his hair.

Guilt filled him.

She'd given him everything, and he was taking the chance of a baby out of her hands. He was asking his friend without her permission. It was on the tip of his tongue to come clean.

Gunner came in, and John was too much of a coward to spoil the moment.

Pulling out of her pussy, he lifted her up in his arms, holding her, showing her that he loved her.

You've got to tell her the truth.

He lowered her into the tub, and followed her in. Gunner moved to her other side, and they relaxed back in the warmth of the water.

"I do love it here," she said.

"Why don't you and John move in?" Gunner asked.

John looked toward his friend.

"I've got plenty of room, and I don't want this to just fizzle out, or for us to try and decide where we want to live." Gunner shrugged.

He glanced at Scarlett. She was biting her lip. "If that is what you both want. Will your boys mind?"

"They love having you cook for them. Believe

me. It beats takeout every single day of the week."

"Then consider it done," John said. He tugged Scarlett over to him. "You finally get that big house I always wanted for you."

She didn't say anything.

Gunner held up the soap, and then words were not necessary.

****

John had to rush into work the following day, so Scarlett came home and decided to start packing. Bennie and Carlos were helping and had already taken some of the stuff with them back to Gunner's home.

She didn't know if she wanted to put this house up on the market. It was her first ever home. After living in a trailer park as a child and then a rundown apartment, this was the first place that had ever felt like home.

Moving in with Gunner was … different. It felt like it was a step away from talking about children.

Yes, she loved John, and she wanted to give him whatever his heart desired. Changing homes, it felt like a part of her was closing off her own dreams of having children. Living with Gunner wouldn't allow for them to talk about the nursery or what they wanted.

"You okay?" Gunner asked, stepping into the room.

She had a photograph album open to her and John's wedding photo. Last night had been one of the most incredible and highly erotic moments of her life. Watching Gunner and John together had been hot, seriously hot, smoking hot.

"Yeah, I'm okay."

He sat on the bed beside her, and he glanced down at the album on her lap. "You looked so beautiful that day. You look beautiful all the time, but that day, you shone unlike anyone else."

She looked at the photo and saw how both she and John looked at each other. "I was so happy. Don't get me wrong, I was nervous. I thought up until the last second that he'd change his mind. That he'd realize he didn't want to marry me."

"He never did though."

"No. Everything is changing so fast. I'm just trying to keep up."

Gunner twirled one of her ponytails around his finger. She had one on either side tied with two bands at the base of her neck.

"Do you not want to move in with me?"

"I do. I'd like to see where this all goes. It feels important that we do. Not just for me and John but for you and John. Did you have any idea that he wanted you? Like the way you do him?"

Gunner sighed, dropping his hand. "No. It wasn't something that ever came up. I guess with me having Cherry for so long and him being with you, it didn't seem important. You were very brave doing what you did last night."

She laughed. "Having two hot men get it on wasn't brave."

"No, but it could have ended differently if you'd misread us."

"I'd been watching you both since that first night that you and I were together. Something felt … strange. I don't know. Like there was an underlying current that I didn't understand."

"And do you understand it now?" he asked.

"I think so. You and John have an attraction to each other that's not easily denied."

He snorted. "We've been denying it for some time."

"Or maybe you both hadn't allowed yourself the

time to think about it." She shrugged. "I'm happy for you both."

Gunner turned her, cupping her cheek. "What's wrong?"

"It's nothing."

"You can tell me everything."

She took a deep breath, nervous about the way he made her heart ache for him. She loved her husband, and truly believed she'd only ever love one man, but when it came to Gunner, she found herself falling for him just as easily.

Slowly, over the past few weeks she'd felt herself drawn to Gunner. Maybe it was because of all the extra time they were spending together. She didn't know, but her own feelings for him wouldn't go away.

"Whatever you want, John and I will work to make it happen. We want you to have everything your heart desires."

Tears filled her eyes, and she pulled away from him, the photograph album falling to the floor.

"I'm sorry."

Gunner picked up the letter that was inside the album. It was confirming the results of John's infertility.

He read over the document.

"You want kids."

"It doesn't matter."

"Scarlett. Whatever you want, it does matter."

She brushed her hair off her face and stared at him. "It's … hard to put into words."

"Try me. I'm a good listener."

She wrung her hands together, and then stopped to look at him.

"Do you have another spare room?"

"Yes."

"You do?"

"I do. There's five bedrooms in that house and two bathrooms. The one between our rooms that is shared. Bennie and Carlos share as well. Then I have a bedroom. It's spare. Is this about the nursery?"

"John doesn't want to talk about it, Gunner. He doesn't want to speak about our options, and I … I want a baby." She pressed her hands against her face, feeling so utterly selfish. "I know, I'm awful."

Gunner pulled her in close, his arms wrapping around her, protecting her.

"You're not awful. Don't cry. We'll all talk about this."

"But you already have kids and you're not going to want any more screaming around the house. I want to get started on either IVF or adoption because it all takes time, and he won't listen." She sniffled. "I'm so sorry about this. We're meant to be packing, and I'm crying."

She heard the sound of a car parking out front and then Bennie and Carlos as they made their way upstairs.

Scarlett tried to pull out of his arms, but he wouldn't let her. He kept her in his arms, refusing to let go.

"Hey, Dad," Bennie said. "Is everything okay?"

"It's fine. There are a bunch of boxes in the fridge. Pack up all the groceries as well."

She knew Bennie hesitated.

Seconds later he was gone, and she wrapped her arms around Gunner. "Did you give him your evil glare?"

"It's the glare I like to give that gets shit done."

"It's a really mean glare though." She sniffed, finding the scent of leather a comfort. "Do you give all of your men that fierce look?"

"Only the ones that deserve it."

She pulled away and wiped at her eyes. "I must

look a mess."

"You always look perfect to me."

"Will our presence in your home cause a problem with your ex?"

"Let me deal with Cherry. She's not going to cause any trouble." He pressed a kiss to her lips.

She melted against him, wrapping her arms around him. Placing her head on his chest, she sighed. "Will you talk to him? I don't think he'll listen to me."

Gunner seemed to tense a little beneath her touch.

"It's fine. I can talk to him."

"Let me do it, Scarlett. I'll talk to him and get him to see sense."

She smiled up at him. "Thank you."

"Don't even mention it."

Chapter Eleven

There was no time to talk to John over the weekend. Between moving them in, and then celebrating, Gunner found a million different reasons to hold off the conversation. Not only that, he was keeping a close eye on the club. Kent seemed to be sticking close, and because of it, Gunner was being extra cautious. His patience was starting to wear thin but right now, he didn't have any proof. Short of having the money in his hands, gut instinct didn't help him. At least he had Scarlett and John's drama to keep him occupied. Her need for a baby had touched him deeply. He wanted to give her what she wanted. Why she didn't consider him he didn't know, but he didn't want her to think about all the times he'd taken her without a condom.

Something wasn't right for Gunner. It wasn't like Scarlett to hold back or to make a deal out of something.

He'd never used a condom with her. He'd filled her with his cum so many times that he'd lost count.

Sitting in his office in his club, he stared down at the latest security footage and saw fucking nothing. Time was running out, and if someone was coming to take his patch from him, he wanted to be ready, and the only way to be ready was to be prepared.

Getting out of his seat, he overlooked the parking lot and saw Kent's bike wasn't there. It was the first time, since Gunner had discovered the missing cash, that Kent had left the clubhouse. This was an opportunity he'd been waiting for. Not willing to miss it, he quickly got into action. Leaving his office, he made the decision, and moved toward the back of the clubhouse where all the rooms were. Some of the boys stayed at the clubhouse, along with the club whores. Not every man had something sweet to go home to like he did.

Finding Kent's room, which was at the bottom of the long hallway, he opened the door, finding it unlocked.

He entered, and quickly closed it behind him. Kent was a fucking slob. Unlike his apartment, which was squeaky clean, this place was a fucking mess. Used condoms littered the floor, and clothes were all strewn around, which made him wonder why. Kent had been sticking close to the club more often than usual. He'd not noticed it before, but it was clear to see now.

The women cleaned on a daily basis. Unless someone asked for them not to. Why didn't Kent want anyone going through his room? This just heightened his suspicions of Kent's motivations.

Moving toward the man's desk, he wrinkled his nose at the overfilled ashtray, empty beer cans, and he was sure he saw puke on the desk.

"Fucking pig."

Keeping Kent as his VP had been important at the time, but right now, he was having some serious fucking doubts. When he'd taken control of the club, there had been a shitload of bloodshed. Even though he'd had doubts about Kent, he still had that belief that with the right leadership he'd be able to change the club. He'd changed it, but Kent still had bad blood inside him. The need for destruction and death was clearly ripe in his veins.

Enemies closer and all that shit started to look overrated.

Opening the desk, he found nothing. Paperwork and notes, along with the odd drawing was all bullshit. Everything was disgusting. He didn't know how the fuck a man could live in this shit. Even during his time in war zones, he'd never experienced this kind of filth.

Once he covered every single work surface and still nothing, he couldn't help the feeling that he was missing something.

Glancing across the room, he noticed the closet. There was no point in not looking at it now. He wouldn't get another opportunity like this again. Going to the closet, he opened it up, and started to rummage through everything. He was surprised to see that the closet was as clean as Kent's apartment. Nothing seemed out of place. Jeans were hung neatly, shirts folded, boots cleaned.

"Come on, fucking think." Looking around the small space, he paused.

There in the back corner he found a box. Pulling it out, he flicked the lid off, and there was the money that had been going missing.

Lots of it.

He lifted the money out, and right at the bottom of the pile was a bag of cartel cocaine. He recognized the packaging as he'd transported some as a messenger. All of his suspicions were fucking true. The only problem he had now, was did Kent act alone? From what Carlos told him, no. There were rats in his club that he had to find, and find them he would. His club fucking depended on it.

His rage knew no bounds as he stared at the evidence of the traitorous son of a bitch. This pissed him off so fucking much. He'd done nothing but steer the club in the right direction, and Kent was going to pull them down. His position within the club would never be fucking taken from him. He'd deal with Kent and all those traitors.

Putting the money back into the box, he put the lid on and left the room.

Making his way downstairs toward his office, he glanced up and saw some of his men laughing and joking. They were going about their business. Some of them had to have known.

"Church in one hour," Gunner said.

He didn't allow them to argue with him. He was the fucking Prez, and he could call church whenever he fucking felt like it. Kent's betrayal would be dealt with, and he wanted to fucking kill the bastard.

Sitting in the meeting room, staring at the patch, the club's symbol carved into the wooden table, he gritted his teeth. He'd gotten this table specially crafted when he became Prez. Before him it had just been one fucking table with no meaning. This was how much the club meant to him. It had given him something to focus on when he'd gotten out of the army. There was no way he was ever going to let that fucker destroy what he'd built. The club was his, and he was going to keep it in the right direction.

His cell phone rang, and as he pulled it out of his pocket, he saw it was Scarlett. For the first time in his life, he turned his cell phone off and ignored the call. Right now, he had to deal with a traitor in his midst.

For an hour he sat there, waiting, preparing. One by one his men started to arrive, and he watched them. Each of them looked so fucking weary as they stared at him, but he didn't give a fuck.

As Prez of the Satan's Demons MC, it was his right to call this meeting, to bring shit to the table, to get them all to vote, but it was his vote that would decide.

One by one they entered, Kent coming in last, looking so fucking smug. Gunner watched him as he looked at a couple of the men. Two of them were old-timers who wanted to be part of the cartel. Another was brand new, not long earned his patch, but that was enough. All of them were going to go to ground.

"What the fuck is all this about?" Kent asked, taking a seat.

"We have a traitor in our midst." He didn't take his eyes off his VP. "Someone who thinks they can steal club money and get away with it. Someone who wants to run with the cartels and get away with it. Someone who wants to take my place as Prez." Again, he didn't look away, but out of the corner of his eye, he saw a couple of people twitch. Some people didn't want him to leave. He knew what he was doing. All of his life he'd been a protector, and he would do whatever it took to protect this club. He'd take his own life to serve it.

He'd given his all.

The moment he killed the son of a bitch who had this club and was working it into the ground, Gunner had stepped in. He'd taken the patch and been sure to make sure the boys prospered from their decision. They all got an equal share. Their families were always taken care of, and life was fucking easy for them.

Every few weeks, he demanded a few club runs for business and to also keep them in the know of what was going on.

Moving his gaze away from Kent, he looked at each of his men.

"What makes you think someone is stealing from the club?" Kent asked.

"I noticed the money not matching up. I saw the doctored sheets, and I had John looking into it."

"Please, John Williams is a pussy. He's so wrapped around that wife of his he can't even see straight," Kent said.

"He's the best damn accountant in the country. He wasn't the only one that was looking into it. I was. I noticed it first, and I brought it to his attention." He glared at Kent. "This is my club, and I have no intention of taking it lightly. The cartels are not the right way to go. You want that shit riding in your town, you're giving yourselves a death sentence." He stood up, grabbed the box, and tossed out the contents in front of Kent.

Kent immediately got to his feet, gun raised. "You think this proves anything?"

"Guns are not supposed to be in the club."

His VP burst out laughing. "You're fucking delusional, Gunner. This club is mine and will always be mine. The cartels are inevitable. You're just too fucking blind to see it."

Gunner saw his men holding down Kent's men.

He couldn't find a way to take on Kent.

"They want me as Prez," Kent said, moving back. "I *will* have it. This club will be fucking mine."

Kent opened the door, firing his gun, making them all take cover. During the struggle, two of the men got away, and Gunner rushed out after them. They were already gone, and he slammed his hand against the door.

They were fucking cowards.

Making his way back toward the main meeting room, he grabbed the remaining men and began shoving them out back of the clubhouse. He took them to the place where he'd taken the life of the previous Prez, and also anyone who thought to wrong the club.

His men, the ones that were loyal to him, had his back, and were by his side, waiting.

Grabbing a gun from Ford, he pointed it at the first man. "Tell me what I want to know," Gunner said.

"Why the fuck should we?" Grayson said, spitting on the dirty by his feet.

Gunner fired his gun at the man's leg, making sure not to hit anywhere that would make him bleed out fast.

"Because if you don't, I'm going to make this as long and as painful as possible. Believe me, I can do this shit for days to get what I want. At night, I'll be here, watching, keeping you men in this exact position. Then of course, the animals will come, maybe rats, or wolves, or I'll starve some dogs. Get them really nice and hungry before I set them on your fucking ass. You decided to stick with a traitor. Kent will get what is coming to him. This is my club, and instead of taking me on, he was a coward. Turning you all away from the club like this is a fucking playground. This is the real world, gentlemen. I don't play by the playground rules, and no teacher is going to be coming to your rescue anytime soon." One by one, he fired the gun so that all the men had matching wounds. "Tick tock, gentlemen. I don't have all fucking day."

****

John was so fucking pissed. Storming into the clubhouse, he saw the women were hanging around, looking bored as shit.

The Prospects were no better.

"Where the fuck is Gunner?" he asked.

"He's dealing with club business."

Ignoring the nerve of the little shit, he walked into Gunner's office, then into the main church meeting place, which overlooked the back of the club. Looking out the window, he saw Gunner dealing with his men.

John didn't give a shit.

Charging outside, he watched as each man drew their gun, but he didn't care.

"John, what the fuck are you doing here?" Gunner asked. His friend's rage was clear to see, but that didn't match what John was feeling.

"Why haven't you been answering your fucking cell?"

"I got proof it was Kent. He's gone with a couple of the guys. I'm trying to get this shit handled. What the fuck is your problem?"

He stared at the four men who were kneeling in the dirt, blood draining out of them, covering the ground. It wasn't something he hadn't seen before, but that meant Gunner didn't know.

"This is important?" John asked.

"Yes, it is fucking important. You think I'm out here having a tea party?"

Grabbing Gunner's weapon, John approached the men. Pointing the gun at the man's dick, he fired. Immediately he went down to the ground, howling in pain.

"If Gunner even shows one of you any mercy, it's going to be without a dick. You may as well start talking." He looked at each of them, seeing the fear in their eyes. But he wasn't interested right now. He had to get Gunner out of here, and to the fucking hospital. "You got a knife?" John asked.

Gunner was already handing him a blade. Stepping up to the second man, he grabbed the man's dick through his pants, and began to run the blade around the flesh, removing it from his body. The pain was clear as his screams filled the air around them. Throwing the dick to the floor, John was careful not to get any blood on him, but when you were removing flesh, that was kind of hard to do.

He moved toward the next guy and stared him in the eye. Lifting the point of his blade to the man's eye, he waited, showing him that he wasn't afraid to insert the point and take out the man's eye.

"Tell me what I want to know."

"Kent wants the club," the man on the end said. "He wants it so badly that he started to do deals with the cartels on the side. They wanted him to start distributing coke, and they gave him a fifty percent cut. The money was fucking incredible, and it was easy work. So easy.

Luring bitches to work for them, getting them hooked on the dough, and all they had to do was earn their money on their backs, and we got another cut of that share as well. Kent promised an easy life."

"How fucking easy do you want your life to be? You want me to wipe the shit from your ass when you go to the toilet?"

The image had John's nose wrinkling.

"You've got two weeks. Kent thought that he could keep doing side orders, and getting it past you, but the time was up. The cartels wanted him to either make good on his promise, or else take you out to prove his loyalty."

"What did they want?"

"The club. They wanted the club running the show, taking over the girls, the drugs, and dealing with the hits that they needed solving."

"He wanted fucking minions. Not such easy money."

"Kent thinks it will be. He's wanted this club for a long time, and he's going to do whatever he can to make you want it."

"Why steal the money?" John asked.

"Gunner was distracted by you and by Scarlett. Kent stole the money and was going to plant it in hope of showing that you weren't fair, that you lied, and that you'd never had the club's best interest at heart." The man John had pointed the knife to the eye spoke up.

"But that backfired. You lock everything, unlike some people, and Kent, nor any of us could get into it."

"I think that's everything," John said. Standing up, he pointed the gun at all four men. One by one, he shot them in the head, and turned toward Gunner. "You were right. You had a traitor in your midst, but now you need to get to the hospital."

Gunner frowned.

"You got a phone call you ignored. That was Scarlett. The school couldn't get in touch with you or with Cherry, so they called Scarlett. Bennie was beaten up real bad and is in intensive care. Someone bashed his head in with a metal pipe, and they had to take him into surgery."

He saw the fear in Gunner's face, and the panicked look.

"We've got this, Prez. We've got your back. Go, take care of him."

Gunner spun on his heel and took off. John was about to follow him when the club stopped him.

"Keep an eye on him, and the family."

He didn't know why, but he believed they were showing him respect. Nodding at each of them, he ran toward the car. Gunner was already inside, and as he sat down, Gunner was already leaving.

"Do we know who it was?"

"No one's talking at the moment. Don't worry. I can make sure they do," John said. "I leave you alone for two fucking minutes and you nearly have a takeover on your hands, and your son in the hospital."

"Not right now, John. You can question me any other time but not fucking today."

John stayed silent as they made their way toward the hospital. When Scarlett had called him, she'd been so fucking scared. It had taken everything inside him not to go straight to the hospital. He, himself, had been in meetings and told his secretary to hold his calls while he dealt with a couple of clients.

The one day that Scarlett needed them both, neither of them had been answering their calls. It was only when she finally convinced his secretary that if she didn't take the phone to him, she'd lose her job, did she actually do it.

Gunner pulled up outside of the hospital, and John climbed over the seats so that he could take control, and park the car.

Once that was done, he entered the hospital and saw Scarlett with red eyes standing beside Gunner. The moment she saw him, she rushed toward his arms, holding him close.

"I'm so sorry for calling like that. I didn't want to do it, but I…"

"I know, baby. I know. I'm so sorry. I just wanted to get done with a few meetings, and then everything went to shit." He cupped her face. "Are you okay?"

"Of course I'm okay. That little boy isn't though."

John held her close and glanced toward the seating area. Carlos was there, staring at nothing. Just sitting.

The anger was there in his eyes.

"What are they saying?"

"He's stable at the moment but critical. There was swelling on his brain, and they had to drain the pressure. They don't know if he'll fully recover. The attack happened so suddenly. They … broke his back. There's going to be a lot of physical therapy, John."

He held her close, and while they waited for Gunner to finish with the doctor, they took a seat on either side of Carlos.

"They waited," Carlos said.

"What?"

"They waited until he was alone. They knew they couldn't take us on together, or with friends, so they waited until he was at his most vulnerable." Carlos's hands were shaking.

John placed a hand on his back, hoping to calm

him down. "None of this was your fault."

"I knew. I fucking knew. I had this bad feeling all day long, and I didn't know what it was." Carlos dropped his head into his hands. "The way they were. I was watching them. Being younger, they don't see me all that much. I'm not as big a threat."

John was starting to think with the rage that Carlos was showing that may not be the case.

"They will all pay," Carlos said. "I'll make sure of it."

"I've got to go and see him. They can only take a couple of people."

"Carlos, go and see your brother," Scarlett said. "You need to."

Gunner nodded, and Carlos stood.

Scarlett took Carlos's seat and took John's hand, locking their fingers together. "Thank you for today," she said. "There's a spare shirt in the car, John."

He frowned, turning to look at her.

"It's faint, but I can see the blood spatter, and seeing as we're in the hospital, I imagine they can as well."

She forced a smile to her lips, and he kissed her before heading out to the car.

Opening up the trunk, he found the bag that held the spare clothes that she always made him pack in case of emergencies. Pulling out the crisp white shirt, he removed his other one, placing it on the car.

Fastening the buttons, his gaze landed on the faint splashes of blood. Scarlett was right. Unless you were an expert there was no way for anyone to notice, but it was there.

He hadn't thought when he got the clubhouse; he'd reacted. His friend had been in danger, his wife was scared, and he'd done what needed to be done.

It's what he'd been doing all of his life, making the calls that others couldn't, like with his wife's pregnancy. He made the call without asking her because he knew deep down, she'd say no, and he didn't want her to say no.

Folding up the shirt, he stuffed it into the bag and made his way back inside. Carlos and Gunner hadn't returned.

"Gunner's going to get his own back, isn't he?"

"Whoever attacked his kid is going to wish they'd never been born, or even heard of the kid's name."

Scarlett looked up at him. "You're going to be by his side, aren't you? At the club."

"I don't know, baby. I know that I can't let him be alone right now. There's danger out there. I don't want you to be anywhere on your own."

She nodded. "You'll tell me everything?"

"Of course. I don't keep any secrets from you." He cupped her cheek and leaned over, kissing her.

****

Scarlett wasn't allowed to go to either her home or Gunner's home. Unless she was taken to the hospital, or to work with an escort, she couldn't go anywhere. She stayed in Gunner's room, not that she'd seen much of Gunner or John lately. They were at the hospital a lot of the time, or John was at work.

Something was going down at the clubhouse, but again, she didn't know what.

Carlos was withdrawn. Gunner wouldn't let him go to school, so she'd gone to collect work. When they'd tried to make excuses for what had happened, she ignored them, or gave them each a piece of her mind, not that it made any difference.

John told her not to worry, that he and Gunner had everything figured out. She had no doubt that it meant they were going to kill whoever had hurt Bennie.

Bennie was still in a medically induced coma and showed no signs of waking up anytime soon.

Rubbing at her temples, she felt the beginnings of a headache.

"Are you okay?"

She looked up to see Gunner in the doorway. It had been a couple of days since Bennie's attack. He looked … dangerous.

"Yeah, I'm okay. What about you? It looks like you haven't really slept much."

She put the book that she'd been attempting to read to one side, and getting to her feet, she made her way toward him.

There was an odor coming from him, and she sighed. "Come on, we need to get you washed. You can't keep going on like this."

"My kid is in the hospital, Scarlett. I've had a lot of work to do. I've got a rogue asshole intent on killing me. Washing has been the last thing on my mind right now."

"And you think working yourself into exhaustion is going to help you in any way? I know you're the big, strong biker, and you don't need help from anyone, but I'm not going to hurt you. I just want to help, and there can't be any harm in that, can there?" she asked, brow raised.

He chuckled. "Fine."

"Good." She took his hand and led him toward the bathroom. Releasing him, she began to run him a bath, adding in plenty of soothing salts to help him.

Turning back to him, she rolled her eyes. "You've got to get undressed for this to work. It has to touch skin."

"Then take my clothes off for me. I won't bite,

much."

Taking a deep breath, she moved toward him. Taking his leather cut, she was careful as she removed it, taking her time. She knew how much he loved his jacket, and she placed it on the radiator. The Prez patch caught her eye as it was so clear.

"Is Kent a real threat?"

"He was VP for a long time. He knows the club business and where we have our fingers into pies that are secret."

"He can't go to the cops though, can he?"

"You think my businesses are not all legit?"

"I'm not blind, Gunner, or stupid. I know the club has deals that I don't want to know about."

"No, he shouldn't go to the cops. There's no reason for him to. He'd get in trouble with the cartels." Gunner ran his fingers through her hair. "So soft."

"And I don't stink."

"No, you don't." His nose pressed to her neck, and she closed her eyes, enjoying his warmth, his closeness. "I've missed you and John."

She smiled.

Once he was completely naked, he didn't make her carry him to the bath. He got in of his own accord, and she took a seat on the toilet, watching him.

"Well, woman, come on, do your duty."

"How rude to assume it's my duty to clean you."

He winked at her, and she made her way to the bath. Grabbing a sponge and bath gel, she worked it into a lather and began to coat his flesh. She rubbed him clean, rinsing off the soap as she grabbed the shampoo.

She took care of his hair, running her fingers through the length then rinsing it. By the time she was finished, she was able to smell something much better than odor.

"There you go, all done."

"I want you to bathe me more often," he said, standing up.

She held the towel out to him with a smirk.

"Seriously?" she asked.

His cock was hard as rock, and an answering pull tugged in her pussy. She wanted him and had been waiting for him or John to take care of her, but they had all been busy.

Gunner took the towel, and as she stepped away, he caught her wrist, stopping her from fleeing. His damp hand came out, cupping her tit. His fingers teased her nipple, which hardened the instant he touched her. She gasped at the rush of pleasure that consumed her body.

Pressing her thighs together, she tried to contain her arousal, but she was wet. The lips of her pussy were already soaked with her need for him.

He took the straps of her negligee and pulled it down her body. Her tits came out as it fell to her hips. With another wriggle, it landed on the floor at her feet, and Gunner groaned. "Now that is a sight I could get used to, and it's so fucking sexy."

His hands lifted up her tits, his thumbs running across the tips, and then his tongue as he bent forward, taking one nipple into his mouth, then the other.

She moaned as he began to move her back into his bedroom.

His touch went to her hips, and he stopped her at the base of the bed.

"Look at me, Scarlett."

She stared up at him, feeling her heart start to pound as she watched him. Licking her dry lips, she placed her hand on his stomach, gliding her hand down, going to his cock.

Up and down, she moved her hand, and then she

sank to her knees before him.

Staring at his cock, she flicked her tongue across the tip, tasting his pre-cum. She closed her eyes as she took him into her mouth. He went to the back of her throat, and she released a little moan, wanting him so desperately. Her pussy was on fire, and she slipped a hand between her thighs, teasing herself.

"I don't want you to touch yourself. That pleasure will be all mine, baby. Not yours. I want your pleasure."

She stopped playing with herself and whimpered as he caught her hair around his fist, and began to sink into her mouth, going as deep as he could go before she started to gag. Gunner took control, using her mouth for his pleasure, and she relished it, the bite of pain as he took charge of her body in only the way that he could.

"Fuck, baby, that feels so fucking good. Don't stop." He drove inside her mouth, and she relaxed, giving herself over to him, letting him do his work. "I can't come. Have to come in your pussy, but fuck, that feels good."

She didn't understand his words, and then she didn't have to as Gunner erupted into her mouth, and she swallowed down every single drop of his cum.

Each wave, each pulse, she moaned around his cock as she did. Only when he couldn't take anymore did he pull away.

He didn't leave her hanging though. He lifted her up onto the bed, spreading her thighs open wide, and his mouth was there, sucking on her sweet spot.

She cried out as he bit down on her clit. His fingers teased through her folds, finding her center, and sliding in deep. He added a second finger, then a third, and he licked her pussy, making her come.

"Am I interrupting something?" John asked.

"There's a condom in the drawer and some lube,"

Gunner said, glancing over his shoulder. She whimpered as he stopped licking her pussy to pay attention to her husband. She shouldn't be jealous, but in that second, she wanted to come. She was so close. "Fuck my ass, John."

Gunner's mouth moved back over her clit, and he attacked it with a fervor that startled her. He kept her at that peak, never letting her rush over the hill. She wanted to come so badly. He only let her when he was ready, and as he did, she came, screaming his name, begging him not to stop.

He didn't give her time to bask in her arousal as he moved swiftly between her legs. His cock found her core, and he slid in deep as he was already hard once again.

She watched as John moved over Gunner. She couldn't see what they were doing, but she knew her husband was working his dick inside Gunner's ass. She held herself open, feeling him tense, and then start to fuck her as John screwed him.

Scarlett didn't think she could enjoy this as much as she did. They gave her something that she didn't even realize that she'd been missing. Watching them together was a thing of beauty, and it amazed her how damn giving they were. Even as they fucked each other, they watched her, and she saw their love and need shining down on her, and she loved them both.

She had tried to fight her love for them, but it was impossible to do so. She loved them both, equally. If there was a chance that they could make this work together, then she wanted a shot at it. With all three of them, they could be happy. Even if it meant being part of the club, she'd do it.

They were her men, the loves of her life, and she'd do anything for them, even give up her need for a baby.

After all, in the back of her mind she recalled them talking about Gunner having a vasectomy, so he couldn't have any children anymore.

Working at the day care center would have to be enough.

Smiling, she felt a wave of peace fill her, and she wrapped her arms around Gunner's neck, kissing him back.

They all came together, their moans echoing off the wall. This was the start of something new, and she'd be sure to make it work.

Chapter Twelve

Gunner ran a hand down his face as he stared at Goldman. It was rather cliché, but he had the man and his security team tied to chairs in one of his abandoned warehouses. He had intended to use the warehouse for something more than torturing people, but right now, he didn't see any other use.

"Bennie woke up this morning," Gunner said. "You see I'm a patient man. I figured that I'd wait, and I'd see who hurt my son. Who hit him over the head with a metal pole so fucking badly that they had to drain fluid because of the swelling. Who kicked him while he was down and broke his back."

"Gunner, I—"

"He's eighteen years old. My son." He stopped talking and looked at Goldman. "You told me you handled it."

"I did."

"Your son acted with his friends."

"I swear to you, Gunner. I'm many things, I grant you. I'm not a fucking saint, but I do have my word, and I don't go back on it. That I fucking swear."

He turned to look at John. His friend stood with his arms folded, looking entirely bored with the situation. His club had wanted him to take John with him. They had seen a side to him when he took out those four traitors, and for the past week, he'd been by his side while he got the proof of what Finn Goldman and his friends had done. He'd also been hunting for Kent. His contacts let him know that the cartels were now hunting him as well.

Kent had made these deals without giving the cartels all the facts. Gunner had already done his meeting with the cartels being sure that his contact, Carlos, had been there. He'd made them aware of the situation within the club.

They had apologized, and then asked if he wanted to extend the friendship. He told them straight the club wasn't looking to expand like that. They had what they wanted and would continue with the runs that were needed, but none of them wanted any jail time, and working with the cartels, that was exactly what would happen.

They would be the ones that were thrown to the fucking wolves.

He was there for his club, no one else. He made sure they were the ones that got the good deals. The club was his life.

"What do you think?"

"Probably telling the truth. Doesn't bode well though, does it?"

"What?"

"He can't even keep his fucking teenage son in line. What good is he to us?" John was fast earning his patch. In the past week, he'd seen the cold-blooded killer come out to play, the man who'd served alongside him in the military, and it was a sight to behold.

"We want Finn," Gunner said.

"He's a boy."

"He's a boy that decided to go against advice and nearly killed my boy. I'm not joking around anymore, Goldman. I want your son, and you're going to get him for me."

He pulled out Goldman's cell phone and placed it against his ear. He'd already clicked "call" for Finn's number.

Gunner told him the location where he needed to be, and Goldman spoke to Finn. While the call was being made, John held the gun to his head, to make sure he didn't do anything stupid.

When that was done, he ended the call.

Dropping the cell phone onto the table, Gunner stepped away from the men and sat down, watching him. His men already had the orders to collect Finn and to bring him to the warehouse.

"How is your boy?" Goldman asked.

Staring at the man before him, Gunner saw that underneath all the wealth and asshole, there was a kind man there. He should have known it. The man had a mistress who he kept away from most of the town so that she didn't get hurt.

"He's … surviving. You know how it is."

Goldman nodded. "Finn's a spoiled fucking asshole."

"You clean up all of his messes?"

"I clean up as much as I can." Goldman sighed. "I figured parenting would be easy, you know? I remember what I wanted from my parents growing up, so I gave it to Finn."

"What was that?" John asked.

"Everything. That was all I wanted. I wanted everything that I could get my hands on. He's not had to work for anything." Goldman shook his head.

"You know, most men would be pissing themselves," John said, smirking. "I'm impressed that you're talking."

"Believe it or not, I'm actually quite comfortable. Hearing what happened with Bennie, I knew you were coming."

It had been easy to take him. Gunner's need for blood was still so fucking strong. Running a hand down his face, he waited. His thoughts returned to Scarlett. This morning she had woken up between the two of them, only she'd gone from smiling to looking really green as she rushed to the toilet. He'd held her hair back as John had been smiling like a fucking asshole.

She'd thrown everything up, and he'd made her go back to bed, hoping she was just sick.

Before he entered this warehouse though, his prayers hadn't been answered as she sent them both a text saying she felt a million times better and was going to work. Billy was escorting her today.

If she was pregnant, that meant John's plan worked, but it also meant that … they had lied and manipulated her, and that didn't sit well with him, not right now.

Glancing at his watch, he was starting to grow bored. He stood up as the door to the warehouse opened.

"Get your fucking filthy hands off me, you piece of shit," Finn said, fighting against the hold that was on him.

Gunner stared at the little punk, and he wasn't impressed by what he saw. In fact, he only saw rage as he looked at him.

Finn looked around the warehouse, and the cocky look disappeared. This bastard had hurt his son. This piece of shit had taken his little boy, and now he had to wait to see if he could walk. The doctors didn't want to rush him as with head wounds, they were quite dangerous, and they wanted him to rest a couple of days before they start testing him.

"You've got a choice, Goldman," Gunner said.

He didn't see a boy when he looked at Finn. He saw an asshole and the enemy.

"What?"

"You or your kid," Gunner said, not breaking eye contact with Finn.

"What? Fuck, your boy had it coming," Finn said.

"He messed up my face."

Gunner stepped right up to the kid. "I'm right here. Let's see what a wiseass you are when you face with someone watching you."

Finn stared at him, but Gunner saw the vulnerability there in his eyes.

"You're not so tough right now without your little clique hanging around."

"Whatever. I can take on an old man."

"Get rid of him," Goldman said. "He's ... toxic. My wife is afraid of him, and my staff is too. He's got to go. There's nothing good about him. I don't want nor do I need him."

"Dad, what the fuck?"

"I warned you, Finn. You were determined to do your own thing, and now you're going to see that there are consequences. There always are some people you can't throw money at. You've got to give them something more, and I'm not dying for you." Goldman looked at him. "You'll make it look like an accident?"

"Yeah, I will."

"Then I say this concludes our business."

Gunner's men grabbed Finn and pushed him down into a chair, keeping him there. Moving toward Goldman's side, he released the restraints and stepped back. He then released the security guards' restraints and Goldman held his hand up. "No. You don't help him. I heard what happened to your boy, and to know it was my son was a shame to me. He shamed my family by going back on our word." Goldman held out his hand. "I'm sorry."

Shaking his hand, Gunner nodded at him, and they walked away.

Either way, if it got out what Finn did, this would backfire on Goldman as well, especially if he'd been the one protecting him.

Stepping up to John, he stared at his friend. "You can leave."

"I don't need to leave," John said. "This asshole hurt you. He hurt your son, and Bennie's going to be in that hospital for a long time. The cruelty he shows, and lack of remorse, I don't care that he's eighteen years old, Gunner. Eye for an eye. I'm here, and I'm not going anywhere."

Gunner wasn't a cruel man. He grabbed his gun and stood in front of Finn. "You're all fucking cowards. The lot of you. None of you can even begin to imagine the shit that I've done."

He was tired of listening to the same old crap. Raising his gun, he pointed and shot Finn between the eyes. Just another body in the endless pile that was gathering.

****

"I don't want to sleep right now," Bennie said. "I just want to go home."

Scarlett pulled back the curtain and let in some light. The doctors had told her that Bennie had been in a bad mood lately, and she didn't blame him. Being locked in a shitty room all day with only the sounds of the machines for company would drive her crazy.

"I'm not asking you to go to sleep." She went to the bag that she'd brought with her. "I want some company." She placed the books she'd gotten from his room on the table. "I imagine it's boring as hell here." She wrinkled her nose. "I've never been good with hospitals."

Bennie chuckled. "Say that to the kid that can't move."

She stared at him. "We're going to make you better."

"I've heard what's been said. I've got a broken back."

"With bed rest, you'll be good as new."

"There's a risk I may never recover. My legs could be useless." Bennie shook his head. "I was heading to class."

She moved up to his side and placed a hand on his shoulder. "You're a strong boy, and you know what? If you can't walk then I'll be here to help you no matter what. We're friends, right? You can help me cook in the kitchen." She took his arms. "There are a lot of people in this world who are in the same situation as you, and they don't let it beat them. Don't let it beat you."

Bennie nodded.

"You know what, you need to take a trip out."

"I'm bed-bound, remember."

"So? I've seen nurses rolling these beds around, and I think it would do you good to get out, to see something else besides this dreadful room." She made her way toward the nurse and talked to her about it. Even though they did advise against it, seeing as Scarlett was willing to stay with him, they allowed it because he was on bed rest, and patients who couldn't get outside, they did allow them to take some time.

They removed several of the wires he was hooked up to, and with the help of the nurse, they made their way downstairs to the seating area. It was cold out, but with all of his blankets, he was warm. She put on a jacket, hat, gloves, and scarf in an attempt to ward off the cold.

Once outside, the nurse's pager went off, and she told them they'd be fine.

"See, the good outdoors," she said, rubbing her hands together and glancing down at Bennie. There were tears in his eyes, but he pushed them back.

"What's Carlos doing?"

"He's at the club. We're not allowing him to go to school just yet. Gunner wanted to deal with the people who did this."

Bennie nodded. "You know what he means by that, don't you?"

"I'm a girl, Bennie, not stupid."

"It doesn't bother you?"

She looked at him, wishing she could see his laughter or his smile. She got nothing. He looked so incredibly sad. "It does, but then I look at you, and you must have been terrified."

Bennie shrugged. "I didn't feel it. They got me from behind. Bashed my head in, and I came to in the hospital. I got lucky."

"That's not lucky. You shouldn't have gone through that." She took his hand and held him tightly.

"You're a good person, Scarlett."

She smiled.

"My mom, she's never cared about us. She only ever cared about what we could get for her. You know with Dad having to pay her money and stuff. She's not even come to visit me." She held his hand just a little tighter. "That's okay. She didn't want us anyway. All the time that we were with us, she'd tell us repeatedly how much she hated us, how we ruined her life. Like it was our fault that she kept sleeping with other men."

"Bennie, it's not your fault."

"I know it's not. Is it wrong that I wished you were my mom?"

Tears filled her eyes, and she smiled at him. "That has to be one of the sweetest things anyone has ever said to me."

He chuckled. "Well, it's the truth. Thank you so much for sitting with me today. I appreciate it."

"Anytime."

They sat out there for another ten minutes, but she cut their trip short as she didn't want him getting ill. She wanted him to see the world once again, and not some room.

Once they were back in his room, he fell asleep and Scarlett got to working. She put some pictures up in his room. Some had been taken recently of all of them together, and others that were much older.

"He asleep?" Gunner asked, coming into the room.

"Yeah, I got the nurse to let me take him out. I hope that's okay. He was really down, and I didn't want it to affect him. He needs to have all of his strength for the challenges ahead of him, you know?"

"Yeah, I do."

Gunner walked up behind her, wrapping his arm around her waist and kissing her head. "Thank you for all of this."

"Anytime. He's going to be here for a while, and I didn't want him to feel lonely, or forget that he's missed."

"There's going to be a guard on his door at all times," Gunner said.

"No word on Kent?" she asked.

She didn't know the complete details of what happened, but John had told her if she saw Kent, to get away from him as quickly as possible and call him or Gunner.

"Nope, nothing. He's gone to ground. It won't take long. My life has a time limit."

She held onto the bear that she found in Bennie's room. Wringing the bear, she quickly placed it on the bed next to him.

"I won that for him at the first fair that he went to. He was three years old. He was a big boy, even then,"

Gunner said, reaching for it.

"I don't want anything to happen to you," she said.

Looking up at her, he frowned. "I won't let anything happen."

"You said your life had a time limit?"

"The deal Kent made, he may not know it doesn't exist anymore, and it put a limit on life." He shrugged. "One way or another, I'll get what I want. How would you feel if John became my VP?"

"That's between you and John. I'd still be here." She sat down in the spare chair, looking at Bennie and then at Gunner. They were similar in looks, and you could certainly see the resemblance to the father in the son. "What does John think of it?"

"I've not asked him. There's an opening, and there's no one else that I'd trust other than him."

She smiled. "That's because he's awesome."

They both chuckled.

"You're feeling better?"

Scarlett nodded. "Yeah, it was really weird. I don't know what came over me this morning. One moment I was sick, and I rested, had some juice, and the next I felt fine. Really weird." She shrugged. "Probably one of those quick illnesses, I don't know. Where is John?"

"He had to go to the office to take care of some business. Don't worry, I've got one of my boys there with him."

"We both know that he can take care of himself, and he doesn't need a caretaker."

Bennie moaned, and his head shifted. She watched him open his eyes and stare at his dad.

"You're here," he said.

"I'm here, son." Gunner stood and moved toward

his bed. She sat back and watched, staying silent. "You're never going to get hurt again, son."

"What?"

"I took care of it. You, Carlos, you'll all be safe. I'll be dealing with the others as well. The ones that were with him."

"Dad," Bennie said. "I could have taken care of it."

Gunner looked at him. "If you think for a second I'd let you take care of anyone in your condition you've got another think coming. I should have dealt with this the last time. I didn't. This shit is on me. Now, I want you to relax, I want you to get better, to get strong, and then we're going to get you to walk again, and you're going to be fine, you hear me?"

Bennie nodded.

She watched as Gunner pressed his head to Bennie's. "I love you, son, never ever doubt that."

Tears filled her eyes. She'd felt that love herself, and if she had any doubts about Gunner's feelings for her, they left her at what she'd just witnessed.

****

Later that night John stood in Gunner's bedroom. He'd dealt with the cleanup of Finn's body, and then gone into work to handle some of his clients and make sure he didn't get behind there. He loved being an accountant. There was something satisfying and constant in his work, and he didn't want to lose anyone.

He didn't need the money and already had a great deal put away in savings, but he liked to work.

"You want me to do what?" John asked.

"The VP patch," Gunner said, holding it up. "It's yours. The club wants you in, John. You don't have to prospect either. You can come straight in as VP. You've proven yourself tenfold. They trust you, respect you, and know you'll do right by the club. There's no one else I want, John. I kept Kent close because I thought it would be the right thing, and look how that turned out. There's no one else, just you."

"You keep on saying that." He took the VP patch from Gunner and stared at it. He ran his thumb across the print and sighed. "I don't know."

"You can do this. If you lose clients, so fucking what. You'll have a piece of the club pie. I swear Scarlett will be set for life, and she'd have the protection of the club."

"It's not about the money."

"Then what?"

"I don't deal with the runs, and the shit I don't want, Gunner. I know you've got your fingers in a lot of shit, but that's not mine." John placed the badge on the bed and shook his head. "The only reason I never joined this club was because I didn't want to have prolonged time away from my girl. I can't do this. I can't do what you're going to want me to do."

"That's it? The drugs and guns, that's your limit."

"I will do everything to protect my family, Gunner, and you're part of that. I don't need a patch to help me make a decision. I've got nothing against you or the club, but I'm not going to be your VP."

Gunner sighed. "You know, I didn't think you'd take this patch but I thought it would be worth a try."

"I'm not going to tell you how to run your club, Gunner. You've been doing a good job of it."

Gunner snorted. "Yeah, that good of a job that I've got a price on my head and a traitor out there."

"We'll find Kent." John had no doubt that they would. They had men everywhere looking for him, and not just club men either.

He watched as Gunner sat down on the edge of

the bed, and for the first time in their life, he actually looked tired.

"Scarlett threw up today," Gunner said.

"I know."

"No, she threw up and then was better."

John was aware of what had happened today, but like a lot of stuff, he'd not had time to process everything, so he'd not given it a lot of thought.

"I went to the pharmacy at the hospital," Gunner said. "I have a pregnancy test for her to try."

"Gunner—"

"She has to know. We can't hide it from her anymore."

John paced the length of the room. This was one of the reasons why he hadn't given it much thought and had refused to think about it.

Scarlett being pregnant gave them all a time limit.

He had to tell her the truth.

"She may not be upset with us," Gunner said. "She's been having sex without a condom and not said anything. Maybe she hoped that I'd get her pregnant."

The sound of a laugh drew John's attention, and there his wife stood. Tears were in her eyes, and she glared at them both.

"What?" she asked. Her gaze kept going from him to Gunner, then back to him. "I'm sure I just misheard that. What the hell are you two talking about?"

John made to step toward her, but she stepped back, holding up her hand.

"I don't want you to touch me right now. I don't want anyone to touch me." Her hand stayed in the air.

"How much did you hear?" Gunner asked.

"You have a pregnancy test for me and that you have to tell me something. Tell me what exactly?"

John stared at her, feeling his heart breaking. He

couldn't stand to see her cry, and yet those tears were real, and he was the one to put them there. "Baby, I can't get you pregnant."

"I know that. I was with you when we got the results. You didn't want to talk about adoption or IVF. You just wanted to pretend that nothing happened."

"I didn't. I didn't want you to go through that."

"Why?"

"Time. I didn't want you to have to wait and risk us being rejected, and then with IVF, the procedure can be painful for some women."

The first of her tears started to drop as she looked at him.

"So, what did you decide?" she asked.

"Gunner has two sons. He's fertile, and I knew the way he looked at you. He loved you. He probably didn't realize that he loved you, but I knew he wanted you, and I wanted you to have his baby, and so I asked him. I asked him to put a baby inside you."

She didn't wipe her tears away as she looked at him. "So you just took that decision completely out of my hands. You didn't think to consult me on how I feel or felt."

"Come on, Scarlett. He was inside you and coming inside you. You must have known what was happening. You're not stupid."

"No, I'm not stupid, but I thought he had a vasectomy, John. I thought he couldn't have kids. I thought this entire thing was you guys wanted to be together because you've been denying yourself for years. I had no idea that he could still have children. Carlos is sixteen, and I remembered you guys talking about it and that he had an appointment. He went out of town."

"I went out of town, but I didn't go for the procedure. I didn't want to. I simply divorced Cherry, and never slept with her. I've bagged my dick up every single time since," Gunner said.

She pressed her hand to her stomach.

"There's a chance you're pregnant, Scarlett, with my baby," Gunner said. "Your sickness this morning and your speedy recovery. I don't want to hurt you, but you need to know."

She sniffled.

"Where's your test?"

John made to step toward her, but she shook her head. "No, I don't want you to touch me."

"You wanted a baby, Scarlett."

"Yeah, I did, and I wanted it to be a choice *we* made. You went behind my back. You manipulated everything to suit your own needs. That's not what our marriage is supposed to be about, John. Wow, and I felt so guilty for bringing you two together when you both loved each other."

Her lip quivered, and he felt like the world's biggest asshole.

Gunner stepped forward, holding out the box. "There's two inside. In case you need to take the two."

She took the box without touching either of them. John watched as she stepped toward the bathroom and wouldn't let either of them near her.

Gunner looked fucking sick, and John didn't feel much better right now. His heart was breaking, but he knew this would happen.

The time kept on ticking, and he and Gunner just stood outside the bathroom, waiting.

Yes, he thought she'd be upset, but he'd intended to tell her face to face, neither of them hiding.

He ran a hand through his hair, his mouth dry.

Finally, after what felt like an eternity, she opened the door. Her face was pale.

"Both of them say I'm pregnant." She wiped away her tears. "I want to go home."

"Scarlett," he said, hoping to get her to see reason.

"No, I want to go home, and right now I don't want to look at you." She glared at him. "We're married, John. We came together and promised to love each other, and to be honest about everything. This … it wasn't … it hurts right now, and I need to go because I don't want to say something that I'd regret."

"You're going to have to take someone from the club," Gunner said.

"That's fine."

John watched as Gunner followed Scarlett out of his home. Sitting on the edge of the bed, he felt like he'd been kicked in the stomach. He'd never felt anything as fucking painful as right now knowing his wife couldn't stand to be near him. He loved her more than anything in this world, and he'd hurt her as well.

Minutes passed before his friend returned.

"Billy and Ford are staying with her," Gunner said. "I've told them to protect her with their lives if they have to."

"I fucked up big time," John said, looking up. "She's one of the best things that ever happened to me, and I screwed it up."

"Then we win her back. That's my baby she's going to have, John. I don't want to miss a moment of that time with her. I'll help you win her back."

John had to have hope. The thought of not being with her killed a part of him inside.

Chapter Thirteen

Scarlett got it confirmed with the doctor that she was indeed pregnant. She smiled for the doctor and the nurse, but she couldn't bring herself to jump for joy. All this time, she'd been wanting to talk to John about pregnancy options, and he'd employed his best friend for his sperm.

Leaving the doctor, she stopped when she saw it was Gunner in the car waiting.

"Where's Billy?" she asked.

"I took over for him. We need to talk."

She stared at the man that she had been falling for. A man she'd cared about and who she knew her husband loved so passionately.

He opened the car door and took her hand, and she slid into the passenger seat. She hated this feeling that was swirling inside her. They were going to have a baby. She had a little human being inside her, growing. All she had wanted for a couple of months was the prospect of getting pregnant, and now everything felt upside down. She couldn't make sense of what the hell was happening in her life.

The happiness that she had been feeling moments ago was gone.

"Will you take me to the hospital? I would like to spend some time with Bennie." She hoped that trying to cheer him up, she'd be able to do so for herself. She didn't want to be a bitch or a bore.

"I'll take you to the hospital, but you've got to talk to me. We didn't want this for you, Scarlett."

"You both organized this without even asking me. I'm now pregnant, and it's your baby. What about you? What do you want out of this?" she asked.

"I want what I've always wanted."

"And what is that?"

"You."

She shook her head. "No, I'm not going to believe that all you wanted was the chance to be with me. I'm not some perfect model or some saint, Gunner. I'm just me. I'm just Scarlett Williams, your best friend's wife."

"Exactly. You love your husband. You're sweet, kind, loving, and I wanted a piece of that for myself, and if it meant I had to put my baby inside you, then I was willing to do it just to have a part of you." He reached out, even as he was driving, and she didn't push his hand away as he placed his palm across her stomach.

Pleasure filled her at his touch, and she closed her eyes. She was having Gunner's baby. He had a right to touch her stomach, and to be part of it.

"Is this what you agreed with John?"

"I told him I wanted to be part of his life. This was before you saw us together or that I could have you both, and I want that, Scarlett."

"What?"

"I want you both. I'm a greedy bastard, and I want you both. Right now, you hate us for discussing this without you, and I get it, I really do, but you're having my kid. Be brokenhearted, but don't keep me away from my child. I love you, Scarlett. I love you, and I love John. I'm going to love our baby when you give birth, and if you want another kid, I'll give you another kid. I will give you everything your heart desires."

Tears fell down her cheeks, and she hated that she was crying again already.

Gunner pulled up in front of the hospital and turned toward her. She couldn't look away from him. The intensity of his stare shocked her with how much he seemed to see. He reached out, stroking her cheek.

She wanted to tell him that she loved him too, but her own stubbornness kept the words locked up tight.

"I'll come and pick you up. We can have dinner or something."

"I'm not very hungry right now."

"I'm not going to leave you alone, Scarlett. I'm not that kind of guy, and I've never been wired that way." He leaned forward, gripping the back of her neck as he claimed her lips.

Once again, her treacherous body responded to his kiss. She didn't want him to stop, and wanted more, always so much more. One kiss was never enough.

"I love you."

She climbed out of the car with his words hanging in the air. She didn't say a word, and made her way up to Bennie's room.

The moment she saw Bennie she forced a smile to her lips, and he frowned. "What's wrong?"

"It's nothing."

"You look like you've been crying."

"I've not been crying. I'm fine."

She kept the smile on her lips as she put her bag on the floor and stepped toward him. Pressing a kiss to his head, she glanced down at the book he was reading. "Is that a romance book?"

"It's a book, and it's kind of cool."

"Okay. You're not trying to impress some girl?"

"No, I'm not. Do you think reading a book could impress a girl?"

"I think so. John always thrilled me when he was able to talk about a book I'd read." The mention of John made her smile drop, but she distracted Bennie by looking through the pages. "Is this for a girl?"

"I know she's reading it. I saw her in school with

it, and seeing as you brought it along, I figured why not."

She was about to answer him when there was a knock at the door. Scarlett looked up and saw a girl on the bigger side. She held some flowers and a card in her hand. It was a large card. Her cheeks were on fire.

"Erm, I hope it's okay that I came. Everyone signed it at school, and we hope you're doing well." She kept stuttering over her words as she talked.

"Come in, Gemma. This is my dad's friend, Scarlett. Scarlett, this is my friend, Gemma."

Scarlett stood up, holding out her hand, and Gemma shook it. "It's good to see you. Bennie could use the company."

She turned to look at Bennie, eyeing the book he had in his lap and nodding her head at Gemma.

He gave her a look that told her to shut up but also confirmed her suspicions. "I'm going to leave you two for a few minutes. Go and grab a coffee or something. Stay, Gemma. I'm sure Bennie is hating my company, me being all old and stuff."

She grabbed her bag and left the room. Looking inside, she saw Gemma take a seat and lean close, showing him the card that had been signed.

He was a good kid.

Leaving the room, she made her way down to the cafeteria. The scents instantly turned her stomach. She quickly left so that she didn't throw up. She found a vending machine and purchased a bottle of water and some cheese crackers.

"Well, well, well, look what the tide brought in," Cherry said.

It wasn't the first fat joke that had been directed her way, and it wouldn't be the last. One bite of cheese cracker and Scarlett realized how hungry she was.

"Are you here to see Bennie?"

"Yes. I bet he's begging for his mommy."

Scarlett raised a brow. She wasn't interested right now. After the evening and morning, she was at her wits' end with bitches and liars. "It took you long enough to care."

Cherry glared at her. "Why don't you just eat your way into a coma or something? Useless bitch."

"I will, thank you. Maybe then I could stop listening to your irritating voice."

Cherry shook her head. "You know, I don't get it when it comes to you. Men like a woman that doesn't squash them, and yet Gunner and John act like shit doesn't fall out of your ass."

"Colorful," she said, wrinkling her nose.

"It's kind of funny though. It has to take two men to knock you up. Makes you wonder if it's because of all the layers of fat that sperm has to get through."

Scarlett didn't say a word. She looked at Cherry, waiting for more, and there was.

"You may walk around town with your kid when you finally get one, but we will all know that it's not John's baby. It'll be Gunner's because he's the only one man enough to knock you up."

All hunger ended as Cherry threw her parting words, and Scarlett stood there in the corridor, alone and feeling completely winded.

She didn't know what to do. She was so confused.

****

John sat at home, nursing a shot of whiskey and waiting for his wife to arrive. All day he'd given her space, and then after Gunner had called him, he'd been determined to see her, to talk to her.

He didn't know exactly what he could say to the woman he loved that would explain why he did what he did.

"I thought I told you that you were to leave her alone," Gunner said.

Sitting back in his sofa, he tipped the whiskey to the back of his throat and glared at Gunner. "She's my wife, and we may fuck each other, but you don't get to tell me what to do." His heart clenched at the shot of pain he saw flash across Gunner's eyes. This wasn't helping either of them.

"She's still got my baby, and I'll let that fucking comment slide for now." Gunner paced the room.

"It's confirmed then?"

"Yes. She went to the doctor today, and there's a baby. Why didn't you listen to me?" Gunner asked.

John shrugged. "I don't take orders from you. I want to see her, try to explain things. To make this work again. We were all having a lot of fun."

"Is that all this is to you? A lot of fucking fun?"

"It's a lot more than that." Out of the corner of his eye, he watched Gunner's anger simmer beneath the surface. His friend was struggling to contain his need for violence. They really didn't need this right now. Not with Kent willing to strike at any moment and the fact Gunner was vulnerable.

John would never wear the patch, but that didn't mean that he wouldn't protect him with his very life.

"We fucked up big time with this. We shouldn't have done this to Scarlett."

"You wanted to fuck my wife," John said. "This worked out great, more than great. We're just having a few hiccups along the road. Nothing a little time won't fix." He finished his whiskey and grabbed the bottle he'd brought along with him. Scarlett was taking forever to arrive home, and his nerves were completely shot.

Watching Scarlett walk away had killed a part of

him, especially as he didn't even know the words that would work to keep her.

"What the fuck are you saying?" Gunner asked, stepping toward him.

Tilting his head back, he looked at his friend. "You wanted to get your dick inside her so bad. It wasn't hard to see. Even your wife knew that you wanted it and had probably been craving it most of the past ten years. I handed you paradise on a plate."

The pain was expected, and so was the violence. It had been a long time since John had needed this to help him deal with his own fucked-up problems.

Gunner's fist in his face was a welcome reprieve from what he needed. There weren't many men out there that could match John in a fight, but he had the one man he trusted more than anything. He was hauled to his feet.

"Why? Fucking why?" Gunner asked, yelling out his demand.

In answer, John brought his head down on Gunner's nose, which threw him back and made him release John.

Gunner's hand went to his nose.

He didn't hear a break, so he didn't for a second believe that he'd broken anything. When Gunner pulled his hand away, he saw that it wasn't broken, but his friend wasn't done, and neither was John. Gunner charged to his waist, pushing him back so they toppled the sofa.

Rolling on the floor, John swung his leg over and slammed his fist against Gunner's face, but even still, he didn't have the upper hand.

Gunner shoved him hard, getting his foot back and slamming it hard into his stomach.

John landed in a heap against the wall, but he was still ready for more.

"It's my baby that's inside her," Gunner said. "I'm the one that knocked her up because you're not man enough to do it."

His rage went to a fever pitch as he launched himself at Gunner. They charged from the sitting room through to the bathroom. The force of being slammed on the table shattered the legs, and the top dropped onto the floor. For a second it knocked the wind out of him, but he'd been told to never give up, to keep on fighting. He didn't have it in him to stop.

Infertile.

Never father a child.

Zero percent chance of fathering a child.

Sterile.

The words rang inside his head, going over and over. He'd tried not to think about them. To ignore the words that had shattered his entire world. Going to Gunner, it had brought together a piece in his life that he'd been missing, but even still, he hadn't thought about why he'd done it.

In the back of his mind, it had always been there.

He couldn't have kids, but he'd not given himself time to even think about it.

Slamming his fist into Gunner's ribs, his friend reared back for a second, giving him the upper hand, but it lasted a second if not even less before Gunner had him around the neck.

"You can't have kids, John. You'll never be able to have them. That nursery up there, it's a fucking sham. That's what it is. A fucking sham."

John clenched his teeth, grabbed Gunner's arm, twisted it, and threw him off.

Just as he was about to slam his fist against Gunner's face the door opened. His attention diverted to watch as Scarlett came in along with her guard, but he didn't look at the man. No, his attention was on his wife.

On her stomach, and Gunner used his distraction to his advantage.

He shouldn't be fighting Gunner or in his home. Scarlett had worked so hard to make it a beautiful home, and he was destroying it.

Even as he thought that, he kept on fighting.

"What the hell are you doing?" she asked, coming toward them.

"Get out," John said, yelling.

He couldn't have her seeing this. He'd not needed this fight in the ten years that he'd known her. She didn't know this was how he dealt with his rage, and how he'd been trying to find other ways of dealing with it for some time. He'd not craved this for a long time though. His life with Scarlett had been precious and still was.

She had given him a beautiful home, and had brought Gunner to him.

"Ford, leave!" Gunner said.

Ford didn't say a word as he turned and left the house.

Suddenly, John's head was locked in a hold, and he couldn't get out of it. He stared at Scarlett, his beautiful wife. A wife that was currently looking at them in horror.

"You see, John, *I* knocked her up, not you. I fucking put my kid inside her."

"Gunner, stop it."

"You couldn't do it."

He hit out, but it wasn't having any effect on his friend. John's throat clenched as he looked at his wife.

I failed.

I couldn't give her everything.

I'm infertile.

John slumped down as the tears started to fall.

Gunner released his hold, and then pulled him into his arms.

"It's okay," Gunner said.

"What is going on?" Scarlett asked.

"I'm sorry, Scarlett." The pain in his voice was clear to hear. He heard it himself. "I'm not a man. I'm half a fucking man. I promised you the world, and I couldn't even give you a fucking baby." He pressed the palms of his hands to his eyes, and just sobbed. Those words were behind his eyelids like a nightmare on repeat. He kept trying to blank them out, but no matter what he did, it was there in the background, mocking him, waiting to take him down. When he came home and he saw that nursery, he only saw his failing.

Gunner had been his salvation most of his life. John didn't intend to break her heart.

"You're a good man," Gunner said.

"I broke her heart. I just wanted her to have everything. I love you, Gunner, and I knew that if anything was to ever happen, you'd take care of her for me because Scarlett has to have a man taking care of her. She's too kind." Realizing his wife was still there, he turned to her and let her see the pain that was inside him. "You're too precious to let go. Gunner deserves your love."

"You deserve it," she said. Her voice was a faint whisper, and tears filled her eyes as she spoke.

"I never wanted to hurt you. We've been talking about kids for so long. I was selfish for a long time, wanting you all to myself. Our nights alone together, wanting to make love to you without having a kid around interrupting us. I saw that you wanted it, and you've waited long enough. So we started trying, and then nothing happened for a long time, and so we went through all the tests, and it's me. I promised you a baby, a big family. I can't give it to you."

"That doesn't make you any less of a man."

"I broke my vows."

"You have never broken your vows to me, John. I love you, not what you can give me. You."

Gunner stood up and helped John to his feet.

John knew that everything Gunner had said, he'd done so to help him, to make him open the dam that had been building inside him, and he'd refused to let go.

"Let's clean you up."

Scarlett reached out, taking his arm. All three of them went upstairs, and it was kind of surreal to have Gunner waiting on him as Scarlett stood in front of him, removing his clothing. He liked the feel of her hands on his body.

"How was the doctor's visit?" he asked.

"It was okay. They confirmed I'm pregnant. I asked if I could stay and wait to see the results, and they put a rush on it. I'm pregnant."

John went to put his hand on her stomach, but recalling the pain in her eyes, he stopped himself.

"Can I?" he asked.

She took his hand and placed it on her stomach. "Yes, you can. You can't really feel anything right now. In time I'll blow up like a balloon."

"I can't wait to see that, Scarlett. I know right now you're hating me, and I took this decision out of your hands, but I wanted to give you everything. If you couldn't have my baby, then the only one I wanted you to have was Gunner's."

"I don't hate you, John."

Once he was naked, they helped him into the bath, and neither of them made any move to climb in.

Together, Scarlett and Gunner washed him, and he was thankful for their attention. Even as he had the two people he loved more than anything in the world, the tears continued to fall. He'd not cried on the day that he'd been told he'd never father children, or after. His focus had been on finding a way to give his wife what she needed, what she craved.

Every night he'd glanced into the empty nursery, and it was like the room was mocking him. Laughing at his failed attempts to make his wife pregnant. All those nights of filling her, of taking her constantly in the hope of getting her pregnant had all been for nothing.

Once he was completely washed, he climbed out, and Scarlett dried him as Gunner got the first aid kit. He didn't fight them as they dealt with the cuts on his hands. He'd seen his reflection in the mirror, and it wasn't pretty to look at.

Bruises were already starting to appear.

After they treated him, Scarlett told him to lie in bed and she tucked him up, pressing a kiss to his temple.

She'd done this many times when he'd been ill with "man-flu" as she called it. He didn't care. For tonight he'd take any attention she'd give him.

****

"Did you have to say those awful things to him?" Scarlett asked.

Gunner picked up the table, resting it against the wall without any pictures on it. Scarlett was placing the shattered pieces of wood into a large sack.

"Yes."

"You shouldn't have been so mean."

"John hasn't cried, has he? He didn't talk to you about what was in that letter. I read that letter, and to a man like him, those words must have completely torn him apart. Still, he kept his shit together. He kept on going to work, dealing with life, and all the time, ignoring what was going on inside him."

"I never blamed him."

"He blamed himself, Scarlett. I remember asking him when he was going to knock you up, and he'd always say the same, not yet, I want her to myself. Not only did he get you to himself, but when you were ready, he couldn't even give you what you wanted."

Scarlett rubbed her temple, and Gunner wanted to go to her, to hold her. Right now, he didn't think it was the right time. She was still pissed at him for the vile words he'd spewed at John.

"Fighting fixed that?"

"John has always been able to keep on going. To push his feelings to one side, and just allow them to fester beneath the surface. In the military, they want that. You don't go on one mission, and come back with some of your friends dead, and they tell you to go and take a break. You get some rest, and you're back out there within a few hours with a bunch of new men. The thing is, it doesn't take long for that fucking dam to break, and when it does, you got to be prepared for it. John hadn't dealt with that letter. He kept pushing it back, seeing that nursery, and back it would push. Over and over, he did that, and you've got to be willing to deal with the consequences of that. He had to respond to that pain." Gunner shrugged. "I never said I agreed with what I did, or what I had to say to him. He deserves more than that, better. I also know John, and in the morning, he'll feel better. He'll be able to handle everything."

They finished picking up the few bits of wood, and he placed all the large broken pieces against the wall with the main table top.

Someone rang the doorbell, and Ford was there with pizza.

"I've got this," Gunner said. "Head back to the clubhouse, take care, and ride safe." He slapped his man on the back and took the pizza into the living room.

He held out a can of soda for her, and she nodded.

"Yes, I can't have wine now." She took the soda, popping it open, and taking a sip. He opened the lid on the pizza, pushing it back. Handing a slice to Scarlett, he took a slice for himself and sat back.

"A girl came to visit Bennie today."

"Yeah?"

"I think he likes her. Once she was gone, he seemed so happy even with Cherry there."

Gunner tensed up. "Cherry was there?"

"Yes, with flowers and looking every part the doting mom."

He glanced at her, and saw she was hurting. "Did she say anything to you?"

"She said a few things, but it doesn't matter. She knows about you being the one to get me pregnant. I don't know if she knows I am, but she mentioned something about it."

He gritted his teeth. "I'll deal with her."

"It's fine. I can deal with it. Honestly, it won't be the first time that I have." She finished eating her slice, licking her fingers as she did. "You won't think I'm a pig for taking a second slice, would you?"

He leaned in and got her one of the biggest. "Eat up. You've got to keep your strength up for two."

Her hand went to her stomach and she sighed. "Everything has gotten so crazy and so messed up."

"That's life for you."

"I don't like it. I don't like my life being crazy like this."

He saw the sadness in her eyes, and he placed a hand on her knee. "It's going to be okay."

"How can you be so sure of that?"

"Easy. I know that you love John more than

anything. You're hurt that we took that choice out of your hands, but for ten years you've been married to him, and you've not forced the issue of kids so you must love him a whole lot, or you've been lying for years."

"I love him more than anything."

"You love me as well."

"I don't like your ego right now."

"It's not my ego. You and I both know that there's something going on between us. I've been honest with you. I love you, Scarlett. I love you, and I love that crazy man up there enough to say fuck it, and to give you my kid, and I promised myself no one else would ever have that kind of hold on me."

"I would never do anything to hurt you," she said.

"I know. Which is why I know you'll find it in your heart to forgive, if you've not already. You're not about holding a grudge, Scarlett. You're about mending bridges, and bringing people together. It's a gift you have that no one else will ever be able to match."

"Now I'm crying again." She wiped away the tears, and he leaned over to take care of the rest, cupping her cheek as he did.

"It's the hormones."

"It can be that quickly?"

"You'll be surprised. Your body won't be yours for a little while, but I can't wait to see it." He moved his hand from her face to cup her stomach. She leaned back, and he placed it where he knew she was going to get bigger. "I want to be with you every single step of the way. When you go and get your first ultrasound, and we hear the heartbeat, I want to be part of it all."

She nodded. "I know John would want you to be part of it as well."

"I didn't give a shit about this kind of stuff with Cherry. She was pregnant, and I left her to deal with all the women stuff."

Scarlett chuckled. "What do you want to tell your boys? I don't want nasty rumors to go around town, and for them to have it thrown at them, used against them out of spite."

"I'll talk to my boys. You don't have to worry."

He heard her gasp as he bent down, kissing her stomach. "I don't even know if you can hear me yet. I bet you're this tiny little bean-looking thing."

She chuckled, and her hand went to his head. Gunner closed his eyes, knowing her touch meant a great deal to him. If she could touch him and laugh, then it meant she didn't hate him. In time she'd get over his and John's agreement if she hadn't done so already.

"What are you doing?" she asked.

"I want him or her to get used to my voice. You see, little bean, you're going to be a little confused because you're going to have two very strong, very sexy dads that love you more than anything in the world. You've got two brothers as well. I don't know if they'll be too cool to be nice, but I'll make them be nice. We're going to have a big family. You see, when you come out, I'm hoping that your mom loves me enough to give her another kid, and another, until she's happy with the family all of us have built together. Like her husband, John, one of your daddies, I love her very much, and I want to give her the family that I know she wants."

Once again, the tears started to fall, and she shook her head. "Don't do this to me."

"I'm telling you the truth. You can hate me, and I'll take everything you can shoot at me. I don't mind. You love me, Scarlett. You love that man up there that is hurting more than anything, and you don't have it in you to hate."

He pressed a kiss to her stomach, then to her lips.

"Do you think you could take a third slice of pizza?" he asked.

"Yes."

"Good." He handed her a third piece of pizza. "I'm going to take some food up to him," he said.

"I'll follow you up. I want a shower."

He locked the house up, taking care with the windows and the doors to make sure they were secure.

Checking on Scarlett, he saw she was already in the shower, and he made his way toward the bed.

John's head was facing the bathroom, and Gunner sat on the floor, the plate with the pizza held up.

"I come with gifts."

John's stomach chose that moment to growl, and he chuckled. "And you can't even lie to me that you're not hungry."

"I'm not that petty." John moved so that his head was resting on his hand, but they were both turned toward the door, waiting for the moment when their woman would enter.

"I know, but just in case you wanted to try and win an argument. I've already got your lame ass pegged."

John chuckled. "Do you think she'll forgive me?"

"She'll forgive us, John. She doesn't have it in her to be nasty or mean. She loves fiercely. She will cry at times though," Gunner said. "We've got to be prepared for that."

"I hate it when she cries."

"Get used to it. I can't kick your ass every other day. We've got to keep you pretty-looking for her."

"Thank you."

"For what?"

"For doing this, for being here."

Gunner turned to look at his best friend. "I know

I've never been open and honest with you about a lot of things, but you should know that I love you. That I want this between all three of us. I want you both, and I'm a man that gets what he wants. You and Scarlett, you're mine now."

"If that's the case then that means you belong to us. Scarlett and I own you."

"Good."

The door to the bathroom opened, and there stood their woman. She wore a nasty-ass nightshirt that had seen better days.

"Can you both … just hold me? I don't want anything. I'd like you both to hold me."

John finished his pizza, and Gunner removed his leather jacket. He made sure to put the gun within reach. Kent was still out there. The threat that he posed was still fucking real, and Gunner wasn't going to let down his guard for anyone.

Taking off his clothes, he climbed onto the other side of Scarlett. Pushing his arm beneath her head, he placed his other hand at her hip.

John moved closer, banding his arm around her waist, kissing her lips.

"I love you, Scarlett," he said.

"I love you too." She touched his face, her finger lightly tracing over one of the Band-Aids that he'd put on. "I hope you don't have to fight like this often."

"I won't, baby." John kissed her lips, and Gunner kissed her neck.

"Sleep, the both of you. We've got a long life ahead of us."

Scarlett gave a little chuckle, but she snuggled between them, and he was able to relax. He didn't know how long it would last.

Chapter Fourteen

One week later

"Any news?" John asked, leaning back in his chair.

Gunner shook his head. They were back at his place. Carlos and Scarlett were in the kitchen, working on dinner together. Carlos had some kind of paper due about healthy eating, and he was learning all the basics from Scarlett.

They were working through their problems. Gunner wouldn't allow Scarlett to hide or to run away from what was happening. Kent was a real threat, and as he'd not been seen, and it was one week closer to the deadline, he knew without a doubt that it would happen soon.

Kent wanted the Prez patch. He wanted the club, and he'd do whatever was necessary to win. His men were out hunting for him, and if it wasn't for Bennie, he'd be out there with them.

"They can't locate him. Kent was always known for being able to hide. No one could ever find him until he wanted to be found. It was one of the reasons I didn't want to fucking lose him."

"How did Billy handle the VP patch?" John asked.

"He didn't feel that he deserved it. With this shit with Kent, a lot of the guys are pissed they didn't see it coming, myself included."

With the time passing, he didn't know what to do. It would only be a matter of time before Kent did strike.

"Billy's a good choice. He's loyal to you and to the club."

"Yeah, and we need that right now."

"I'll always have your back," John said. "Without a doubt."

He nodded and took a seat. His leg bounced as he listened to Carlos and Scarlett in the kitchen.

Sex hadn't resumed among all of them yet. She was no longer staying in her home, and she shared their bed every single night. Gunner was just happy to hold her, to feel her in his arms.

"Any news on Cherry?"

His ex-wife had tried to get their son moved from the private ward where he was. Gunner had made sure the doctors were aware that under no circumstances were they to change Bennie's medication or his arrangements without consulting him first. Cherry had also been removed from the list of people who were allowed to see Bennie.

Afterward, he made sure his wife paid him a visit.

Staring at John, he made sure his friend got the message. "Cherry won't be a problem anymore."

John looked at him and nodded.

He had found out that his ex was a traitorous little bitch. She was prepared to use her own son as leverage against him to get more money. It was why she'd tried to move Bennie.

Gunner had found the evidence, and he'd dealt with her how he dealt with all traitors. Killing his son's mother didn't bother him. Her death had been a long time coming. He only hated that he'd put Bennie and Carlos through enough pain before he realized how much of a fucking bitch she actually was. It seemed rather fitting really. He'd made her beg for death long before he'd given it, and now she had a permanent place within the club—only she was six feet under for that privilege. She was buried on club property and would remain there for a long time.

He'd pulled the trigger and watched her fall back into the hole he'd made her dig. There had been no feelings of happiness, just acceptance that she was gone, and he'd done what he'd needed to do.

"Are you okay?" John asked.

"Me, I'm more than fine. I should have done it a long time ago." He could no longer trust her though. Bennie was in a vulnerable position, and he made sure that there were men to watch him. He made sure to see his son several times a day.

Scarlett was always there as well, to cheer him up. With Finn gone, and the boys who helped him dealt with, Carlos had returned to school.

Everything was getting back on track, and he just needed to deal with the one loose cannon in his life, and that was Kent.

Soon, he'd show himself.

Scarlett entered the room, and she offered them both a smile. "Dinner's ready."

Carlos was at the table looking nervous.

"You cook this?" Gunner asked.

"Yeah, it wasn't so hard when Scarlett showed me everything that was going wrong, you know. It was kind of fun."

"My son likes to cook?" Gunner smiled as Carlos's cheeks heated.

"There is nothing wrong with a man wanting to cook. A lot of girls think it's pretty sexy," Scarlet said. "Ignore him."

Carlos chuckled.

He took a bite of the baked chicken spaghetti, and he was quite impressed with his son's skill.

"This is really good," Gunner said.

"Thank you."

"See, I told you. Stop stressing and allow yourself

to relax," Scarlett said.

"There's something I want to tell you," Gunner said, looking at his son. He knew he'd have to talk to Bennie soon, but with Scarlett and John there, he didn't want to leave it. "You know that Scarlett is pregnant."

"Gunner?" Scarlett dropped her fork to the plate.

"No. We made a mistake with waiting, and I'm not going to wait another second."

"I know she's pregnant, Dad," Carlos said. "She vomits in the morning and she doesn't make coffee anymore, and she has those fruity things that she seems to like so much."

"The baby is mine," Gunner said.

He reached out taking hold of Scarlett's hand, refusing to let her to run. He was tired of people running.

Carlos stared at her hand and smiled.

"I know," Carlos said. "I know that you've been seeing Scarlett and John. That you've got some kind of poly relationship going. Bennie and I both know. It wasn't hard to guess with you guys eye-fucking each other all the time."

Scarlett gasped.

"I did tell you my sons were not sweet and innocent."

Carlos burst out laughing. "Far from it. It'll be cool to have a brother or sister. Are you guys moving in here?"

Scarlett looked at John. "It's a beautiful place," Scarlett said, picking her fork back up and stabbing at her plate.

"This place is bigger, and you'll love it. We can start working on the nursery," Gunner said.

"Bennie and I started on it," Carlos said.

They all left the dinner table and followed Carlos upstairs to the spare bedroom. Gunner stepped in, flicking on the light, and indeed the room was completely different, and he'd not even entered this room in some time. The walls were a pale yellow, and there were different drawings that he knew his kids had done.

"We kind of figured what was going on, and to show that we hold no hard feelings or anything, we did this."

Gunner saw tears in Scarlett's eyes, and he moved to her side, wiping them away. He hated to see her cry, but at least he knew these were tears of happiness.

"I can't believe you did this." She sniffled.

"Do you like it?"

"It's beautiful."

There was a crib in the center of the room, and she walked up to it.

"That was mine and Bennie's. It was in the attic. Bennie got it down and fixed it up like that. You might want to check over it though before the baby comes," Carlos said.

John moved up behind them, touching her back.

"We can make this work, Scarlett."

She nodded. "I can see that. People in town are going to be harder to please."

"Screw them," John said. "Half of them have secrets of their own. Let them whisper. We've got to do what makes us happy, not what makes them happy."

He pressed a kiss to her neck, and Gunner stroked her hip.

Opening his arms, Carlos stepped toward him, and Gunner hugged his youngest son. Everything was coming together. He only hoped that he could keep everything working even with the threat he faced.

****

Time was ticking.

John knew with very second that passed, the deadline for Kent grew closer. Even though the cartels had agreed with Gunner's plan and told them straight that Kent was going to die, that didn't mean the threat wasn't real.

Each night, he slept with one eye open, making sure his loved ones were protected at all times. He'd even started to place guns at different locations around the house. When Gunner and Scarlett had been out, and he'd been left to his own devices, he'd checked every single part of the house to see where anyone could enter, where they could hurt the people he loved.

During the day, between meetings, he took the time to catch up on sleep. It was the only other way he knew he could recharge his batteries.

He'd just closed his eyes when there was a knock at the door. Running a hand down his face, he got to his feet, clearing the tiredness from his eyes.

Opening the door, he saw it was Gunner.

"Hey, man, what's up?"

"I just thought I'd come to see how you were. I know you've not been sleeping all that well."

"I'm fine. How's Scarlett?"

"I dropped her off at the day care center. Bennie is with a physical therapist."

Bennie was making an excellent recovery. His young age and determination had moved him toward the next stage of getting better. Thinking about Bennie brought him back to the memory of Finn.

He'd done a lot in the past few days to help his friend.

"What are you going to do when the boys start asking about Cherry?" John asked.

"Tell him that she had to go. They've not asked about her, and when I saw Bennie this morning, he asked to keep her away, that he didn't want her near him."

John nodded. "Everything feels so fucked-up."

"You still not talked to Scarlett?" Gunner asked.

"Not since she saw me break down. Every time I try, she finds an excuse to leave the room or to walk away. I've never known her to be the kind of woman to not fight back. I hurt her deeply."

"You're going to have to make her listen to you," Gunner said. "That's what I did. I made her listen. I wouldn't go anywhere else."

John smiled. Each time she walked out of a room, he let her. The only time he'd gotten close to her was at night. He probably should have spoken then, but he'd just been happy to have her in their bed, in his arms.

"She'll come around."

"You don't sound so sure about that," John said. He ran a hand over his face. He was fucking exhausted. Sleepless nights no longer appealed to him. "When do you think this fucker is going to hit?"

"Kent? It could be any day now. I've been riding around, pretty much put a target on my fucking back. I was hoping that as we got closer to the deadline of him needing my dead body, he'd lose his shit, and I'd be done." Gunner blew out a breath. "I guess he's a lot more patient than I fucking thought. You need to get some sleep."

"No, I can't sleep. Not yet."

"What use are you to me if you can't even aim straight?"

The phone on his desk started to ring. "My secretary still out there?"

"Yeah, she told me to come right on in. Your door was closed though."

"I don't want anyone just walking in," John said. He'd not wanted Gunner to see that he'd been using his office to catch up on sleep.

Grabbing his phone, he listened as his secretary spoke.

"Someone called Kent is on the line, sir. He said it's urgent."

John turned to look at Gunner. "Put him through."

Pressing the speakerphone button, he waited.

"Hello, John," Kent said. "I'm hoping Gunner is there with you. I've seen him visiting you a lot more, and let's just say I've got two special somethings in your life right now."

There was a loud scream to be heard, and then Scarlett's voice.

"Leave him alone!" she yelled.

John's blood ran cold.

Another scream, and Gunner paled.

"Carlos, are you okay?" Scarlett asked.

"Your son's a little fucking pussy, Gunner. Can't even handle a few broken bones. You know what, I think I'm going to take him piece by fucking piece."

"What do you want?" Gunner asked.

"I want you both here, at the warehouse. Come alone or I will tear the baby out of your whore, and make sure she can't have any children. You try anything funny, I will make your lives a living hell."

Kent hung up, and John grabbed the phone, throwing it across the room. He was so fucking angry.

"She was at the fucking day care center!" John gripped the edge of the desk, his rage consuming him as fire filled his blood.

After everything they'd been through, he couldn't allow Scarlett to get hurt.

"We don't have time for us to lose it right now," Gunner said.

"He's got her and Carlos, Gunner. You do realize the risks right now? You've got to know them."

"I know them, John. I fucking know more than anyone that he could kill her. That he could take away two of the most important people to me. Bennie's in the hospital. I lose his brother, I've got to tell him what happened. I'm not having that conversation. We're not doing this," Gunner said. "Will you help me get our woman back, and my son, and if anything happens to me, promise me you'll take care of them?"

"You don't even have to ask," John said.

He would protect Gunner with his life, and there was no way he'd let anything happen to him.

They left his office, and he told his secretary to cancel all of his meetings and to take the rest of the day off.

John climbed into his car, and Gunner sat in the passenger seat.

"You got any guns in this car?"

"They're in the duffel in the back."

"How long have you been carrying guns around?"

John smirked. "What makes you think I ever stopped carrying them around?"

"You wear a suit to work."

"So? My best friend is the Prez of an MC, and you're known for fucking people off. I got prepared and stayed it. The suit is just a front."

"Like a superhero."

"I'm not a superhero, Gunner. I'm long past that fucking status."

They rode toward the warehouse, and once outside, John parked the car. Today could see his life ending. He may not live to see his wife give birth, or to share in the love of a family.

"If I don't make it today, I want you to tell

Scarlett that I'm sorry. That all I wanted to ever do was give her everything. I don't want her to hate me or what we've done."

"Shut the fuck up and get out of the car. No one is dying today but Kent and whoever he has with him."

****

Scarlett kept trying to tug her hands out of the rope. They had tied them too tightly, and even though she'd cut her flesh, she had to get to Carlos. He was curled up in a ball on the floor, his leg at an odd angle.

Kent and two men she didn't recognize kept pacing the floor.

"What if they don't come?" one of the men asked.

As time started to pass, she saw they had all started to look a little scared. Kent was barely hanging on by a thread. When he'd taken her, she'd been throwing trash out in the alleyway. It had taken her by surprise when he'd caught her and bundled her into a car. She didn't even realize he was there. When she was in the car, she saw they had Carlos. They'd bound and gagged him.

Carlos had looked at her and seemed to try to ask if she was okay.

He was such a sweet kid, and no matter what she tried to do, they had hurt him. She'd wanted them to hurt her rather than hurt a boy. That's all Carlos was, a young boy.

Tears kept falling down her cheeks as she watched.

Blood was pooling beneath his leg that Kent had stamped on until she heard the echoing of a break along with Carlos's screams.

"They'll both come. We've got these fuckers here. They'll come."

"I've heard that John's not to be messed with," the other one said. "That Gunner wanted him as VP."

"John's a fucking pussy. He's about as scary as my fucking granny, and she's fucking dead. Shut up."

He kept saying *fuck* over and over.

"Is this all about taking Gunner's place?" she asked.

Her voice was croaky from her screams.

She wouldn't stop screaming, and Kent had struck her across the cheek, stunning her. She'd not screamed again, but her voice hurt, as did her face.

Keeping her hands close to her stomach, she hoped that he didn't try to take away her baby. Even though she'd been hurt by learning what Gunner and John had done, she didn't want to lose her baby.

She loved her baby already, and she couldn't wait to meet him or her.

"That club deserves better than Gunner." Kent spat the words. "He thinks he's all high and mighty. Served his fucking country. He don't know shit of the stuff I've done for that club." Kent pressed a finger to his head. "He don't have the brains to take it to the next fucking level. He's a fucking pussy, and all pussies need to go to ground."

"This coming from a man who's hurting a sixteen-year-old child who's bound up. Yeah, you'll be a better choice for the club."

Kent bent down and glared at her. "You think you're so smart, do you, whore? You've got those two wrapped around your finger. Willing to do whatever to keep you safe. You must have a pussy made out of gold." He reached out, stroking a finger down her cheek. "Once I get rid of Gunner and John, I'll kill the kid, put him out of his misery, and then I'll get rid of that piece of shit inside you. Once that club is mine, I'll get you to how I want you. I'm going to have to starve you a bit because I don't like my bitches fat. I'll see just how fucking hot your pussy is."

He grabbed the back of her neck, pulling on her hair as he did that. She cried out and tried to pull away from him.

His lips pressed against hers, and she bit him.

Kent jerked back and slapped her face, left and right, before releasing her.

"I'll make you beg for my cock, and you'll see. You'll wish you never fucking turned on me, whore!"

He was about to kick her, but the door opening stopped him. She watched as John came in, gun poised at Gunner's head.

Her heart picked up at seeing her two men, but then shattered as she watched them both. They looked pissed off, angry, and ready to kill.

"What the fuck is this?" Kent asked.

"This is simple. You want him dead, right? You want the fucking patch?" John asked. "I want to know what your deal is."

"What?"

"How do you get your cartel deal, Kent? You got to have his head or something?"

"You're not kidding anyone."

John pointed his gun at one of the other men, and she gasped as with a single shot the man went down.

Bang.

Kent now had his gun raised, pointed at both her men. With them focused on each other, she wriggled toward Carlos.

"Are you okay?" she asked.

"Yes. It hurts." Carlos covered his face.

"I know, honey. I know."

"Scarlett," Carlos said.

"Yeah?" She glanced up to see them arguing. They were talking about Gunner's death, and Kent and the guard were advancing.

"I have a knife."

Her gaze went back to Carlos.

"What?"

"In my jacket." She reached into his jacket, which was hard to do with her hands together. It was one of those pocket knives. She couldn't open it. Her hands were shaking. Even though Carlos was shaking, he took the knife from her and flicked it open. "You've got to help them."

Feeling fear unlike anything she'd ever known, she kissed Carlos's head. "Don't die."

Moving over him as if she was protecting him, she saw Kent and John talking, coming to some sort of agreement. Kent was so close, and she was behind him. She had to do this fast for it to count.

Since her pregnancy, her balance had been off lately, and waves of dizziness would overcome her.

If she didn't do this though, John and Gunner could end up killed.

Carlos looked at her, and she saw that he didn't have much longer. He was bleeding, so pushing all of her fears aside, she gripped the knife tightly. Turning around, she stood as fast as she could. With her hands tied it made it awkward, but putting all of her anger, her fear, her rage into her attack, she plunged the knife into his neck. She pulled it out, and before he could react she did it again.

This time, he spun around, shoving her away and knocking her against the wall.

She didn't see what happened next.

The sounds of gunshots rang around the warehouse.

When it was over, John came to her. He rolled her over and held her tightly. "Don't ever do anything so fucking stupid again," he said.

"I didn't want him to kill either of you."

"Gunner and I had a plan."

"If it meant one of you dying, it was a stupid plan."

John had the knife, and he sliced through the rope. She threw her arms around him. "The club is going to clean up the mess. We've got to get Carlos to the hospital."

She didn't wait around. John took the lead, helping her into the car. Carlos was already in the backseat. "I've already called the club. They're going to take care of the bodies," Gunner said. "I'm so sorry, son, I had no idea they'd come for you."

"It's okay, Dad," Carlos said.

"You've got to stay awake. We'll get you to the hospital, and everything will be fine."

John was behind the wheel, and completely disregarding the speed limit, he got them to the hospital in record time. Before he even parked, she got out with Gunner as he carried his son into the hospital.

They were immediately transferred to another department, and she stood there, feeling completely weak.

John came in, and he did what he always did best. He ordered everyone around. He got a doctor to check her over even though she argued that she was fine. John wouldn't take no for an answer.

After running several tests, the doctor gave her the all clear, and they were back in the waiting room.

She wanted to go up and see Bennie, but she didn't want to worry him.

John took her hand, and she held him tightly,

squeezing him back.

"I don't know what I'd have done if anything happened to you," John said. She pressed her head against his shoulder. "I know you're angry with me right now, and I have no right to ask, but I hope one day you can forgive me for what I did."

Looking up at him, she smiled. "I do forgive you, John. I can't stay angry at you for too long. I know why you did it."

"You're not angry at me anymore?"

"No, I'm not."

He cupped her cheek, and she didn't pull away. "You didn't want to talk."

"I wasn't ready to talk. Maybe I've been too stubborn, but I love you and Gunner. I want to make this work. For us to have a family together. I do want to try that. Do you think we could? Do you forgive me?"

"There's nothing to forgive, Scarlett. I love you, and I'm sorry. I just wanted to give you everything."

"I do have everything."

Scarlett held him close as they waited for Gunner. An hour passed before he came out, and they both stood.

Gunner cupped her face, tilting her head back. She knew they got a couple of weird looks, but fuck them. This was her life, and she intended to live it how she wanted.

"Is he okay?"

"He's fine. He's out for a couple of hours. They've repaired the break, and he's got a cast on. He'll be joining Bennie in some physical therapy, but other than that, he's fine. Are you okay?"

"Yes, I'm fine. He didn't really hurt me. A few bruises, but other than that, I'm good."

"Thank God. I can't fucking lose you. I won't."

"You won't lose us, either of us. We're here to

stay, Gunner."

His gaze went to John, who nodded.

"We're all good?"

She chuckled. "Yeah, we're all good."

****

Six months later

Gunner rested his head on Scarlett's stomach, trying to listen to the sound of his little girl. She had already kicked him in the head, and Scarlett couldn't stop chuckling. They were out in the clubhouse's garden. Carlos stood at the grill with John and Bennie and several of the guys.

Scarlett was on bed rest though as she'd been doing too much at the day care center. Their little girl was growing faster every single day. He'd already seen the blurry ultrasound pictures, and he knew his girl was going to be a looker.

In the past six months, life had changed a lot for him. John and Scarlett had sold their house, and now lived with him and his boys. He was there for every single step of the way. John was by her side as well. After Kent's attack, their life together got back to normal. Scarlett forgave him and John. On the club front, he'd made some changes as well. He'd removed all of his deals with the cartels including transporting. Since Kent's betrayal, he'd been working on deals closer to home, and keeping drugs out of his town. He didn't want any of that shit in his life.

Gunner had also made the club vote. He'd told them about his relationship with Scarlett and that he was fucking John as well. They both belonged to him. He wanted the club to take a vote to keep him as Prez, and it had been unanimous in keeping him as their Prez. They didn't give a fuck who he screwed just so long as they stayed in dough and Scarlett baked cookies for them.

"How are my two girls today?" Gunner asked, pressing a kiss to her stomach.

"We're doing okay. Mommy's fat, though."

"Mommy's not fat. I kissed every single inch of her just last night, and I didn't find any extra bits."

She threw her head back, laughing.

"Can you two be less gross?" Bennie asked.

His eldest son had made a full recovery. It had taken him some time to learn to do things slowly, to pace himself. He had ended up in the hospital a few times because of this, and Gunner had been pissed at him.

In the end, Bennie's back was fine, and he was even looking at going to college in the fall. He was catching up on all of his classwork, and he also was dating the girl whose name Gunner couldn't fucking remember. Still, they were cute together, and for his birthday, he'd gotten Bennie lots of condoms with the warning that he didn't want to be a granddad.

Carlos had also recovered, and it hadn't taken as long. He was fully healed, and the short kidnapping hadn't affected him too much. The first week after the attack, he'd woken up in the night screaming, but Gunner had stayed with him, and made sure he was safe.

No one hurt his family.

Gunner glanced out toward the far field. There was a reason the clubhouse had a lot of yard. There were a lot of secrets buried on this land. Secrets of the club.

"I don't think it's gross," John said. "It's cute." He dropped a kiss to Scarlett's lips, and joined them.

Billy had taken over manning the grill.

Getting up, Gunner helped Scarlett to sit up, and they enjoyed their food together. They were one big happy family.

Scarlett gasped and quickly grabbed both of their hands, placing them on her stomach. "Do you feel that?"

Gunner kept his palm across her rounded stomach and waited. There it was, and he smiled. "She kicked. Our baby girl kicked."

Bennie and Carlos moved closer and their hands were on her stomach.

The look of wonder in their eyes matched his. He'd never taken the time to care about them when Cherry had been pregnant.

"She's going to be a little fighter," John said. "Just like her mother."

"She's not going to need to fight," Carlos said. "Bennie and I can take them. Dad, what are you going to do about dates?"

Gunner stared at his boys. "She's not going to be dating. It's as simple as that."

Scarlett shook her head. "If our daughter wants to date, then she will date."

"That baby is part of me, and I know what men think, and it's not pretty."

"I don't care what you say. Our little girl will be dating if she wants to."

"Yeah, she can date," John said. "There's nothing wrong with having a chaperone or four."

Gunner smirked at his friend. "Or the entire club. I like it. Our little girl will always be protected."

"Don't worry, Mommy will be here."

He'd never felt so fucking happy in all of his life. He had his boys, his best friend, the woman he loved, and the club.

****

"Come on, baby, you can do it. You can push," Gunner said.

Scarlett whimpered, holding both of their hands. John and Gunner had been determined to be part of the birth together. She'd read about the pain, and she whimpered as she felt it completely suckered her. "I can't. It hurts." She collapsed on the bed, needing a few seconds.

Her water had broken two hours ago, and the contractions had immediately started. The doctor between her thighs told her to give one more push, but she shook her head.

"You've got this, baby," John said. He kissed her head. "Let's meet our daughter. Come on, sweetheart."

They were waiting for her, and with tears in her eyes, she sat up again, holding their hands as she pushed again.

She listened to the doctor as she kept on telling her to push, and then one final push.

Scarlett's heart nearly stopped as she heard the sound of the baby cry. That was her little girl, her baby.

"A beautiful baby girl," the doctor said.

John and Gunner at her back as the doctor placed her daughter in her arms.

"Well done, Mrs. Williams."

She was still John's legal wife, but at the clubhouse as a way of Gunner's men accepting his relationship, they had married her to both of them in the eyes of the club. That had been a really special day for her.

Their relationship came with all three of them.

"She's so beautiful," she said.

The pain was lessening as she stared at her little girl.

She leaned back so Gunner and John could have a look.

"Our baby girl," Gunner said.

She rested her head back. She knew it didn't matter on whom. She loved both of her men equally. They always held each other no matter what.

Staring down at her daughter, she knew that she'd never stop loving them.

They were bound together for eternity, and there was no better place to be.

Epilogue

Eighteen years later

"Mom, seriously! I want to go to prom, and Dads, both of them, are making me take a club Prospect with me. How is that fair?"

John smiled as he finished eating his mashed potatoes. He'd been late at work, hoping to miss this outburst, but he was in agreement with Gunner. Emily wasn't going out dating anyone on her own.

"Gunner!" Scarlett called his name, and John looked up as his wife came into the room.

The other man in question turned the corner, and John watched as he held their youngest child.

Besides Bennie and Carlos, they also had four daughters. Opal, the youngest, was in Gunner's arms.

Scarlett's hands went to her hips. "We agreed."

"No, you suggested, I didn't respond. I don't know who this boy is."

"Mom, seriously, Drake is, like, one of the biggest nerds in school."

"I heard you tell Bennie that he's the hottest nerd in school, and last time I checked that still meant he had a dick."

Scarlett glared at him, taking Opal. "Fix this," she said, turning to him.

"I'm eating cold mashed potatoes," John said.

"That's because you wouldn't come home."

John loved to come home more than anything in the world. Between Gunner and Scarlett, they had given him a huge family. All together they had six children, and also two grandchildren, who were nightmares.

Scarlett left the room, and he watched Gunner and Emily face off. He'd been to all of their kids' births.

Emily being their oldest, she did hold a special place in his heart as she'd helped to bring them all together.

"Dad, please, I'm sensible. I want to go to prom, and I want to do so with Drake. He's nice, and we study together all the time."

"Wait?" Gunner asked. "Your date is glasses-wearing Drake?"

"Yes. He's around all the time. He fixed your computer for you."

"Oh," Gunner said. "That's fine. Sure, he can take you out."

Gunner sat down at the table, and John smirked. He looked incredibly hot when he was smug.

"What did you do, Dad?"

"I didn't do anything."

"Ugh! This is not fair." Emily stormed out of the room, and Gunner turned to John as Scarlett came back into the room, brow raised.

Opal was shaking a rattle in her arms.

"What did you do?" Scarlett asked.

"Oh, I happened to tell Drake that if he put a finger on my daughter that I have a special hole dug at the back of the clubhouse for losers like him. I even got the two new prospects to dig me a hole. I have to say, kid has got balls. I showed it to him. Told him to respect my girl and her family otherwise he'd be saying hello to the earth up close and personal."

Scarlett shook her head. "And he still asked her to the prom. Damn, that boy is a keeper." She sat down in the chair between them.

John finished his food, and took Opal from her arms, kissing her on the head.

"Why are you crying, baby?" Gunner asked.

"I'm just so happy. Can you believe that our little girl is going to prom? Where did the past eighteen years go?"

John crouched down and kissed her lips. "We've been so gloriously happy." They had found their happiness together, all three of them. They'd fallen in love, created a family, and were now building a future. With Opal on his hip, Gunner took Scarlett into his arms, and John watched his two lovers embrace.

This was what he'd always hoped for, and he was the luckiest son of a bitch in the world.

The End

www.samcrescent.com